# Atop an Underwood

## ALSO BY JACK KEROUAC

The Town and the City

On the Road

The Subterraneans

The Dharma Bums

Doctor Sax: Faust Part Three

Maggie Cassidy

Mexico City Blues

The Scripture of the
    Golden Eternity

Tristessa

Lonesome Traveler

Book of Dreams

Pull My Daisy

Big Sur

Visions of Gerard

Desolation Angels

Satori in Paris

Vanity of Duluoz: An
    Adventurous Education,
    1935–46

Scattered Poems

Pic

Visions of Cody

Heaven & Other Poems

Pomes All Sizes

Good Blonde & Others

Old Angel Midnight

The Portable Jack Kerouac

Selected Letters: 1940–1956

Book of Blues

Some of the Dharma

Selected Letters: 1957–1969

# Atop an Underwood

EARLY STORIES AND OTHER WRITINGS

## JACK KEROUAC

Edited with an Introduction and Commentary by
### Paul Marion

VIKING

VIKING
Published by the Penguin Group
Penguin Putnam, Inc., 375 Hudson Street,
New York, New York 10014, U.S.A.
Penguin Books Ltd, 27 Wrights Lane,
London W8 5TZ, England
Penguin Books Australia Ltd, Ringwood,
Victoria, Australia
Penguin Books Canada Ltd, 10 Alcorn Avenue,
Toronto, Ontario, Canada M4V 3B2
Penguin Books (N.Z.) Ltd, 182–190 Wairau Road,
Auckland 10, New Zealand

Penguin Books Ltd, Registered Offices:
Harmondsworth, Middlesex, England

First published in 1999 by Viking Penguin,
a member of Penguin Putnam Inc.

1  3  5  7  9  10  8  6  4  2

"Count Basie's Band Best in Land: Group Famous for 'Solid' Swing"
first appeared in *The Horace Mann Record,* February 16, 1940.

Grateful acknowledgment is made for permission to reprint excerpts
from "Blues in the Night" by Johnny Mercer and Harold Arlen.
© 1941 (renewed) Warner Bros. Inc. All rights reserved. Used by
permission. Warner Bros. Publications U.S. Inc., Miami, Florida.

LIBRARY OF CONGRESS CATALOGING-IN-PUBLICATION DATA
Kerouac, Jack. 1922–1969
Atop an Underwood : early stories and other writings / Jack
Kerouac : edited with an introduction and commentary
by Paul Marion.
p.  cm.
ISBN 0-670-88822-2
1. Beat generation—Literary collections.   I. Marion, Paul.
1954–   II. Title.
PS3521.E735A92   1999      98-20052
813'.54—dc21

This book is printed on acid-free paper. ∞

Printed in the United States of America
Set in Bodoni Book
Designed by Betty Lew

To young writers everywhere

As I am, so I see.
—Ralph Waldo Emerson

Are you he who would assume a place to teach or be a poet here in
the States? The place is august, the terms obdurate.
—Walt Whitman

Always considered writing my duty on earth.
—Jack Kerouac

# Contents

## Part Two:
## An Original Kicker 1941

# Introduction

When Jack Kerouac burst on to the American scene in 1957 with his Roman candle book *On the Road*, he had been a writer for more than twenty years. He later defined what it means to be a born writer: "When the question is therefore asked, 'Are writers made or born?' one should first ask, 'Do you mean writers with talent or writers with originality?' Because anybody can write, but not everybody invents new forms of writing." The clarification was rooted in his understanding of the word *genius* as meaning "to beget." Along with creating more than twenty books, Kerouac knew he had invented a new way of writing, fusing local talk, blown jazz, a scribe's eye, relentless self-examination, the grammar of dreams, memory glee, and gloominess about our short lives.

For someone who felt he was born to write, Kerouac spent his youth "busy being born." And so this is Jack Kerouac's book about becoming a writer and an artist. Unlike *Some of the Dharma, Book of Blues*, and other books of his published since he died in 1969, Kerouac had not prepared the manuscript of *Atop an Underwood: Early Stories and Other Writings*. He did, however, leave an enormous cache of writings in carefully organized files, the source of this book and others to come. His papers are an extraordinary record of an artist's development.

*Atop an Underwood: Early Stories and Other Writings* takes its title from a book of stories Kerouac imagined publishing in 1941. Readers of Kerouac's novel *Vanity of Duluoz: An Adventurous Education, 1935–46*, will recognize the title because he brings it into his story about Jack Duluoz growing up in America. After working all day in a gas station in Hartford, Connecticut, Duluoz would head back to his digs: "I was happy in my room at night writing 'Atop an Underwood,' stories in the Saroyan-Hemingway-Wolfe style as best as I could figure it at age nineteen." Kerouac's readers have long wondered about the real stories written in Hartford in the fall of 1941. Do they exist?

Kerouac's proposed introduction for *Atop an Underwood* describes the book as a sixty-story collection. One handwritten table of contents for *Atop* includes twenty-five story titles, and another list has six. From the same period Kerouac left two other lists. "Stories for *Blame It on the Heart*" numbers forty-two titles, some of which overlap the original *Atop* contents, and "Stories" has forty-eight titles, repeating a few of those on the *Atop* list. An inspection of the author's papers showed that only fifteen of the stories exist; the surviving ones of that period would have made a short collection.

In an essay entitled "Au Revoir à l'Art," written in November 1944, Kerouac assessed his writing output since 1939: "Poems, stories, essays, aphorisms, journals, and nine unfinished novels. That is the record—600,000 words, all in the service of art—in five years." Interviewed by Barry Gifford and Lawrence Lee for *Jack's Book: An Oral Biography of Jack Kerouac*, writer William Burroughs recalled meeting Kerouac in mid-1944: "Jack was quite young at the time. He'd done an awful lot of writing. He'd written about a million words, he said." About eighty thousand of those words are published here for the first time.

This book includes the Hartford stories and then some, looking backward to Kerouac's earliest efforts in Lowell, Massachusetts, and past the Hartford period to work he was doing through his twenty-first year—just before he encountered the writer friends with whom he was to make history. The writings include stories, excerpts from novels, poems, essays, sketches, plays, and other work from 1936 to 1943. The contents vary more than the other published collections of Kerouac writings, *Lonesome Traveler* and *Good Blonde & Others*.

It is startling to see how early Kerouac began writing about America, adventurous travel, spiritual questing, work, family, and sports, to name a few subjects that occupied him. From the start Kerouac's writings usually centered on his experience. He wrote a novel when he was eleven, a lost manuscript he referred to in *Visions of Cody* as "Mike Explores the Merrimack." Biographer Tom Clark comments on the early "Merrimack" novel: "The same basic story of a tantalizing power that removes one from humdrum existence and takes one on a remarkable voyage can be found underlying almost everything Kerouac wrote for the next 18 years, up to and including the best known of all these fantasies of life, *On the Road.*" An impressive work that survived is the football novella he wrote at sixteen, which opens with a wayward college athlete walking along a railroad track in the American heartland.

As self-deprecating as he was about some of his early writing (dismissing, for example, the stories written in the fall of 1941) Kerouac was proud enough to say the work was "a great little beginning effort." From the résumélike autobiography that kicks off *Lonesone Traveler* to his memory-laden author's note in the anthology *The New American Poetry,* he recorded his first steps as a writer.

In 1943 Kerouac identified his major artistic project: "Long concentration on all the fundamental influences of your life will net a chronological series of events that will be open to use as a novel— for a novel should have a sort of developing continuity, if nothing else. [. . .] [Please see note on editor's ellipses on page xxi.] Your life and every other life is stuff for great novels, providing the treatment is good." By 1951 he had refined the concept: "*On the Road* is the first, as the French Canadian novel will be the second in a series of connected novels revolving around a central plan that eventually will be my life work, a structure of types of people and destinies belonging to this generation and referable to one another in one immense circle of acquaintances."


In a notebook kept when he was barely twelve, Kerouac lists writing as one of his talents, along with cartooning and billiards, and reading as his hobby. Whether handling metal type in his father's printshop or soaking up stories told by his mother and aunt on long walks, he was hooked on words. On those walks he heard his family's Franco-American or "Canadian French" language, a malleable form of talk with creative blends, rapid musical sounds, and lively inventions. In his 1941 story "The Father of My Father," Kerouac describes it as "one of the most languagey languages in the world. It is unwritten; it is the language of the tongue, and not of the pen. It grew from the lives of the French people come to America. It is a terrific, a huge language."

Kerouac's friends describe him as an imaginative and restless kid, though quiet and mild-mannered too. He was a stand-out athlete on local fields and a talker on night porches. Kid Kerouac saw adventure everywhere. He was brave enough to scale Lowell's iron bridges. Jack entertained his friends with stories, mimicked radio characters, and improvised roles. He was as proud of his chess victories as he was of his sports heroics. He is also remembered as a keen observer and an intent listener.

By his early-teenage years Kerouac was writing and designing at-home sports newspapers. His reading expanded from French versions of the Catholic catechism and the Bible, *Rebecca of Sunnybrook Farm*, and serial magazines like *The Shadow* to, by the time he was seventeen, Jack London's adventure novels. He moved on to Walt Whitman's poems, the writings of Henry David Thoreau, and stories by Ernest Hemingway, William Saroyan, and another 1930s luminary, Albert Halper of Chicago and New York City.

A prolific author of the Hemingway–Thomas Wolfe generation, Halper produced a dozen books about people of his day—urban, ethnic, working people. This book reveals for the first time the crucial impact of Halper's potent writing on Kerouac. In particular, Halper's story of a young writer who wants to write "a big raw slangy piece of work" and who feels "a locomotive in [his] chest" resonated deeply with Kerouac.

In a poem written when he was eighteen, Kerouac described how he would "nibble at some sweet Saroyan" for dessert when he fed his head with books. He and his friends were also impressed by the dramatic products of the polymath Orson Welles. Young Kerouac once listed Wolfe, James Joyce, and Welles as the "Greatest Modern Poets." His writing voice gained definition when he absorbed the sounds, rhythms, and visions of Wolfe, Joyce, Herman Melville, and Fyodor Dostoevsky. He praised Wolfe and Joyce for their "deeply religious feeling for beauty" expressed in artful writings that surpassed the makings of a poet. Together with a poetic prose, the hyperlocal detail, urban texture, self-focus, and "cosmic regionalism" (in the words of scholar Harry Levin) of Joyce excited young Kerouac. A 1942 novel set in Lowell (titled *The Vanity of Duluoz*) had the markings of Joyce's "Stephen Hero," an early version of *A Portrait of the Artist as a Young Man*. Shakespeare, Homer, and Tolstoy ranked high on Kerouac's lengthy reading list. He made notes to "delve into Chinese and Hindu thought," along with Celtic and Breton folklore. In his early twenties he veered toward Arthur Rimbaud, William Blake, and Goethe, going so far as to burn some pages of his writing to prove his artistic fire. He broke through to his own style in his late twenties, with a spontaneous prose form that flowed from jazz method, new ideas about word sketching, and creative interplay with friends like Neal Cassady, Allen Ginsberg, and Burroughs.

Kerouac found creative people and the arts in Lowell, even as the Great Depression brought economic woe to the city; about 40 percent of Lowellians had accepted government assistance by the mid-1930s. His father had introduced him to the performance world with stories about entertainers on downtown stages. Jack attended meetings of the Scribblers' Club at Bartlett Junior High School. He and his friends were great movie fans, and Lowell had the Crown Theatre, the Royal, and others. His gang danced to big band music at the Rex and Commodore ballrooms. In 1940 he and others formed a dramatic group, the Variety Players, and produced a radio play. Friends like Bill Chandler, Bill Ryan, and John ("Ian") MacDonald wrote, drew cartoons, and listened to Beethoven. In *Lonesome Traveler*, Kerouac writes, "Decided to become a writer at age 17 under influence of Sebastian Sampas, local young poet who later died on Anzio beach head." Sebastian's older brother Charles, a journalist with the *Lowell Sun*, stoked the ambitions of Jack, Sebastian, and others. The elder Sampas was also mindful of Lowell's literary heritage. Nineteenth-century Lowell, the model textile mill city, had a cultural buzz for a long moment. Charles Dickens wrote about Lowell in his *American Notes for General Circulation*, Emerson delivered twenty-five lectures in the city, and Thoreau chronicled the region in *A Week on the Concord and Merrimack Rivers*. Kerouac's own Franco-Americans had distinguished themselves as journalists, publishers, and music composers.

Kerouac was friendly with Michael Largay and other writers associated with *Alentour: A National Magazine of Poetry*, a modern poetry journal published in Lowell from 1935 to 1943. In the unsigned 1940 essay "New England Thought" from *Alentour*, a writer describes the Concord River sliding past nineteenth-century houses of poets and philosophers in Concord, carrying "a twig Emerson may have once broken from a branch" toward the Merrimack River in Lowell. But the once-humming mills are closed when the twig at last drifts into sight: "[. . .] perhaps a boy playing barefooted by the edge of the river picked up the twig, long from Emerson's hand, and planted it that later it would grow into a tree, bringing life to the ruins. And then because workers were idle and had time to listen, perhaps the birds would come to the tree to sing." Kerouac heard the song in the trees. He read Emerson's essay "The Poet" and Thoreau's *Walden* and later imagined living in a hut like Thoreau, high atop Christian Hill overlooking Lowell. Analyzing himself in 1941, Kerouac explained why he was a poet: "He is a man, so he does the most man-like thing and writes for his fellow men."

Kerouac recoiled from what he viewed as spirit-killing millwork in his hometown, but he did not flee Lowell in 1939; he built on what he had accomplished there and stepped forward to pursue artistic and material success. Though he was awarded a "scholastic scholarship" to attend Columbia University, Kerouac was required to spend a year preparing for the rigors of the Ivy League. Accordingly he attended the Horace Mann School, a private school in New York City. While there in November 1939 Kerouac wrote to fellow Lowell High School football hero Ray Riddick, who had been graduated ahead of him and starred at Fordham University. Kerouac asked about free rides with Lowell truckers making the run from New York: "As I'm going to Columbia next year, and then for four more years, it would be convenient for me to start knowing my Lowell brethren truck drivers." He planned to keep town and city linked.

At Horace Mann, Kerouac combined his interests in sports and writing and then moved to Columbia, where the American romance of Thomas Wolfe defeated football dreams. He had sought New York as the nation's cultural nucleus. Athletic recruiters from Boston College and Duke University could not compete with Manhattan's theater, jazz, and publishers. He mixed with the sharp upper-class students at Horace Mann, joined the drama club, and dug the city's music scene. With his friend Seymour Wyse, he heard jazz greats at the Savoy Ballroom and Apollo Theatre. In prep school and college he composed themes on Dante, Virgil, Milton, and other giants. At Columbia he shared his writings with Eugene Sheffer, professor of French, and studied Shakespeare with Professor Mark Van Doren.

*Atop an Underwood: Early Stories and Other Writings* is arranged chronologically to chart Kerouac's artistic development. The time window closes in late 1943. Kerouac's girlfriend and soon-to-be wife Edith Parker introduced him to the Columbia University student Lucien Carr in 1944, and that led to meetings with Ginsberg, Burroughs, and others in an alternative, avant-garde crowd on the fringe of the Columbia campus. Kerouac, Ginsberg, and Burroughs were to become the leading writers of the Beat Generation, a label Kerouac applied when asked in 1948 by his friend and fellow writer John Clellon Holmes to describe their contemporaries. He was referring to a generation of young people with no illusions about their identity and place in the world; these men and women expressed "a weariness with all the forms, all the conventions of the world. . . ." Later he associated *beat* and *beatific,* emphasizing the spiritual values he honored. *Atop an Underwood* is a roots document for the Beat Generation, whose beginning Kerouac sees in the family house parties and gleeful neighborhood life of the 1920s and 1930s. Kerouac's first published use of the word *beat* appears to be in a passage near the end of his first published novel, *The Town and the City* (1950), in which he describes Liz Martin, the "hip-chick" and part-time New York nightclub singer, "wandering 'beat' around the city in search of some other job or benefactor or 'loot' or 'gold.' "

The selections are weighted toward the period from 1941 through 1943, reflecting the contents of Kerouac's archive and the artistic complexity of the work. Part One covers the years 1936 to 1940, beginning with a feature from one of his handmade horse racing newspapers, and follows him through his first semester at Columbia University. Part Two includes work from 1941, a prolific year for Kerouac as the result of a productive summer in Lowell and a fantastic burst of writing in Hartford in the fall. In Part Three, covering 1942 and 1943, a maturing Kerouac pushes to create more complex works. This section has an extended excerpt from Kerouac's novel *The Sea Is My Brother,* a version of which was written in March 1943 and dually titled *Merchant Mariner.* The collection finishes with stories drawing on his merchant marine voyage to England later that year.

By August 1943 Kerouac could articulate his goal: "My only ambition is to be free in art. This is a moral synthesis. To be free in art is like the refueled, repaired, reconditioned, and 'fit' ship that I have signed on, and which is ready to sail in 4 hours from now. From there on, the ship is on its own, but it suffers from no drawbacks other than those in the essences of nature and supreme reality."

Not yet "free in art," he acknowledges that he has a responsibility to help with family living expenses and owes a debt to his generation: "I must take part in the sacrifice of my generation,

[ xix ]

otherwise I should not seek their love in the future. It is an ethical matter, of great importance, and of spiritual & social significance." Wondering how to meet his goal of being "free" upon returning to America, Kerouac lists options for earning money: "(a) By finishing the [sea] novel, (b) Going to Hollywood to write, (c) Getting a newspaper job, (d) O.W.I. work overseas, (e) Continuance as seaman."

This book should help answer how and why Kerouac became an artist. His ideas about love, work, and suffering can be traced back to his apprentice work. At nineteen years old he was already remembering his life—he had an acute sense of loss. The early writings help us understand a North American author who was a cultural free trader with Canada and Mexico long before a continental vision was called up on political screens in the United States. His roots in the industrial, multiethnic milieu of early-twentieth-century society connect him to millions of Americans. Taking his life as legend, he asserted his standing as a representative person of his time and revealed the passion, struggles, and dignity of one life. As improbable a candidate as he may have been, Kerouac achieved his goal of becoming an American author.


*Atop an Underwood: Early Stories and Other Writings* was shaped to meet the interest of readers new to Kerouac and those familiar with his writings. I took a documentary approach, piecing together an untold story. This collection represents only a portion of Kerouac's early papers, excluding letters and notebooks. For example, there are student essays that I set aside. Favoring examples of Kerouac's imaginative writing, I chose not to include school assignments, letters, notes, fragments of poetry and prose, and most of the commentaries on social, political, and economic issues. Although I was limited to excerpting the few longer works of the period, I used selections from two novellas and a novel as evidence of Kerouac's gift and ambition. Until now only a few examples of Kerouac's writing before 1944 have been published, most notably the letters in his *Selected Letters: 1940–1956*, edited by Ann Charters, and two short stories ("The Brothers" and "Une Veille de Noël") reprinted from the Horace Mann literary magazine.

Some of Kerouac's stories went out under the names of classmates. In "Short Story," from 1940, he boasted: "I've written plenty of short stories in my day, I would estimate a number of nearly 80 all of which were no good, and of which 60 of them sold for a buck apiece to my dauntless school chums in the private school. They used them under their own names and got better marks." Photocopies of his miscellaneous writings for student newspapers and journals have been circulated over the years.

I had access to original holographs and typescripts in the Kerouac archive. These works were created before Kerouac adopted the technique of keeping breast pocket notebooks and larger student notebooks in which he wrote prose and poetry that he later typed and sometimes expanded upon. The manuscripts do not show extensive revision. It is possible that Kerouac discarded some of the first drafts, but unlikely given his pattern of saving papers. The manuscripts are not marked "1st draft," "2nd draft," etc. Not all manuscripts were dated, so at times I had to date works by relying upon details in the text, typewriter font, writing style, position in the author's files, writing tool, paper stock, and other factors. Further research may yield a finer-tuned chronology for the sequence of writings within the larger time periods presented here.

My comments are in italics preceding the selections. Within Kerouac's text editor's ellipses are shown within brackets: [. . .]; all other ellipses appear as they do in the original manuscripts, including those with multiple ellipsis dots. Dashes and quotation marks are standardized throughout. Kerouac's underscored words have been kept. Obvious misspellings were corrected, but unusual and perhaps intentional misspellings were kept. I maintained line breaks as they appear in Kerouac's texts for all poems, short sketches, notes, vignettes, and prose poems, whether the original was typed or handwritten. Novel excerpts, stories, plays, essays, and long sketches appear in standard lines. With untitled pieces, I assigned a title (shown in brackets) taken from the first line or two of the composition.

For the most part I let Kerouac speak for himself. Using source material from the author's archive and excerpts from his published works and other commentary on Kerouac's literature, I have tried to help the reader understand the origins and implications of the writings.


In the mid-1980s I worked with federal, state, and local officials; community leaders; and Stella Kerouac and her family on the planning and installation of the Jack Kerouac Commemorative, a sculptural tribute in Lowell with thousands of Kerouac's words blasted into reddish brown granite. The artwork by Ben Woitena stands in Kerouac Park, a downtown green designed by the landscape architecture firm Brown and Rowe. Lowell regularly recognizes Kerouac through scholarly and creative activities and the annual "Lowell Celebrates Kerouac!" literary festival. There is a Kerouac Street in San Francisco. Kerouac conferences have been organized in the United States, Quebec, and Europe. Orlando made a writer's residence of an old Kerouac cottage. Naropa Institute in Boulder dedicated a writing school to his ideas. *Life* magazine and *The Times* of London named him one of the most important figures of the twentieth century. The result of all this activity is more people discovering Kerouac. I am elated every time I drive by the Kerouac Commemorative and see somebody reading one of the stone pages that will stand for centuries. May this book live as long.

Paul Marion
Lowell, Massachusetts
March 12, 1999

# Part One

# Pine Forests and Pure Thought
# 1936–1940

# from Background

*Kerouac wrote this "Background" for prospective employers in late 1943, while living in New York City. He was seeking work as a script synopsizer in the motion picture industry, believing that the experience would help him write his own scripts and establish contacts in the movie business. Parts Two and Three of this book open with subsequent passages from Kerouac's short autobiography.*

I was born in Lowell, Mass., in March of 1922. Shortly before my birth my father had begun a small theatrical publication known as the "Spotlight Print," a unique weekly filled with news, comments, anecdotes, editorials, and advertisements dealing with the theatre and cinema of that time around Lowell and Boston. At the age of eleven, I spent most of my time after school in my father's printing and editorial offices, dashing off publications of my own on the antique typewriter, using the hand press for headlines and cuts. This early association with the printing and publishing business soon enough stained not only my blood but my hands and face with ink. My father's incessant stories about playing poker with George Arliss, with the Marx Brothers, with John Barrymore, and many other "troopers" during his days as an advertising man for the RKO Keith circuit in New England filled me with an early dream of the theatre.

At twelve, I printed a novel laboriously into a nickle notebook dealing with the adventures of a runaway orphan down the Merrimack River. At thirteen, I was busy turning out cartoon strips, handprinted racing form sheets, and a club newspaper. It was also at this time that the Lowell Sun published a "column" of mine written in father's office predicting the outcome of the Louis-Braddock fight to the round.

A year later, I was in High School trying out for the football team. A senior at sixteen, I had by that time so distinguished myself in athletics and studies to draw the attention of several colleges and football coaches for a scholarship, chief among them being Lou Little of Columbia and Frank Leahy, then Head Coach at Boston College. I chose Columbia, but since I needed more math before I could enroll there, Little arranged to send me to Horace Mann School here in New York, where, during the course of the year, Frank Leahy paid me a visit and tried to persuade me to go back to Boston College. He told me then, in 1940, that he might eventually leave B.C. for Notre Dame, but that he would take me to South Bend with him. "Now," he said, "let's go out and dine and see a good show. What would you like to see?" "William Saroyan!" I cried.

We went to see "Love's Old Sweet Song," and Frank seemed to enjoy it thoroughly. But, for my part, the performance was marred by the presence of a certain gentleman behind Leahy and me, and to this day I cannot tell whether or not it was a coincidence, or that the gentleman in the back row, the Freshman football coach at Columbia University, was surreptitiously tailing us.

At any rate, I stuck to Columbia: New York was too exciting to leave, and was too closely identified with boyhood dreams.

At Horace Mann, I was an out-and-out killer: star on the football, baseball, and chess teams, I earned money writing sports news for the New York World-Telegram (a job I got through Lou Miller, scholastic sports editor), turning out English papers for lazy but wealthy fellow students, and tutoring French. I wrote feature articles for the school weekly (mostly interviews, one with Glenn Miller), took an active part in the Dramatic Club, wrote several articles on jazz, which earned me the title of "jazz critic," appeared each quarter in the Horace Mann Quarterly with a short story, and, although I played baseball and football on the teams, wrote up the games, and often my own successes, the following day. In general, I earned good enough marks and made a sufficient impression to rate the status of "good citizen" from the prim, severe Dean. (However, at graduation exercises, finding myself the only member of the class sans culottes blanches—the irony of economic determinism—I spent the afternoon reclining under a tree behind the school thinking about Whitman and Saroyan, whom I had just begun to admire.)

At home in Lowell that summer, two old pals and I made elaborate preparations to stage a three-act play in a small town in the outlying suburbs. I wrote the script, the other was to take the leading role, and the third undertook a producer's duties. In the end, our mutual money shortage made short shrift of our attempts, but we did manage to put on a 15-minute play over the local radio station. These pitiful efforts may sound ludicrous to an outsider, but I cannot forget the enthusiasm with which we pitched our projects; nor can I forget the morning we three went to the old swimming hole in the pine woods to see the sunrise, after a long night of discussion, planning, writing, and drinking of coffee. For, later on, the "producer" was at Bataan, the "actor" is at present in Italy with the Fifth Army, and the "writer" spent many long, cold months in the North Atlantic.

The following Fall, at Columbia, I returned a kickoff against Princeton Frosh 85 yards to the Princeton 5-yard line and was carried off the field with a broken leg. I was actually glad; now I would have all of my time to myself and for studies. I wrote movie reviews for the Columbia Spectator, covered the varsity track team in the winter; ran a one-man typing agency, did some more ghost-writing, was elected Vice-President of the class, tutored French, and worked as private secretary for Prof. Eugene Sheffer of the French department. I helped Prof. Sheffer edit and translate his French textbook, typed out the whole manuscript, and even ventured definitions for his daily Journal-American crossword puzzle. We became fast friends; I wrote voluminously and took all my plays and stories to him. At this time, I had begun to read Thomas Wolfe and would spend entire nights roaming New York until dawn. I wrote and wrote, sending stories to all the better magazines (New Yorker, Esquire, Harper's, etc.), but without success [. . . .]

# Repulsion May Race Here in Exhibition Feature!! Mighty Kerouac Gelding Would Attract Many Fans; Don Pablo, Mighty 1935 Champion, May Race Repulsion!

*The following is a back-page feature from the* Daily Owl *of February 6, 1936, a twenty-cent horse racing newspaper from Pawtucket Racetrack created by thirteen-year-old Jack Kerouac. The front of the two-sided, hand-printed sheet is headlined "3 Day Meet Launched at Pawtucket." The long subhead reads: "Vermont Oval has the Finest Crop of Jockeys, but no High-Class Horses; Col. E. R. Bradley Brings out Six of his 3-yr. old Maidens; Lewis, Morriss, Myet at Track; Kerouac, Tortar Barns Present!" Between 1936 and 1938 Kerouac produced an amazing array of sports news publications filled with reports on real-world and make-believe sporting events and characters. Among these "newspapers" were* Romper's Sheet, Sports: Down Pat, Racing News, the Sportsman, Turf Authority, Jack Lewis's 1937 Chatterturf, the Daily Ball, Sports of Today, Jack Lewis's Baseball Chatter, and the Daily Owl. The publications were either carefully printed in pencil or typed as single-spaced sheets (without errors). In them we see the teenaged Kerouac as sports reporter, columnist, and statistician, consumed with the texture of the different contests and colorful personalities. His peppy writing style and intricate records lift these early efforts beyond the hobby-time doodling of a typical boy. Interestingly, some of the publications are long, densely typed sheets filled top to bottom like later manuscripts Kerouac produced.*

Pawtucket Park, Montpelier, Vt.:—Repulsion, mighty son of Khorasan, 1936 Champion candidate, is expected to stop here on his way to Sarah Springs for the distinguished Spring meet and Preakness. Don Pablo, great gigantic 1935 King, may also stop here and Jock Dennis hopes it will be in time for Repulsion's race. This match would attract at least 16,000 race goers, figures the little owner of Pawtucket.

Down at Sarah Springs, the colorful scene of fair ladies and rich gentlemen, flying banners and of course the historical Derby, Spotlight and yearly Preakness.

These three stakes may compare with the Vermont Derby. Although the class is lacking for that race, it is going to be a historical feature.

Even last year, men were chatting about this time (in February) about the Massachusetts Derby. Well may they talk about the Vermont. Repulsion, widely known as the fastest runner ever put out since racing history began, will attract many. Ranking as the world's champion, Repulsion should win the small race in which he will race in here but Don Pablo may be on hand, but yet the latter has had a serious leg injury.

Today, E. R. Bradley's highly touted Lena Cardoza will start in the Pawtucket Hi-Stakes with Onrush, Brevity, Sisowen and other stars. Rustic Joe, Mac Tortar's entry for that race and Boake Dobbin's Blue John are the old boys that will start. Blue John, a clever veteran campaigner can easily beat the field of ten. Rhodius, Mac Tortar's sensational three yr. old that improves with every start, is making his first start since racing in the Hopeful in December. Boake Dobbin's Brevity, another highly touted colt, also will have something to say.

# from Football Novella

*The following excerpt carries familiar Kerouac motifs: American road voyager, wayward collegian, and football hero. Kerouac sent the manuscript of this novella (written when he was sixteen years old) to a reader with a note addressed "Dear Margaret," most likely Margaret Wiley, one of the professors of his friend Sebastian Sampas at Emerson College in Boston. Kerouac explained to Margaret that he stopped writing just before the undefeated State U. team was about to face State College in the climactic Thanksgiving Day game. He then attached to the novella sixteen pages from another story, with the character name changes scratched in, and outlined the climax on another sheet. At this point in the story the coach had moved the main character, Bill Clancy, to a running back position:*

With a great bull-like, madly determined, tormented run Bill Clancy charges down the field with <u>tears of fury in his eyes</u>. He just doesn't want to be stopped. They hit him several times; he shakes them off. One Trojan tackler gets him by the neck and becomes momentarily his streamer and banner, and drops off. Big State linemen, particularly Bill's friend George Baker, throw great body-blocks that clear Bill's path, and he makes it down to the goal-line by crashing over with four men (two from each team), on him and in front of him: they all fall over the goal-line. Touchdown . . . State 12, Trojans 7. The run characterizes Bill's general determination throughout the story.

Harrison McCoy himself is so moved that he makes up with Bill in the lockers, so that after the game, amid wild celebration of a great hard victory (as distinguished from all the easy victories heretofore), McCoy himself suggests Bill & Barbara join him and his new girl to the ball. The human solution is everyone forgetting grievances, and rival lovers finding themselves appropriate mates. Which is also the way Clancy wanted it . . . because earlier he "doesn't like to fight with anybody."

*In a notebook entry from February 15, 1950, Kerouac described the emerging central figure for his novel* On the Road *as "closer to Bill Clancy, the football-hero-hobo I wrote at sixteen; also closer to Wesley Martin of 'The Sea is My Brother' [. . . .]"*

## CHAPTER ONE

Old Chet Hingham was the first to see Bill Clancy. At least, he was the first member of the Brierville township to see him.

It was a sultry August afternoon, and Old Chet was sitting at his usual post at the railroad crossing, reading the Brierville News. As he remembered it, he also had a copy of the State University Crier with him, which Scotty Cobb had just brought him that morning.

Way up the tracks, Old Chet could see a tiny speck come crawling along. After a few minutes, he could make out the figure of a young man with a pack on his back, walking the rail like an expert. A few more minutes elapsed, and Old Chet could hear the tune of "My Wild Irish Rose" come drifting over the rails.

At first, Old Chet had told the story later on, he didn't pay much attention to this bum. But when he had approached the crossing to such an extent that Old Chet could make out the sun-burnt, clean cut features shaded by an old felt hat . . . . Old Chet took an interest and put down his paper to study him as he passed by.

But he didn't have a chance to do it quietly. The young fellow stopped and addressed Old Chet: "How do you do. Could I possibly get a drink of water inside that box of yours?"

"What box?" asked Old Chet, disturbed.

"Why that thing you live in, I suppose. It's right in back of you. Can't you see it?" And he had the audacity to point out Old Chet's cherished railroad shack with his finger.

Now, Old Chet Hingham was pretty particular about his railroad crossing shack. It wasn't big, nor was it fancy. . . . but Old Chet had been working in front of that shack for twenty-eight years. And inside, it graced the finest gate-tending equipment in the county. Naturally, Old Chet fumed immediately.

"Look here, you scoundrel, what makes you think you have the right to call this shack of mine a 'Box.' I ought to be several years younger; I'd teach you a lesson or two!"

The young man had a charming smile, and when he turned it on, Old Chet Hingham couldn't help but like him a little bit despite his disparaging remarks.

"If you want a drink of water, just wait outside here," Old Chet finally said. "I'll get you some."

"Thank you very much," the young man had said, the smile still creasing his bronzed face. "I'll need it."

From inside, while he filled a quart bottle full of water, Old Chet called out: "Where you from?"

"Nowheres," had been the calm answer. "I'm just drifting along."

Old Chet came out with the bottle of water.

"You mean to say that you haven't even got a home!"

"Well, not exactly," said the younger, draining the bottle in record time.

"Well, where is your home?" queried Old Chet suspiciously.

"I was born in Arkansas," answered the bedraggled youth. "I left home a couple of years ago to go on my own hook."

"What did your Paw say to that?" asked Old Chet, sitting down on his stool in front of the shack.

"He died before I was born, and my Maw died when I was five years old. Instead of sticking around with my aunt and my sisters, I figgered it would be better for them if I jest drifted off. Nobody even noticed it much."

Old Chet got to like the boy from then on. He was interested, and wanted to know more: "What you been doin'?"

"Well," smiled the youngster, seating himself on the ground and leaning back on the shack, his eyes pointed to the sky. "I've been drifting for four years now. Up in Vermont, I was cuttin' trees. When I passed through Virginia, I worked on a tobacco farm. I can remember the job I had on a wheat ranch in Kansas. I don't reckon it would be very interesting listening, all those four years. Except maybe one year."

"What was that?" asked Old Chet, carefully studying the youngster.

The latter took out an old corn-cob pipe and began to fill it.

"Believe it or not," he went on, "I went to College."

"You don't say!" ejaculated Old Chet. "Why, we have a college right here in Brierville. State University."

"Have you? Well, this college I went to was out in the Middle West. One day I was throwin' rocks over the river, I forget which one. A whole day I had been standin' near the highway, tryin' to get a ride. Well, I took a little rest and got throwin' rocks for the exercise. A man in a nice coupe stopped and watched me for a while. When I turned around, he offered me a ride. The next day, I was all set for College. He was the baseball coach out there, and he said I had the best throwing arm he had ever seen. I played centerfield in the Spring on the team, and got sick of college in June. I stuck it out till the Freshman year was over, and I took to the road again. I wonder what Coach Billings must of thought of me!"

"And you didn't like college?" asked Old Chet.

"No, not much. I stuck it out for a whole year, and then I hit the road. I travel by hitchhiking and hopping freights."

"Must be sort of exciting."

"Well," said Bill Clancy, puffing his corn-cob pipe. "I figger I'll stick to drifting until I feel like settling down on a permanent job."

"How on earth," asked Old Chet, "do you manage to eat three meals a day?"

"Sometimes I stop in on a town and wash dishes in a restaurant for a couple of days or so. I get myself up enough money to eat for a few weeks, and leave. I don't like to stay in the same place long."

Up the tracks, the 2:57 was coming, heralded by a long mournful wail which traveled over the rails toward the two men at the crossing. Old Chet got up leisurely and went to work on the controls. The two long poles, striped black and white, dropped down parallel to the rails. For the first time, young Bill Clancy glanced about him and inspected Brierville. The train roared louder and louder until it thundered across the crossing, throwing a wind which knocked Bill's felt hat from his head.

When it had disappeared around the bend, Bill got up with his pack in his hands.

"Thanks a lot for the drink, Mister," he had said. "Now, if you could tell me where the restaurant is around here, I think I could stand a few days of this little burgh . . . ."

"Just down the street," said Old Chet, smiling for the first time. "Good luck to ye!"

"The same to you," shot back Bill. According to Old Chet, Bill Clancy had crossed the tracks and headed into the center of Brierville lustily whistling "My Wild Irish Rose."

"I swear," Old Chet had said. "That kid is going to do something big right here in Brierville. I have a feeling he will . . . ."

Old Chet swore he'd said that, that very same sultry afternoon.

[. . .]

## CHAPTER SEVEN

The day of the Blaine game had arrived. Thousands of cars, down for the game from the big industrial towns up north, were milling about the streets of little Brierville.

Blaine College, a set-up for the big State juggernaut, had arrived the night before after a trip of 400 miles. The team had stayed at the inn.

Nesmith Stadium was the scene of excitement. Just before game time, with the gridiron all spick and span, white lines and goal posts intact, the bands began to blare and the crowd began to arrive.

When State's brilliant blue and white colors came out on the field, worn by two dozen husky football players, the roar went up from the stands. The cavernous maw which had enveloped the players in practice now seemed to be turbulent with life.

The starting lineup began to run through their paces, a short signal drill. Then the backs began to punt and pass, and the linemen running about. Bill Clancy, who was to start at right guard, was thoroughly awed by the vastness of the big football scene. His roommate, Manny Martin, ran beside him at right tackle.

"Wassamatter, Bill? Excited, nervous?" said the rangy tackle.

"I dunno," muttered Bill, running his stubby hand through his brown hair. "It sure is a big crowd."

"Wait till the rest of it arrives. As a matter of fact, wait till the big game of the year on Thanksgiving Day!" replied Martin.

"Who's the team then?"

Martin said with a very suggestive expression: "State College!"

Coach Bob Alexander and Assistant Coach Joe Neal stood nearby, watching their charges dash about. The other team, Blaine, had now come out on the field. The stands continued to fill up, until Bill thought they would burst with corpulence.

Bill Clancy, however, had little to worry about. Barbara Barnard and he had been seeing plenty of each other in the past week, after that first official meeting at the Town Hall dance. Bill could still remember the dances with her, and the walk home, and the joking about their first meeting.

And when Bill had met Barbara on the campus, she had greeted him warily. Harrison McCoy, originally known as her beau, had now stepped into the background in favor. And this was known all over the University.

As a result, the enmity between Bill Clancy and Harrison McCoy—both of them strong candidates for All-America—had become a real feud. Both of them were angling for the same girl—and both of them had disliked each other at the first meeting. The natural result was a seething hatred on the part of McCoy, an uncomfortable dislike on the part of Bill.

Now, the game was almost ready to begin. George Baker, who had been elected captain of the varsity eleven just a few days previous, was towering over the officials and the Blaine captain out in the middle of the field. A team which has a hugely proportioned captain like George Baker always has a psychological edge over the other team. The coin was tossed, and State was to receive.

Coach Alexander got the team lined up and sent them through a final short signal drill.

The moment Bob Alexander's State eleven began to run through their plays, newspapermen in the stands immediately sensed the odor of champs. The pressbox was afire with excitement. The radio hookup man was excitedly jabbering away.

"What may prove to be the year's finest football eleven in college ranks can be seen down on the field this fine afternoon, running through its paces like a perfectly geared machine."

The backfield, composed of Felix Henderson at the quarter, who had now forgotten the first day of Bill Clancy's football career and had become one of Bill's finest friends; Harrison McCoy, the highly heralded halfback; Ben Barnouw, the passing ace; and Lou Ginelli, the big Italian fullback line-plunger, was called in by Coach

Alexander for a final word. The linemen then received their instructions, after which the entire eleven joined hands before going out on the field to receive the kickoff from Blaine.

Barbara Barnard was seated up in the stands with her father, Professor Barnard, and with Scotty Cobb. She and Scotty had become inseparable, although hardly in an amorous way. Among others in the vast crowd were Big Gertie, Old Chet Hingham, and the faculty of the University. Almost everybody in Brierville was in the stands.

And then the kickoff. The ball, gyrating end-over-end, came down on State ten yard line, where Big Lou Ginelli picked it up. He returned it to the forty-seven yard line, plunging straight ahead, with the State team blocking beautifully. And so the State football season had begun.

On the play, Bill Clancy had had a huge lump in his throat just before the kickoff. As soon as he had seen the ball go sailing over his head and beyond him to the State backs, he had sorted out a Blaine man to take out. And this he did. He hit him head on, flattening the unsuspecting Blaine player out on the green, and falling on top of him to hold him intact.

The game was on. The highly vaunted State University team was ready to show whether or not it was the mighty team it has been predicted to be, even against the weak Blaine eleven.

On the first play, Harrison McCoy was in the tailback. But the ball was snapped to a short back, Ginelli, and the latter plowed into the Blaine line like an elephant through the jungle grass. He made six yards before crumpling underneath the weight of four men.

Second down and four to go.

The team came out of its huddle and snapped into its formation with a fancy dancelike step. The glistening white helmets flashed in the September sun. The blue jerseys, with large white numbers and white stripes on the sleeves, lined up in a perfectly geometrical formation. The Bob Alexander shift had a beauty and grace about it that made the team look like a million bucks.

The brown ball, brand new and just beginning to pick up a little dirt, went spinning back to Harrison McCoy. The guard, Bill Clancy, pulled out. The right side of the line cross-blocked as Bill pulled out, accompanied by Ginelli and Barnouw. The three of them darted toward the Blaine left end, bowled him over, and went on to the close back. Behind this steam-roller blocking pranced Harrison McCoy, his long powerful legs cutting up the gridiron. He swept around the fallen end, past the bewildered close back, and down the sidelines. Right ahead of him ran Bill Clancy. Now, McCoy was on his own, and had already gained 12 yards. He went down the sidelines until almost pushed out of bounds by two pursuing Blaine backs, whence he cut back suddenly and flanked toward the left. One of the Blaine linemen dove frantically and hung on to McCoy's foot. McCoy stumbled forward, and finally crashed to the ground. Otherwise, he would have scored a touchdown; the field ahead of him had been clear.

The ball was now on the Blaine 30. First down, and ten yards to go. State again came out of its huddle, and went into their graceful shift. The ball went back to Ben Barnouw, who began to sweep the end. It was the identical play which the varsity had tried out that first day in practice, and which had resulted in a sixty-four yard jaunt on the part of McCoy. Barnouw suddenly faded from his end run, flipped a neat pass to quarterback Henderson, who in turn lateraled to McCoy. The latter had a clear field down the sidelines, and as he dashed down in a straight line, the lane began to narrow with potential tacklers. By the time McCoy had reached the 18 yard line, he was confronted by four Blaine men. With a lightning cut, McCoy veered to the left and flanked the men, heading for the goal-line in a long diagonal sprint. He reached it with plenty to spare, going over standing up.

State 6, Blaine 0 . . . . and the game was hardly two minutes old.

Felix Henderson converted the point, making the score 7–0 in favor of State U.

The crowd went berserk, and the newspapermen began to typewrite wildly. The radio announcer began to take on an "I told you so" air. Truly, the vaunted greatness of State University had been no exaggeration.

The afternoon went on, and the gridiron was dug and marred and mauled by the scuffling elevens.

When the sun was going down in the West, and the football fans all had that tired, happy look in their faces; when the stands were painted by the russet glow of sunset—the score was immense!

State—54 Blaine—0. And through the keen air of the evening sunset, there was the blast of a gun, ending the game. Seven touchdowns! Seven successful conversions by the drop-kicking Felix Henderson. And out of the seven touchdowns, five were chalked up by the Galloping Ghost of the new season, Harrison McCoy.

In the chilly locker rooms, Bill Clancy shivered as he hauled off his sticky uniform. His body gave out steam, his feet were cold. His ribs ached with exhaustion, and his head felt hot and stuffy. Under the hot shower, Bill let out a long sigh of relief; the prickly sensation of the water sent waves of comfortable blood through his wiry frame.

Milling fans filled the locker rooms, talking, gesticulating, watching the State heroes. Bill Clancy paid little attention to them, and turned on the cold water. The invigorating effect made him yelp, and he darted from the showers to his locker where he dried himself vigorously.

All dressed and with the hair slicked, Bill Clancy began to feel like a human being again. As he was fixing his tie, he nodded and smiled at the people who were surrounding him and talking all at once. He could make nothing out of it, and let them talk on.

"What tackles you made today, Clancy!" an old grad was saying. "You almost killed the entire Blaine backfield!"

"Thanks," Bill mumbled, picking up his canvas bag and hanging it in the locker.

"You were terrific!" piped someone else.

"Thank you," smiled Bill.

Outside, the sun had gone down and the stadium was literally empty, except for the scattered remains of enthusiastic fans. Bill shuddered as a cold Autumnal blast came down the mussed up gridiron and hit him in the face. There were cuts and bumps here and there on his face, and his shoulders ached. All in all, as Bill walked along toward his dormitory room, he felt somewhat weary, but happy.

There was to be a victory dance in the evening, and Bill could think of nothing but meeting Barbara there. Wearing a topcoat and felt hat, Bill strode along through the falling leaves and reached the dorm. A big yellow Fall moon was beginning to peep over the little houses of Brierville.

As Bill was about to enter into the hallway of his dorm, he noticed a figure approaching him from the sidewalk. Bill waited, until he could make out the tall graceful form of Harrison McCoy. [. . .]

# Jack Lewis's Baseball Chatter

Baseball Chatter *(this is Number Two, U.S. Cop. 1938 Reg. Pat. Off) was one of young Kerouac's many sports publications. In this write-up, as in stories in his 1938 baseball sheet the* Daily Ball, *he reports on the doings of the teams in his imaginary league: the Boston Fords, New York Chevvies, St. Louis LaSalles, Pittsburgh Plymouths, Philadelphia Pontiacs, Chicago Nashes, and others. This issue of* Baseball Chatter *stands out for the slice-of-life reporting by "Jack Lewis," a departure from the insider talk about standings, trades, star players, and the like. Lewis's dispatch opens like a short story and develops into a scene with characters, dialogue, and setting.*

Bob Chase was meditatively chewing gum and twirling apple seeds with his thumbs out of his tenth story window, when I came in with a greeting. Genial Bill Mahaffey, who used to sit in Bob's chair in the Chevvy office, would have been quite a contrast to the heavy browed, fiery eyed, and square jawed young man; Bill is a tender faced, portly person, and very enigmatic. But young Robert of the Janke men sat there and mumbled a greeting, and smiled cynically before beginning his talk.

"Howaya, Jack," said he. "I guess us Chevs are confounding you boys, hey?" I [calculated] they were.

"Well, don't always be too sure about anything; anything may happen to anything, and that's pure, common sense." Bob spat in his golden spittoon, and leisurely went on.

"Look at those LaSalles of Marty Sloane's. Now there's a real strongly loaded club—loaded with hitters and pitchers that are a revelation. But once they go on a losing spree, they're just like any other club. Take us—we were hot on the trail of the Plymouths, until they beat us the other day. They got hitters and pitchers, but they got the way of winning and they are rolling."

I wondered about the Chevs.

"We were a-rolling when we met the Plyms, but they were too— and they had a better team." Then Chase sat up in his chair and pointed a thick finger at me, saying: "That boy Pie Tibs is a real hitter—and that goes for Lou Badgurst and that Gavin kid, Tod. And Ed Stone is a better pitcher than he ever was today, and you remember how good he was one season back, with Harry Packfall's old Buicks. Yup, those Adams boys are going to town, but don't take your eyes away from my club, either."

"Say," he enthusiastically cried, "I got a pitcher that is a pitcher, and I mean that rookie Maxfield. He's got speed and control, and boy he's going to win games for us, and I don't mean maybe. And look at the way old Ed Steele and old Texas Davidson are macing that apple; and the Kelley boys, and my young catcher McGregor; and my other chuckers, especially old Joe McCann—say, we got a team that will press those Plyms to death, and don't be surprised of anything that happens here in New York—anything." And with a knowing smile, Bob spiraled an apple seed out into the spring air, down to the street where trod hopeful Chevvy fans.

# [One Long Strange Dream]

*In 1939 Kerouac described this dream to his great and good friend from boyhood George J. Apostolos. They had met in Pawtucketville after the Kerouacs moved to that Lowell neighborhood in 1932. Kerouac routinely recorded his dreams, and this appears to be the earliest surviving dream transcription. In 1961 he published* Book of Dreams, *a singular volume in American literature. In the foreword he writes: "The reader should know that this is just a collection of dreams that I scribbled after I woke up from my sleep—They were all written spontaneously, non-stop, just like dreams happen, sometimes written before I was even wide awake—[. . . .]"*

George, one hour ago, I woke up from a strange sleep. I had fallen asleep at 6 o'clock in the evening, following a Sunday afternoon dinner. I slept till 8 o'clock. During this slumber, I had one long strange dream. It was one of the most magnificent dreams a man has ever dreamed, although I hardly recall what it was about. All I do know is that my subconscious mind worked with the outside world while the dream world wove about me in a maze of stunning and mysterious and moving events.

My writing this brings to mind the time you wrote and told me about a similar situation of yours, when you had slept one day and had awakened, and had gone down to get my letter, and had proceeded to write to me and describe the mysterious mood which occurred.

This dream of mine contained characters which I am sure included you, and also someone else, and I hope you don't think this is a joke, but it was Ernie Noval. But the point is this, it was so well-woven together and my sleeping mind told it to my soul as I slept

[ 19 ]

and I distinctly recall noting this as I dreamt. One of the incidents in the dream was that my mother was sick, and that I was hysterical and you were there to comfort me. My explanation for this, however, is the fact that the picture I saw last night called "Andy Hardy and Family" in which Andy's mother was sick must have caused this event. However, I do remember that there were other events which occurred and which were perfectly Welles in character.

The main idea of me telling you this is the mood which I was in upon awakening. I sat in my big arm chair and stared at the fireplace and contemplated the most penetrating meditations I had done in a long time, possibly since I sat on your wood pile in Lowell a few weeks ago and studied the board which you pointed out to me and upon which you had told me the white cat had stared at you for nights.

Slowly, my mind unwound itself from my unearthly thoughts, and I picked up a book which I had given to me yesterday, called "How to Learn." As I read it, the materialistic world returned to me, and I unconsciously made it known to myself that I would make this book my second bible. My first bible is the Holy Bible, because of the fact that I am about to make a concerted study in religion soon, and put down my conclusions of it along with its effects and consequences. However, back to my mood. As I made my way out of it, I looked at the clock and saw that it was 8 o'clock. I jumped up and put on WABC. On came the music which seemed to fit my mood, and soon, Orson Welles' tremulous tones came over the ether announcing that he was presenting Jane Eyre. Thus, I enjoyed a program as I haven't for a long time.
[. . . .]

# Count Basie's Band Best in Land; Group Famous for "Solid" Swing

*In addition to publishing short stories in Horace Mann's quarterly magazine, Kerouac wrote regularly for the campus newspaper, the* Horace Mann Record, *in 1939–40. He covered the sports teams and contributed articles on music, including pieces on the jazz critic George Avakian (a Horace Mann graduate) and bandleader Glenn Miller.*

"I want guts in my music!" Count Basie once said publicly. "No screaming brass for me," he had added, "but I do want plenty of guts in my music."

And so, without any screaming brass, the Count managed to weld his unit into a terrific gang of soloists and ensemble players. Much to the dismay of most of our present day "swing" bands, they cannot be terrific unless they tear off some deafening brass measures to send the jitterbugs out of the world. Count Basie's swing arrangements are not blaring, but they contain more drive, more power, and more thrill than the loudest gang of corn artists can acquire by blowing their horns apart.

Possibly, excepting Duke Ellington, the Basie band is the most underrated and greatest band in the country today. Unlike the vacuous phraseology of pseudo-swing bands, Basie's stuff means something. As for solo work, there is no greater assortment of soloists to be found on any one band-stand.

Taking these stars apart, we can well realize why the Basie ensemble is the best in the land. Since the old days in Kansas City, these boys have been jamming together, causing a magnificent blend of musicians familiar with each other's peculiarities and ideas, and a subsequent precision of play.

To begin with, the Count has the greatest rhythm section in the history of jazz, and this has helped his other great musicians to improve. The Count himself is an outstanding soloist. He is a thrilling player with tremendous ideas. He ranks at least third among the best pianists of the swing world. The rest of his rhythm section is composed of Jo Jones, Walter Page, and Freddy Green.

## JONES FINISHED DRUMMER

Jo Jones is the most finished drummer in existence. It is interesting to note how he keeps the beat going when he takes a solo on his hides, unlike the ordinary drummers who stop all activities when they set sail on their riflings. Freddy Green's steady guitar work has been unparalleled in jazz since the days of the old school guitarists. When Freddy Green starts his rhythm going, in unison with Walter Page's mighty bass-playing and Jo Jones chimes in on the drums, you have the rhythm section that every maestro dreams of.

But that is only half of it. The Count's soloists are all good, especially Lester Young, Dickie Wells, Harry Edison, and Buck Clayton.

Lester Young, who is now rated along with Coleman Hawkins on the hot tenor, is the Count's outstanding soloist. Lester uses a different riff on every chorus, and his enormous store of ideas enables him to take an unlimited number of solos. His phrasing on jump numbers is unequaled, while he is highly proficient when it comes to blues. It would be safe to say that Lester Young is actually popularizing the tenor sax, an instrument which the ordinary jitterbug cares little for, because he would prefer a screeching trumpet a la Clyde Hurley. Young's playing may turn the trend of public interest to the tenor sax, because he is really a master-mind with that horn of his.

Besides Lester Young, Buddy Tate plays the tenor in the first chair. Tate is a stylist, and has an individual style definitely distinct from Young's, which adds a touch of variety to the Basie reeds. Earl Warren and Jack Washington are the other two saxists, each of whom are better than average. Lester Young is also a terrific clarinetist, but he rarely plays it except to mess around someone else's solo in the background. The same for Washington's alto yet to be heard.

Harry Edison, a powerhouse trumpeter, with a choice individuality of ideas, is featured in the brass section. His marvelous control, and the thrilling manner in which he delivers his trumpet solos makes him the equal of Buck Clayton, the other trumpet ace.

# CLAYTON RANKS WITH BEST

Clayton, who has improved a great deal in his long stay with Basie, has beautiful tone and some wonderful ideas. Clayton ranks, in fact, with the greatest trumpeters of all time. Al Killian, who recently joined the band at the Golden Gate Ballroom, has taken Shad Collins' place as lead trumpeter. Collins had been an amazing high note trumpeter. Ed Louis, a good hot player, occupies the other chair.

However, the thing which makes Basie's trumpet section what it is is the definite clash of style, provided by Edison and Clayton.

Dickie Wells, probably ranking alongside of Higginbotham, Keg Johnsen and all the other great slip-horn men, is the man who provides those stirring trombone passages for the Count Basie orchestra. Dickie has a torrid accent on his phrasing, and is purely hot. It was unfortunate that Ben Morton had to leave the Basie band last month, but Wells will carry on. Vic Dickerson replaced Morton. The other trombonist is Dan Minor, the veteran first chair man. Morton had been Basie's straight player and hot man before leaving.

One could pick up a dictionary and cast all the superlatives in existence upon the Basie group, but it still wouldn't suffice. Words cannot explain the meaning of Basie's music, both to the listener, and to the good name of swing. A marvelous drive, borne by the assurance of over-talented musicians, makes this group what it is—the last word in music.

Supplied with an amazing group of soloists, Count Basie's orchestra has all the necessary harmonious technique and life conducive of REAL swing bands—and we do mean Basie.

(This is the first in a series of articles dealing with the nation's leading swing orchestras, written by Jack Kerouac and based on theories and opinions derived from Seymour Wyse, Donald Wolf, and the author himself.)

# Go Back

*The next five selections were written by Kerouac in the summer of 1940. In May 1955, working on what became his Buddhist document* Some of the Dharma, *Kerouac referred to these early pieces: "[. . .] I should have been told to stay home, in the sandbank, in the woods, praising Nothingness as I had done that Summer layin around the grass with dogs and Walt Whitman and grass 'tween my teeth, and I guarantee you there would have been no torrent of suffering—Everything I did as a kid was instinctively right—[. . . .]"*

One night I sat on the curbstone of a street in the city and looked across the road at a little rose-covered cottage which was rickety, like the fence around it, and it looked old, not Colonial, but old. That's where I used to live, I said aloud to myself in a tone of yearning. I tried to sigh like they do in plays, but it was a fake one. I didn't want to sigh, but I tried. The thing I really wanted to do was weep, but I couldn't do that either.

The city was all about me, and the electric lamp above me, and the house was there and my memories flashed through my head and the scene before me supplemented them. I, small and dreamy, dashing about—over that banister, up that old tree of mine, around the yard, through the back fences . . . . . . and the shed with the old organ in it, and the sounds I used to hear and now they are dissolved, their scientific sound waves far away.

I saw a man walking toward his destination and I felt bad. He was hurrying, and I was sitting thinking about the past. The dream I used to have . . . . . . snow, tinkling icicles, laughter, sunshine, sleighs . . . . . . and the nightmares too. And the man was hurrying and I was sitting quietly, staring at my old home.

The old cat, I thought, a bundle of bones now, somewhere. The cat who used to sit right there on the porch, placidly enjoying his digestion.

Later on, I left and I went toward the house before that, where my brother had died. Here, the memories were now vague and childish. I was three and four there, three and four years old.

I remembered the high snow, my sandwich, calling for my mother, weeping, all. Myself . . . . . at the church . . . . . unabashed, they burying my brother. Why do you cry, I ask my mother and sister. Why do you cry? Why?

Now a man comes up the street and walks right into my old house.

Zounds, I say. Zounds! You hurry while I stand here, trying to recapture the past. And here you are, brushing it aside, the past of tomorrow, which is the present of today, you are brushing it aside as you stride along, intent on your cheap present practical and physical desires and comfort. You fool! Wait, don't hurry.

Get out of my old house!

And then on the way home, I think about the fool and the other fools, and myself a fool. Hurrying away the past of tomorrow, like I had hurried away the past of today, in the past.

Fools, I think. Myself a fool. I must take it slow now and look at the present and say to myself: Look, John, hold the present now because someday it will be very precious. Hug it, and hold it.

And just yesterday I was sauntering home thinking about the future. The future! What a fool, I, myself, a fool, hurrying.

# Nothing

I am going to write about nothing. Nothing at all. Did you ever think hard and say, what is nothing? Nothing is really nothing at all to try to figure out.

Look, a comet comes down from nothing crashes into the earth and the earth is scattered to the winds of nothing in little pieces and suppose I survive and you survive and we begin our journey through nothing.

How would you like that? I would like that if I could be conscious of it. It would be a great experience to travel up and down and to the left and the right through nothing at all and just keep traveling around and seeing nothing but distant stars and feeling nothing 'neath my feet and just flying about through nothing.

If I could live through it I would enjoy it. But soon I would get hungry and I would want to eat something but there is nothing in the line of something in nothing, so that I would starve to death and then I would be traveling through nothing but then I myself would not know about it so that I would not enjoy it. Because enjoying is a sensation of living, as you know, and to enjoy you must live and all that, etc. And so it amounts to nothing, nothing, nothing. And soon I guess things would get at me and I would soon dissolve, and then absolve into nothing and become part of nothing.

I know some day I will be nothing. (Think hard I say to myself. Think very hard and consider yourself nothing.) I will be nothing someday because I will be part of the dust of the earth which will scatter to the winds of nothing (not the four winds of the earth, but the sextillion winds of nothing) and I will scatter and fly about through nothing and be nothing. Maybe—a million years from now. And I will be nothing. I try to think hard and imagine myself nothing, but I am too much alive to think myself nothing so that despite the fact that I know its inevitability, I feel as if I'll always go on, but I know better.

And when the dust of the earth will scatter to the winds of nothing, then even the particles of dust themselves will begin to dissect themselves and they themselves will emulate the earth's big act of dissolving and dissolve themselves. Then the particles of the dust particles will in turn dissolve, and this process will continue a million billion times over and over again until the particles will become so small that they will not be far from nothing. Then when eternity ends, the process of making all the particles of the earth into nothing will have been completed. And so I say eternity will never end, because that is what it means. So I look at it this way: When I look into the sky and see nothing (space is nothing) I should kneel down and weep with joy at the marvelousness of such perfect nothingness. Can you imagine how many billions of aeons nothing had to go through before it reached its stage of nothingness? I imagine it because I just found out that the earth will never quite completely be nothing.

# A Play I Want to Write

*Eighteen-year-old Kerouac wrote about the "spontaneous burst of passion" that would make him "rush to [his] typewriter" and the idea of writing about "life as life is." In capsule form this essay describes the technique and vision that occupied him for the next thirty years.*

This summer, I am going to write a play and I don't quite know what it will be right now but I know it will be done at my very best, which I am afraid isn't much. As far as I'm concerned it will be satisfactory to myself at least, and I shall have the pleasure of reading it in future years and think and say: I wrote that when I was 18 and when I wanted to become a playwright because it was the most interesting, fascinating, marvelous, romantic way of making money anybody could invent. So I will write this play.

My mother bought me a looseleaf book with a thick bunch of papers inside which I will be able to extract to type on as I evolve my play, and then put them back when the magic words of man will have been imprinted on them. On the outside of this unimportant looking little black book I will stick a paper on which I will write this: Kerouac's Works, and above that I'll have the name of the play, which I will try to make as vague as possible.

The setting for this play will soon hit me in the face. I am waiting for the moment this summer when I shall be sitting or walking, but all the same breathing, and suddenly I will start with a jump and say: What a setting for a play!

This play of mine will have to be a spontaneous burst of passion which I will develop all of a sudden, then I shall rush to my typewriter and begin to extract pages from the book and begin writing my full-length three act play. When I shall have had finished it, and have had smoked about two packs of cigarettes which I don't inhale but just smoke because they help me write, then I shall read it to myself at night by the lamp and when I finish it I will say: Now I will let my father read it, and my better friends, and finally Pete Gordon of New York City and if he likes it, then I will send it to Mr. Golden or Mr. Harris or someone on Broadway and I will net a quarter million dollars and pull in the Pulitzer Prize and the Nobel Literature prize for $50,000.

$16.83 I collected today for my salary, selling subscriptions for the newspaper. I was sitting in the car with the check in my pocket and I was riding along with the fellow who takes care of the Sun insurance and a little child between us and I thought: I will write a play about life as life is and I will wait till it hits me in the face before I write it. Then I will rush to my typewriter and write it. So hold on to your seats. It will soon come and I feel terrifically exuberated right just now.

# Concentration

*One of the busier streets in 1940s Lowell, Moody Street be-
gan in the shadow of City Hall, ran past Little Canada,
crossed the Merrimack River, and continued into Kerouac's
section of the Pawtucketville neighborhood. The street was
named for Paul Moody, a master mechanic of nineteenth-
century Lowell. Its bars and rowdy enticements made it a
favorite destination of military personnel on leave during
World War II. It was the model for Rooney Street in Kerouac's first novel,* The Town and the City. *Kerouac renders
the sensations of Moody and finds earthy and other-world
glory in the beer, steak, fiddles, and men. In "Essentials of
Spontaneous Prose" (1957), Kerouac writes: "Begin not
from preconceived idea of what to say about image but
from jewel center of interest in subject of image at* <u>moment</u>
*of writing, and write outwards swimming in sea of lan-
guage to peripheral release and exhaustion—[.]" In his
essay "The Great Rememberer," John Clellon Holmes says
Kerouac wrote "astonishing sentences that were obsessed
with simultaneously depicting the crumb on the plate, the
plate on the table, the table in the house, and the house in
the world [. . . .]"*

*In 1958, Kerouac wrote to Elbert Lenrow, his former
teacher at the New School for Social Research in New York
City, telling him about the recent appearance of his aes-
thetic statement "Essentials of Spontaneous Prose": "My
new theory of writing, my old original one of boyhood actually, is contained in* Black Mountain Review *no. 7 just
out [. . . .]"*

I shall now write about Moody Street.

Furthermore, I shall concentrate. Even further, I want to say right here and now that it will be a poor job because I haven't my typewriter propped up on a little table on the pavement of Moody Street with the milling things and people all around me—and the smells of beer and beer and beer. But I will attempt. A little concentration may do the trick.

Beer and beer and beer and sizzling grease in a pan with a pat of steak and sizzling and sizzling and grease and beer and now and then, liquor. Noise and noise and cars, and gutters filled with cigar butts and matches and dusk and god's earth and little children running about oblivious and men with white shoes with women without white shoes. And now music with fiddles and beer is acridly predominant and laughter laughter laughter only a little bit of weeping here and there, though hushed and under. Undermining filth. Undermining filth and undermining horror. Weeping—not of little children, only of old men and middle-aged women—oblivious of their weeping. Young men very young with life and being men and living and walking and breathing and most of all thinking and talking. Most of all, talking. And occasionally other young men, very rare young men, laughing with pure joy at the fiddle music and the beer and the middle-aged women and laughing with the little children. And then these young men weep, until the beer is inside them and then the beer is man and man becomes flush with joy and ambition and he talks—but now, most of all, he thinks.

And the cars and the music and the beer; the gutters, the little children, the old men, the middle-aged women, the fiddle music . . . . . . and all sorts of things and sounds.

And these unusual young men. I remember one night when they were men with beer in them and they entered the gay barroom and they drank beer. Later, they told everybody that they were God.

Can't you see, George was saying to the man in the lavatory who stood swaying with half-closed eyes. Can't you understand that you are God. God! Do you hear, God!

And I espied another and I took him by the lapel and I say, And you too are God. All of you are, but you do not realize it. Laugh and smile, and close your eyes. But do not weep for your own sakes. You are all Gods.

On the way out, forcibly, a fat woman leaning against the car, alone, waiting—and George is saying, You are God's receptacle. And I was dubious, for a woman is man, only a female. But George is stubborn and regards them as God's (man's) receptacle, and I don't know, but I do know the sounds and smells and beer beer beer and little children joyful, oblivious, really weeping.

# We Thronged

*Kerouac noted that the following was a "story of the nights with Sebastian Sampas (Anzio) and Wm. Chandler (Bataan)" and was written in June 1940. William Chandler was a casualty in the battle for the Bataan Peninsula in the Commonwealth of the Philippines in 1942, soon after the United States entered World War II. Sebastian Sampas died in March 1944, after being wounded in the Battle of Anzio on the western coast of Italy. Kerouac opens Chapter Three of The Town and the City with an extended description of the same episode described below: "'We thronged!' shouted Peter triumphantly."*

It was midnight and so we talked about eternity and infinity and the government and Reds and women and things and even plays. You won't sleep out in that field with those two fellows, said my mother, so we had to take the blankets we had sneaked and pile them in a corner and sleep in the house and so we talked all night instead of sleeping, and then at 3:30 A.M. we set out.

The morning mist fascinates me, and once before I wrote about it. Now it was hanging around the woods, dripping its fingers about and hugging the ground, and making it wet. We walked through it and recited poetry and shouted. When we got to the stream, which was wide enough to swim in, the sun was just beginning to make the Eastern sky red. I ran up the hill like a deer and stood with arms folded and feet wide apart, like a Knight I thought, and waited for the sun. They stood on a hill which was lower than mine so that I was king of the world. I looked and waited.

Just before the sun came up, Sam began to sing The Road to Mandalay, and we were in the New England forest but he sang it well. And I thought of Mandalay, which I had never seen. Then I looked up and bent way back and saw the sky and said, spaceless. Then I felt how solid New England was under my feet and I jumped hard on it to make sure that it was solid—then I looked up at the sky and said, spaceless and unsolid.

The world is round, I said aloud and Sam sang, Come ye back to Mandalay. And I said, New England. Solid New England. Did you ever know how solid New England is, or even Arizona. Stand on the Arizona ground and look up and then bend back far and look up some more and you'll realize. So I stood and listened to the song of Sam and the song of the birds, and Bill he sang too. I started to sing Mandalay too, but then I stopped singing and yelled out, Solidity. And Sam said, Solidity and Bill sang some more.

Oh, then the sun came up and it painted things red and the wet ground, solid under my feet, remained thus and the sky remained endless and even scattered—yes it was scattered all over the place. It was supposed to be endless, but it seemed to end where the sun came up, but I know better because I took Geography and I am 18 anyhow and so I knew and I thought about the solid ground and how we had thronged, the three of us, through the gorgeous woods to see the sunrise. On the way back, I paused to sit on a tree which hung out over the water and I looked into it and said, Lucidness. And when the sun filtered through some leaves Sam said, Chambers of beauty. We walked home and I picked flowers like a fool but I smelled the solidity of their odor so I picked them. Then we saw two women walking to church which was two miles away and I said, Fear.

# [A Day in September]

*This story prefigures Kerouac's 1942 novel* The Vanity of Duluoz, *with Richard Vesque standing in for Robert Duluoz. Lowell is cast as Galloway, the name Kerouac maintained for his hometown when he wrote* The Town and the City *from 1946 to 1949. Vesque reappears as a character in the later story "Famine for the Heart." The name is right out of Kerouac's deck of character-name cards. In 1950 he wrote to Franco-American poet Rosaire Dion-Lévesque of Nashua, New Hampshire: "I'm very glad and honored that you wish to write an article about me for* La Patrie, *especially as it will be written by a man whose name is the same as my mother's maiden name and who comes from the town of my ancestors."*

*Vesque has William Saroyan's short stories in his bedroom. Many of Saroyan's early stories feature introspective but fired-up artistic characters and deal with city life and ethnic American families. In a winning letter written to Saroyan in 1942, Sebastian Sampas explained that he, Kerouac, and their friend Bill Chandler in 1939 had discovered Saroyan's first book,* The Daring Young Man on the Flying Trapeze, *and asked Saroyan to write a note of encouragement to his admirer Kerouac: "God! If you could read his manuscripts to see the stuff he has got."*

*In the preface to* The Daring Young Man on the Flying Trapeze, *Saroyan offered rules for writers: (1) "Do not pay any attention to the rules other people make [. . .]"; (2) [. . .] "write the kind of stories you feel like writing. Forget everybody who ever wrote anything"; and (3) [. . .] "Learn to typewrite so you can turn out stories as fast as Zane Grey." He added: "Try to learn to breathe deeply, really to taste food when you eat it, and when you sleep, really*

*to sleep. Try as much as possible to be wholly alive, with*
*all your might, and when you laugh, laugh like hell, and*
*when you get angry, get good and angry. Try to be alive.*
*You will be dead soon enough."*
    *Writing in* Archetype West: The Pacific Coast as a Lit-
erary Region, *William Everson places Saroyan and Ker-*
*ouac in the "school of naked experience," an approach to*
*writing that he links back to Jack London. Everson de-*
*scribes Saroyan as "a kind of precursor to the Beat Gen-*
*eration, advocating the 'Go, go, go!' philosophy. . . ."*


You would hardly expect a day in September to be colorless, humid,
and depressing. On the other hand, you would expect a day filled
with the happy tang of the fall, the keen bite of the leaf-blown
winds, and people wearing the dapper autumn clothes of the brown
and green, and feathered felt hats, and well-cut topcoats blowing
and whipping around your body in the wind. But, reflected Richard
Vesque, what a man expects in life never seems to be what he is re-
warded with. You might say, he thought, that anticipation is what
makes you feel happy. But if anticipation is always to remain below
the actual standards of realization, how can a man be happy in such
a world?
    And such was this day in September, a wet day with a long gray
face. And, to make it worse, the wetness of this day was only a sug-
gestion, a provoking dampness from yesterday's rains; you might at
least be assuaged by a neat downpour of rain, glistening streets,
dripping eaves, gurgling gutters; a resolute water-shedding that
made you feel like reading a book in the parlor, snugly content inside the heart-warming ramifications of man.
    But, no, there was no rain. The heavens were swept by large gray
clouds, with an even grayer background. The streets did not glisten,
but were damp and steaming. Everything was damp and steaming.
    Richard walked past the city library and looked at its moist
granite-blocked structure, a looming castle of books, as dreary and
joyless as the day. But inside, Richard could picture the reading
room, strewn with tables and chairs and busts. And in one particular corner, where the bookshelves seemed thickest and most forbid-
ding, Richard's own nook.

All the way up the street, he could see the familiar shamble and lean of objects which you have been looking at all your life: storefronts, telephone poles, filling station pumps, bakeries, trees rising from cement sidewalks, extinct trolley tracks, fences plastered with posters, barber shop poles whose limitless energies had fascinated his stare since childhood. And above all this hovered a gloomy, tasteless sky.

A man may be walking up the street like this, completely wrapped up within himself, and satisfied in his solitary observations. And in such a state of mind was Richard as he strode up the street, his wet soles making an irritating crunch as they ground into the sand on the cement. A man may be doing just this, and in such a case, be truthful and completely himself, with no quarter to ask and no desire to tyrannize anyone. He is just walking on a street in America. But suddenly he is accosted by an acquaintance, and immediately this man is no longer truthful and philosophic and meditative; he has to apply himself to the other individual in such a way that he becomes partly submerged within the other's ego-universe, and in so doing, loses his own private dignity.

"Hello Richard," is the greeting.

Richard whirls, looks at the accoster, recognizes the features, thinks for a brief second, and then finally says: "Oh hello Walt!"

"How you doin'?" asks Walt, not really wanting to know.

"Swell."

"Still goin' to school?" asks Walt, the accoster.

"Yeah. I'm a Post Graduate in High this year."

"What are you studyin'?" is the next query.

"Accounting and shorthand. I'm going to Galloway Commercial College next year." Richard answers these questions politely and in a friendly manner, although he has no real desire to be friendly. But way down deep within him, he feels the necessity of making the other fellow feel good.

"Good!" ejaculates the other. "Good goin'."

"What are you doing, working?" asks Richard, knowing that the half-way mark of the conversation has arrived, and knowing that this question is as inevitable and necessary in social contact for him as death, taxes, and war seem to be inevitable and necessary for mankind.

"Yeah. I'm workin' in the Nostrand," is the answer.

The Nostrand is a by-word in Galloway; it is a large cotton mill.

"Day-shift?" asks Richard kindly, showing by his expression that he hopes it so.

"Yeah."

"Good!" says Richard. "Good thing you're not on the night shift."

"You said it, Dick," agrees the accoster.

And now comes the pause. Both sides have given short accounts of their contemporary progress. Life, at this very moment, is hinging on jobs, day-shifts and night-shifts, school, how one is doing, and studies. Life, that rich adventure, is narrowed down to a few terse sentences and obliging smiles; it has lost its grand luster, it has become nothing but a sidewalk conversation, looking into a mill-hand's fretful eyes, smelling the smoke of his cigarette, noticing his oil-stained overalls, and being open for the outpouring of the mill-hand ego-universe—a universe of the terror and death of early morning, of walking to the mill in the cold morning drawing from a cigarette butt, of the tin lunch-box, of the terrible maw of the mill with its full-faced heat and aromatic dyes, of walking home in the sunset, of a supper tasting cotton, of standing on the corner and dis-cussing the Red Sox, of going to bed because you have to get up early to go to work.

The pause is just long enough, and to the experienced mind of Richard, it means the end.

"Well," smiles Walt, the millworker. "I'll be seein' you Dick. So long!"

"So long!" smiles Richard, turning up the street to resume his walk. "Take it easy."

And now life broadens suddenly and swiftly. Life is no longer the ego-universe of the millworker. It is the ego-universe of Richard Vesque, and consequently, so much better and greater and more ap-propriate. The ego-universe of Richard Vesque is the greatest ego-universe of all time.

Walking home from school, it seems to Richard Vesque that he must hurry. There is no reason for it, because it is two o'clock in the afternoon and there is no one home, but nevertheless Richard walks swiftly and eats up the distance eagerly. Something prods him to hasten; he knows there is nothing at home but the kitchen with food in it for him to eat, and an empty, silent house. Yet he hurries as if he had an appointment with someone that he must keep. And, as a result, he suddenly finds himself at the foot of the staircase leading up three flights to the flat. He opens the mailbox, locks, and slams it. He starts to climb the stairs. At each floor, he turns wearily with hand on the banister post, and begins another ascension. Finally, he stands before his door. He is heaving and panting, and there is a clammy sweat on his face. The banister itself is clammy. The gray light outdoors finds its way into this hallway and renders it dark-gray, sad, and dimly sullen. Richard sees this, and unlocks the door leading to his home. He walks across the threshold and closes the door, and then crosses the flat to his room where he literally tears off his clothing and flops onto his bed, almost nude, with a tremendous sigh. At this gray moment in life, Richard thinks that he cannot make it; that he is not equal to life, and will soon have to give up; it is too hot, too humid, his hair is too often in his face, he is too skinny, it is too gray and gloomy and discouraging outside, there is no great symphony of conquest ringing through the corridors of his world, only a long series of dull days. Life is too funereal, too painful, and has no rewards.

Richard lies there on his back, wearing only a small pair of trunks, and stares at the cracks in the ceiling, noticing how they resolve themselves into shapes of mountains. It is two o'clock in the afternoon, the house is empty, and life drags on.

There is a copy of William Saroyan's short stories on the bed. Richard picks it up, reads a few lines, and drops it again. His eyes are too heavy and his mind too despondent; he couldn't read a page if he had to, even Bill Saroyan. Richard closes his eyes and feels his nude body begin to cool, until finally his body begins to be coldly clammy. It clamors for the need of warmth. Richard moves his tired bones, slithers in bed, and then stays limp.

"I can't make it," he says out loud. "I'm going to die like this, freezing in a cold, empty house, at two o'clock in the afternoon on a gray day."

Five minutes of staring at the ceiling and thinking of nothing, and then Richard finally rolls over and over to the edge of the bed, and then swings his legs down. With a crazy little cry, Richard begins to dance around the room, and then with a mad whimsy, takes a swan dive back onto the bed where he lies with his face submerged in the pillow. He yelps into the pillow, and then he makes ominous dragon growls. Then he rolls over and over until he again swings his legs over the edge of the bed. He stares at the floor, sighing through his teeth and making crazy sounds come out of his throat.

"I'm crazy," he concludes, beginning to dress.

Dressed, he goes to the kitchen and opens the pantry door. He finds a box of crackers, takes it down. He finds some peanut butter, and some cold milk in the ice box. With a knife, he butters the crackers; he pours the foaming milk into a glass, and seats himself at the table, putting a newspaper under his meal. It is the funny page, and as he eats and drinks, he studies the comics carefully. Even the funnies are gray and colorless, but although their world does not cry with color and dazzling light, their deeds are romantic. Richard turns on the radio to an all-day recording program, and listens to the announcer making his commercial with a trained, enthusiastic, precise voice. And then the music comes on, and the empty house is filled with music, but it's only from the radio. Life is still gray; the music is joyful, but it is a sad joy that does not go beyond the radio, and fails to penetrate the invincible gray wall of life. It is a music that is thwarted, yet goes on self-sufficient and self-satisfied.

Richard goes to the window and looks down the street. A yellow bus goes by and a man comes down the street on a bicycle. A newspaper boy is untying his pile of papers, his wagon ready. Somebody is coming out of the barber shop, yelling back into it and laughing as he goes across the street to the Club. Inside the Club, Richard thinks, he will have a glass of beer to celebrate his new haircut. Richard presses his nose against the window pane and crosses his eyes. "What a screwy world this is!" he says out loud. "There's nothing in it. Everything is gray, even my eyes."

Richard gets up from the chair and goes to his room. He lies down on the bed and drowses off, saying: "To hell with it. I'm going to sleep it off."

And he does.

# [I Know I Am August]

*Kerouac notes on this typescript dated 1940 that the first five lines are a version of Walt Whitman's (from the long opening poem of the 1855 edition of* Leaves of Grass, *later titled "Song of Myself") and the remainder of the poem is his writing. In a journal entry from June 4, 1941, Kerouac writes: "Again got up late. Read more Whitman—great man, regardless of what they say. True, he may be an old sensuous wolf, but his philosophy of individualism cannot be beat—although his democracy is inapplicable. [. . .] Here's something from Whitman that is deathless:*

> *I know I am august*
> *I do not trouble my spirit to vindicate*
>   *itself or be understood,*
> *I see that the elementary laws never*
>   *apologize.*

*Also, about man:*
>   *WHO GOES THERE?*
>   *HANKERING, GROSS, MYSTICAL, NUDE . . . .*

*My next reading will be London & Wolfe."*

*In 1950 Kerouac wrote to New England poet Rosaire Dion-Lévesque, who had published a French translation of Whitman's* Leaves of Grass: *"Whitman was my first real influence; it was on the spur of reading Whitman that I decided to cross the country."*

I know I am august
I never trouble my soul to vindicate itself;
I see that the elementary laws never apologize.

What is this blurt about vice and about virtue?
Evil and reform of evil propels me, I stand indifferent.

There is a great song ringing through the pavilions of
    life:
Is this a paradox or is [it] a fact?
I believe the former is so.

I am no judge of Life's immutable whimsies,
But I do know that it is fraught with richness and with
    death;
And so perhaps it is better that this be no Utopia,
For what a gray tale of nothingness we could unfold
To the progeny untold
That would follow to do the same in turn.

I am a Man;
You are a Man;
We are all Men.
Thus I stand, and thus you stand, the Lord and Master
Of the domain called the Universe.

It is in times like these that I feel like taking a swim.

Sincerity is the pole-star by which I steer;
I see it here and I see it everywhere—
Even in the spiritless eyes of tired laborers
I see a spark of it.
I accept sincerity because it tops all things;
I shall have no part of the mundane.

Gluttony?
I do not believe in the word:
I am as sensate as a gourmand king,
And perhaps more. I need with a will, and fill them
    likewise.

My food is often that of books,
For in them I find the steak and the beef for my famished
    brain;
And oftentimes, for dessert, I nibble at some sweet
    Saroyan.

My pipe sends odors and aromas of delicate nicotine thru
    my nose;
Thus, I never hesitate to light it in order to enjoy further
This heaven of fine sweet smoke.
They tell me that life will be shortened, and I listen
    attentively;
But in a moment I desire my nicotine, and so I light my
    pipe
Without any regard for their solemn warnings.

# Radio Script: The Spirit of '14

*In June 1940 Kerouac and six friends (George J. Aposto-*
*los, William W. Chandler, James F. Cuerden, Frances R.*
*Hayward, Sebastian G. Sampas, and Raymond E. Walsh)*
*organized the Variety Players Group, for which Kerouac*
*wrote this script. The group was probably modeled on Or-*
*son Welles's radio drama ensemble Mercury Theater on the*
*Air. The announcer in the play explains that the author is*
*Jack Kerouac of Columbia University, and although Ker-*
*ouac did not start college until September 1940, the play*
*may date from the summer before his freshman year. It is*
*possible that he wrote it as late as the spring of 1941, sev-*
*eral months before Japanese warplanes attacked U.S.*
*forces at Pearl Harbor, on Oahu island of Hawaii, draw-*
*ing America into the widening world war.*

THEME
    ANNOUNCER: This evening, the Variety Players present
a short dramatization of the play called "The Spirit of
'14," written by Jack Kerouac of Columbia University,
and directed by William Chandler, President of the Variety Players Group.
    MUSIC: SOFT, WHILE ANNOUNCER SPEAKS IN A
NARRATIVE TONE
    ANNOUNCER: The scene is not an elaborate one. We find
ourselves comfortably settled in a comfortably squalid
barroom. Seated at a solitary table in the corner is a Legionnaire, sipping spasmodically from a glass of beer. He
seems to be expecting someone. The bartender pays absolutely no attention to him, as if he weren't in the room.
But there is a noise outside (NOISE OF HALF-DOZEN

VOICES FROM WITHOUT) and the doors of the bar-room open violently (SOUND OF VOICES LOUDER ACCOMPANIED BY SOUND OF OPENING DOOR) allowing in a group of happy young people.

JIM: Hah! We've found just the spot. C'mon kids! In we go!

VOICES: HUBBUB OF LAUGHTER, MERRIMENT, STAMPING OF FEET, SHOUTING.

JIM: Hey Bartender! We're starting off with six beers— shoot 'em right up!

BARTENDER: (FROM DISTANCE) Righto!

ANNOUNCER: (WITH THEME PLAYED SOFTLY AND HUBBUB OF YOUNGSTERS AS BACKGROUND) Our solitary Legionnaire seems to have found the party he was waiting for. He sits up straight and watches the youngsters.

JACK: Margie, you play the piano! We'll form a chorus and sing the Alma Mater! . . .

SOUND: (AFTER SHORT PAUSE, WHICH IS FILLED BY HUBBUB) PIANO PLAYING TYPICAL COLLEGE ALMA MATER SONG

VOICES: ALL SING FURTIVELY AND JOYFULLY

ANNOUNCER: Our Legionnaire stands and stares at the group of singing school youngsters. He nods his head slowly.

JIM: Hey, pipe the Legionnaire, Jack. Let's go over and talk to him, . . . . . . he seems to be down in the dumps. Here, bring him a beer . . . .

JACK: Okay.

SOUND: HUBBUB AND SINGING GOES ON

ANNOUNCER: The two college students approach the solitary table, where sits the solitary Legionnaire. . .

JIM: (SHOUTS LIGHTLY) Buck up, soldier! Here's an extra brew.

LEGIONNAIRE: Thanks.

JACK: I guess it was sorta peaceful before we got in here, huh? Cigarette?

LEGIONNAIRE: Thanks.

JIM: Here's a light. How do you like our women—not bad hey, or are you allergic . . . . (LAUGHS)

LEGIONNAIRE: I like Kipling's description of a female.

JIM: What did <u>he</u> call them?

JACK: "A rag, a bone, and a shock of hair . . ." or something like that . . .

LEGIONNAIRE: Just about . . .

JIM: C'mon Jack, let's go back and throw some ice down Ann's back. She'll tear for sure!

JACK: Wait a minute, Jim. I want to find out something. Legionnaire, do you think we'll get in this war?

JIM: WAR? Oh man, how I'd like to get at one of those Nazis?

LEGIONNAIRE (SHARPLY): It <u>would</u> be an adventure, wouldn't it.

JIM: I'll say—it'd be one honey of a vacation from school.

LEGIONNAIRE: Yes. I can just picture it.

JIM (BOLDLY): Hah! I know what you're thinking about, soldier. Well, listen, I'm not afraid of any Nazi nor any war . . . .

LEGIONNAIRE: Neither was I.

JIM: There you are.

JACK: I dunno . . . . I worked pretty hard to get to college. I'd hate to leave now to go to war and fight.

LEGIONNAIRE: Fight whom?

JIM: Why, the Nazis.

LEGIONNAIRE: (LAUGHS LONG AND LOUD) Nazis! You won't be fighting Nazis. You'll be fighting the dregs of imperfect humanity. Did you ever hear of the perfect social system?

JACK (EAGERLY): In some of Wells' Utopias . . . .

LEGIONNAIRE: Wells' Utopias are Wells' Utopias. That's where you stop boy scout.

JACK: Oh no, I don't stop there. I know they are pure fantasy . . . .

JIM: Cut it out! Both of you are breaking my heart. I'm going back to the party. C'mon Jack. He's shell-shocked or something.

LEGIONNAIRE: (QUIETLY AND OMINOUSLY) No, I'm not shell-shocked. I'm just plain shocked.

JIM (SARCASTICALLY): Shocked at what—my "impertinence" (MIMICS SCHOOL TEACHER)

LEGIONNAIRE: No, kid. Not at you. Not at anyone. I'm just shocked at it all.

JIM: (FRANTICALLY): What all?

LEGIONNAIRE: Everything.

JIM: Oh a Communist, hey?

LEGIONNAIRE: Communists don't get shocked by things . . . . they shock them.

JIM: Oh well, whatever you are, I'm going to have another beer.

LEGIONNAIRE (FIERCELY): I'll tell you what I am!

HUBBUB STOPS COMPLETELY FOR FIRST TIME IN SKIT, LEAVING A HEAVY SILENCE.

Go ahead all of you! Stare at me to your hearts' content. I'll tell you who I am! And what I am! I'm the "Spirit of '14." No doubt you've heard of the Spirit of '76. Well look me over. I'm the Spirit of '14.

JIM: So what. (BREAKS SILENCE, AND CAUSES SNICKERS AND SIGNS OF A RETURN TO THE JOYFUL HUBBUB WHICH HAD BEEN HALTED BY THE LEGIONNAIRE'S CRY.)

JACK: Shut up, Jim.

JIM: Why should I? And who are you to keep me from . . . . .

LEGIONNAIRE (IN A DEAFENING ROAR): War! (HUBBUB AGAIN DIES TO NOTHING) War! I'm the old man himself. I'm war! Look at me. Here's where my left hand used to be, way back in '14. Do you see this cute little stump? There used to be a fine, five-fingered hand sticking out from there once upon a time. Sure! I'm war! I can tell you all about it because I'm war! I can tell you about war better than the industrialist or warmonger who's caused it for his own sleazy private gain—because I'm war. He's only my creator. I'm the masterpiece that's bringing OH'S and AH'S from your European bulldogs. I'm that intangible masterpiece called war! Look at me.

VOICES OF GIRLS: I'm scared of him. Let's get out of here . . . .

MARGIE: He's crazy or something.

JIM: Shut up you empty-headed women. This guy is saying something that takes a hold of me in the insides like . . . .

LEGIONNAIRE (GASPING AND COUGHING): (ROARS) Yes! I am war! (COUGHS) I was born in the good old U.S.A. like a lot of you, but I was molded into a graceful sculptor's dream in 1914 so that I could satiate the wild creative desires of society's foppish misfits.

*Someone crossed out the closing lines of dialogue on the surviving copy of this undated radio play. The following lines are included with that advisory and with the intention of providing the final scene from one version of the drama.*

Misfits! (LAUGHS LONG AND LOUD, THEN COUGHS.) Misfits. I should say misfits when there is no word to describe such a miserable creature . . . . (GASPS) . . . Well I'll tell you . . . . I'm war . . . . . and for the good of you, and all the others—all the world to boot—I am going to show you what should be done with me.

VOICES (SCREAMS OF ANGUISH, FEAR, RIOT).

SOUND: (LOUD REPORT OF GUN, DEATHLY SILENCE FOR TWO SECONDS, AND THE HEAVY DROP OF THE LEGIONNAIRE'S BODY UPON THE FLOOR.)

JIM: He's shot himself! (FRENZY BREAKS OUT IN BARROOM)

MUSIC: (GOOD POWERFUL MUSIC BREAKS OUT FULL FORCE FOR FIVE SECONDS, AFTER WHICH IT FADES AND THE ANNOUNCER SPEAKS SADLY)

ANNOUNCER: Young Jack, with a glass of beer still shaking in his hands, stands over the body of the Legionnaire and looks down at him . . . .

MUSIC: (MUSIC TURNS FROM POWERFUL EFFECTIVENESS TO SOFT, SAD STRAINS)

JACK: Whatever the papers say, Legionnaire, I know the cause for which you died.

JIM (FEARFULLY): Suicide!

JACK (FIERCELY): Suicide? I should say not. It's something you'll never understand.

MUSIC: (AUGMENTS IN VOLUME)

JACK: No you'll never understand! God, but there's been a mistake somewhere, some time—I don't know . . . . .

THEME: ENDS WITH FLOURISH

END

# [I Remember the Days of My Youth]

*In this 1940 piece Kerouac recollects skipping high school
classes to spend time in a homely, rank hangout on a river's
edge. The invented terms and weird spellings like* fructifications, desolacy, *and* defigated *add to the texture of the
piece. This is a description of the "Club de Paisan" (in
French,* paysan *means "countryman") that Kerouac later
wrote about in* Maggie Cassidy: *"We began hitting the
Club de Paisan poolhall which was a shack in the Aiken
Street dump behind the tenements of Little Canada—Here
an old ninety-year-old man with perfect bowed legs stood
by a potbelly stove with an old French Canadian red Indian handkerchief to his nose and watched us (red eyes)
tossing nickels on the torn pool table for who gets the
break."*

I remember the days of my youth which were spent in a rickety
rendez-vous, days when school bore the promise of boredom pain
and effort, days which cried for romantic idling in secluded shacks
along the river dump. We used to play hookey from school in those
days. Days lashed by the white fury of New England snowstorms;
and a squalid, scattered conglomeration of shacks alongside the
frozen fructifications of the river dump. On those wild days in New
England, when the white sky seemed scattered with down-coming
black snow crystals, we used to wend our way down through the
frozen mass of houses which comprised Little Canada. We would
approach the Club, which was nothing but a hastily constructed
clap-board structure. In the desolacy of the storm, the broken sign
which announced the name of the Club in French seemed to be
indicative of crude, raw escapism; an escapism not of comfort or
warmth, but an escapism which howled and yearned inside the

muggy, snow-melt streaked boards. The old stove, leaning to the left, would glow with fierce heat, but the corners of our rendez-vous were as cold and bleak as the Tibetan peaks. And there was filth: Filth on the floor, in the form of cold, forgotten beans, probably fallen out of someone's plate the night before; old cigar butts, their once clammy bits now grown hard and darkly brittle in the New England cold; tobacco ashes; caps from liquor bottles; and in the tiny, nauseating toilet there was on the floor around the bowl a gangue of frozen, crispy puke and urine-seep—and in the corner, a small brain-like pile of convoluted dark-brown man-waste—if one were to poke this unholy mess of defigated matter, he would find that the crusty, dark-brown integument covered a deep-orange core of wet stuff which smelled of old cheese and acid, rank fermentation.

There was an old pool table, its green broken here and there by cue-tips. We would enter this bleak shack, put our coats on the hooks and feel ourselves shiver within our sweaters. We would run to the cue-rack for the straightest cue, and that once procured, we would rub their leather tips vigorously and happily with blue chalk.

"My break!" we would yelp happily, inside our frozen, damp shack.

"Let's toss!" Skunk would cry happily, pulling out a penny.

Skunk! How well I remember him.

He would toss the penny up and let it fall on the hard green table.

"Heads I break. Heads it is. My break."

There was an old man in that shack who used to open it up in the early New England dawn. While we were shooting pool, he would sit by the old stove and mumble to himself. An old French-Canadian with the most ridiculously bowed legs imaginable—short, convex stumps of bone and flesh, upon which he swayed about unsteadily but with firm resolution. We called him, affectionately, "Le Pere." The father.

# from Raw Rookie Nerves

*This excerpt from a twenty-five-page novella illustrates Kerouac's avid interest in baseball. He played ball with his friends in the neighborhood and in organized leagues with the local American Legion team and at Horace Mann. For most of his life he played a solitaire-style card game of baseball he had devised, keeping careful records on games and player performances. His baseball writing is represented with the best of the genre in the anthology* Baseball I Gave You All the Best Years of My Life, *edited by Richard Grossinger and Lisa Conrad. In the final scene of the novella, rookie second baseman Freddy Burns sparks a triple play that gives his Blue Sox a place in the World Series. Following is his bumpy road to big-league success.*

## CHAPTER FOUR

Lefty Hargraves was in a fine fettle that shimmering September afternoon. From the moment he stepped up to the mound, the fans in the stands could feel the spell of an old master. All over the country, rabid baseball fans clung to their radio sets, admiring the wonderful pitching performance. The first three men to face Hargraves in the first inning went down, two of them popping up to Joe Young at third, and the other striking out. Like a smooth machine, with every cog perfectly oiled and coordinated for action, Old Lefty Hargraves put away the three men and calmly strode off the mound. A long, pleasant roar of approval from the fans accompanied him to the shade of the dugout.

"Working smooth, Lefty," said Manager Joe MacNeill. "Keep him in there Kishy." To Freddy Burns he said nothing. The young rookie, his nerves raw with fear and awe, sat on the bench and quietly enjoyed the whole thing. His first appearance on a big league diamond had been uneventful, but in the least, perfect. He looked forward with apprehension to his first trip to the plate—he was to be up seventh.

"Well, well, rookie," said Nick Vickers, leaning back indolently in his seat and grinning at Freddy. "How does it feel to be a heap big Big Leaguer?"

"Swell," answered Freddy, smiling freshly. "Just swell."

"My my," said the burly red-head, acidly.

Freddy Burns turned to look at the big second baseman, and let it drop with a shrug of his raw-boned shoulders. He began to think about the ball game again. He watched the Blue Sox lead-off man, Joe Young, roll out to the pitcher. Pat Gordon, on the mound for the Falcons, wasn't starting off any too badly.

The Blue Sox left fielder, Hank Brunis, came to the plate and laced out a sweet single. Clean and neat; dropping into left field, the white pellet bobbing around the outfield. The crowd liked it, and wanted more. Bib Williams, long and dangerous, came up. He popped up a high foul, which catcher Freddy Fletcher gathered in near the Commissioner's box seat. The clean-up man had been Nick Vickers all during the season. Now the Blue Sox depended on center fielder Paul Tibbs. He was a good man, looking shabby in his uniform, standing at the plate left-handed, waving a long bat.

Tibbs was fast, and one of the best men in the league. The first pitch from Pat Gordon came near to his head and he dropped in the dust. On the next one, he leaned with abandon, and there was that undeniable clouting sound. The white pellet arched to deep right, and simultaneous with the Falcon right fielder's thrown-up arms in despair, the ball disappeared in the maze of bleacherites, appearing once as it took a hop off the stands. A true home run.

When Tibbs crossed the plate, one brown hand on his visor, the other clasped in the bat boy's, Freddy Burns felt his old hero-worship come back to him. All his youth, he had worshipped these Big League stars—especially when they trotted around the bases with the roar of the crowd in their ears and a home run under their belts. And now, as in a dream, Freddy Burns could feel the hot breath of Tibbs himself as he sat panting beside him, accepting the congratulations of his teammates with a quiet complacency.

Tony Zaven, the shortstop, struck out quietly and went to his post at the short field. The teams changed positions. Freddy was beginning to feel better, and he went out to second base feeling more like his old self. One thing disturbed him: on his way out, Nick Vickers had said something incoherently, and the others had laughed. Freddy could feel his ears burn. He could not understand it. He tried to push it back to the bottom of his mind. Manager MacNeill had given him an encouraging smile.

And there he was, Old Lefty Hargraves, working like a million, and with a two-run lead to carve on.

Like a bolt out of the blue, Freddy watched Lefty's first pitch come bouncing back to him, hissing sibilantly as it cut towards him in wild capers. A real "grass-cutter." Freddy put out both hands and took a few steps. The ball took a mean hop and caromed off his shoulder, and into short right field back of him. Error! said the official scorer. Man on first.

"It's okay, Freddy. Forget it. Bad hop!" Shortstop Zaven was talking to him amidst the roar of the fans—that roar which sounded like the sea itself—booming with maddening persistency.

"Come on, you. Wake up!" This came from the Blue Sox bench, and Freddy could recognize the rasping tone of Nick Vickers' voice despite his fear.

Now he was afraid—actually afraid. His error . . . . his and his only . . . . and there was a Falcon on base.

[. . .]

The ball game went on. Old Lefty Hargraves quietly went about his way, and emerged from the inning, still unscored on. Three pop-ups. The old knuckler was working today. And now that the second inning was half over, Freddy felt a new fear as he strode to the dugout—he was to be up in this inning. He . . . . Freddy Burns . . . . standing at the plate in a Big League ballpark, waving his bat . . . and a big time pitcher like Pat Gordon up on the mound, looking at him disdainfully.

Right fielder Johnny McRae was up first, and he made things worse for Freddy by drawing a walk. As Freddy picked out a 34 bat, Nick Vickers said something from the dugout. There were a few snickers, and a growl of remonstrance from Manager MacNeill.

"Leave the kid alone, Vickers," said Joe MacNeill.

Freddy Burns walked the Long Mile to the plate. Thousands of eyes were on him . . . on the way he held the bat . . . on the way he wore his cap . . . and Freddy Burns could feel all these things. He stepped into the holes in front of the white plate, and looked askance at Pat Gordon, cool and calm on the mound. Gordon nodded at his catcher, and Freddy could feel the Falcon catcher, conspiring behind him.

The first pitch came down, nice and big and low. Freddy swung, and to his dismay, found out too late that it would curve away from his bat. He finished his swing awkwardly, missing by a half-foot.

Whistles accompanied his miss, as if it were something sensational. A sensational miss, thought the fans.

Freddy, now in a lethargy of fear, let the next two pitches go by and was informed by the umpire that he was called out on strikes. Heavily, he walked back to the shady dugout and sat down, all eyes on him.

"What a flop!" he thought. "What am I doing here!"

Nick Vickers leaned over and poked a sardonic face before Freddy's: "Wassamatter, bush leaguer. Don't you feel at home."

Freddy felt the repugnance of the red face, topped by a fiery mop of red hair. He could feel his fists harden, but he kept his temper. This was Big League ball, not a street brawl. Vickers was probably just sore at his being barred from playing for a week, and the fine to boot. Freddy repressed a surly answer, and smiled. Hank Daniels, on the other end of the bench, smiled also. The next two Blue Sox went down in order, and the second inning was over.

As a matter of fact, the game was over as far as the records were concerned. For seven innings, Old Lefty Hargraves toiled in the broiling sun, keeping his white-wash intact. The game ended in favor of the Blue Sox, 2–0. Thanks to Paul Tibbs' home run, and Old Lefty's inspiring pitching performance. After the ninth inning, he was escorted off the field by some wild-eyed fans to the showers. Old Lefty Hargraves, a ten-year man in the Big Top, had come through just once more!

And Freddy Burns had managed to beat out a roller in the seventh inning, which made him feel better as he took a shower. Beating out a roller was a hit in any man's league, he thought. Even though he had muffed two grounders in a row in the fifth inning. Luckily, his miscues had no effect on the score, although coming close to it. And he had struck out the first and second times up, walking the third. And through it all, Freddy could hear Nick Vickers' biting sarcasm, lashing out at him after each miscue or bad play. [. . .]

# CHAPTER FIVE

[. . .]

The bomb exploded in the eighth inning [of the second game of the doubleheader]. The Blue Sox came to the dugout for their turn at bat. The shade thrown by the center field stands, where Big Bill Lacey had deposited his home run in the early innings, began to lengthen and deepen. The big crucial game had quieted down, and the Falcons were calmly efficient in their effort to hold the lead. Andy Robb was working like Hargraves had done in the first game. It might probably result in two white-washes, both ways, thought some of the fans.

In this quiet baseball scene something happened. Freddy Burns sulked to his seat in the dugout, and found the leering face of Nick Vickers in his face.

"Listen, Busher, now that you know where you stand around here, you had better get the hell off this ball club tonight!"

Freddy Burns looked up quietly, tiredly. He had played 17 innings of ball, and he was weary.

"I'll do whatever the manager, Mister MacNeill, tells me," he answered quietly.

"Yeah!" Vickers spat. "Well, I'm telling you right now. So don't you forget, Punk!"

Freddy looked out at the ball field, at the diamond, the scene of long and dusty, the nervous, scared afternoon. Then he looked at his agitating heckler. The bombshell burst. Freddy jumped to his feet.

"Look! I don't know why you hate me, but I do know that you're just a pain in the . . ." and instead of saying where the pain was, Freddy Burns whipped a hammy fist right flush into the red face to emphasize his point. The result was uproarious.

"Red" Vickers, the terror of the League, staggered back, blood streaming out of his big nose. His blue eyes fired with rage. Like a bull, he charged forward, both hands closed into big bony fists.

There was the dull, sickening impact of bone on bone—Vickers ran right straight into a perfect uppercut—and that was the end of his afternoon. He lay there on the dugout cement, breathing hard, knocked out cold!

[. . .]

# Where the Road Begins

You embark upon the Voyage, face eager, eyes aflame with the passion of travelling, spirits brimming with gaiety, levity, and a flamboyant carelessness that tries to conceal the wild delight with which this mad venture fills you. You sit in the train, and you begin to feel yourself eased away, away, away . . . . . and the gray home town is left behind, the prosaic existence of 18 years is now being discarded into the receptacle of Time. You are now moving along more rapidly, and the old town slips by in level undulance. You see the old familiar things: streets with time-worn names, houses with barren roofs and upthrusting chimneys, staring tiredly at the same old sky, the same old heavens, the same old ashen emptiness. You look at all this and you tingle. You can feel a shudder of expectancy course through your tense, vibrant body. Your eyes swell with what you think is joy. You envision the Big City—and you squirm in your seat happily.

"I hope you have a nice trip on the way over, John," your old pal said to you at the station. "And be sure to study hard, now, and get some good marks at College. And write to me!"

"Sure, Fouch," you told your old chum. "I'll write some tremendous documents and tell you all about College in detail."

And then you remember with poignant inklings of a new regret the mist in your mother's eyes as she fluttered her kindly hands all over your coat, brushing off specks of dust and infinitesimal strands of hair with a meticulous nervousness and a taut hopelessness that kindled a hot fire within your inner entrails. You don't know just what to call this hot fire which had burned your very eyes and caused them to unleash molten love in searing rivulets. Probably, you think, it is because you are leaving your Mother for the first time!

As a matter of fact, when you left your loved ones at the station, you didn't know much—all you knew was one thing: that you were leaving home, and going to College, and that a new and glittering existence awaited you, far-off and shimmering and towering into clear, lucid skies, shrieking out into space with an exultant triumph!

"Ah!" you say now, seated in the roaring train, the last remnants of your old home-town suburbs scattering by in sparse bits, as if completely blown to non-existence by the fact that you are leaving it. "Ah!" you repeat to yourself, "Now I am heading toward my goal—and I am hurtling through the land to my destination. I am no longer immovable. I am now alive!" You dream of these fond sayings with a puerile, knowing smile.

Ah, my poor little madman, still a child, why don't you open your eyes and look about you in the train. Look carefully at your fellow passengers. See those seamy, lined expressions; those tallow grimaces of mobile resignation, weariness, and impassiveness. These fellow-passengers of yours, little madman, why don't you study them carefully. Why don't you remove the mist of youth from your unassailed, unpummeled young eyes! Why don't you do this! Why must you wait for Life to beat it into you with its blunt hammer, its vulpine leer glutting above you with a fresh new triumph!!!!! But wait . . . . .

Now, it is four months later, and there is a blinding blanket of snow covering the earth. A train is wailing its mournful whistle across the alabaster wastes, and our little madman is seated in the train, going back home for Christmas, four months of College under his belt.

He is thinking of the City Hall clock, as it has winked in the night for eighteen years. He is thinking of the smell of his cellar at home; of the murmurous hush of the river at night; of the wail of the winds through the backyard trees . . . . . and then he jumps with a delighted start! For the train has begun to slow down, and he sees the familiar old Mills, stolid and bowed in the blanket ebony of the night sky, silhouetted against the whiteness of the snow. To him, they look as though they have been patiently waiting his arrival. He feasts his eyes upon them, but leaves his thirst only partially satiated. Now the train is really slowing down, and our little madman takes up his grips and rushes down the aisle. There is more to come, more miracles to be beheld, and more wonders to stun him!

"Homeville!" croaks the conductor in his wooden weariness, going to the door of the train and spitting out into the night air. Our little madman stands behind the conductor, eyes riveted upon the broad blueness of his back, the maddening bulk of this man thrust between himself and the glorious happiness which awaits him at the station.

Now! The train is easing to a crawling stop, and you wait while the torturous engineer blasts all the atoms of your existence with his damned preciseness! Slow, slowly—please get out of my way, Mr. Conductor, I want to see my old Home Town, I want to consume the sight of it, to masticate it, to slurp up its blood . . . .

At last, the blue-uniformed conductor swings down to the platform, and everything is unfolded to your clouded gaze. You see a group of old familiar faces, and you think of God as you watch the radiance and warmth sing up to your very soul. You see all that God-like essence come up to you from the dark night, and your Faith is redeemed. You see God before you, emblazoned in all those loved faces like a starry tarpaulin. The all-encompassing, all-loving God!

With all the nonchalance that you can muster, in an effort to betray your College experience, you step down from the train, your hands trembling wildly. You kiss the lovely cheek of your mother and sister, and you shake hands warmly with your father, a stout stone of integrity; and you clasp the wiry hand of your best pal.

[Y]ou realize that a man can take a train and never reach his destination, that a man has no destination at the end of the road, but that he merely has a starting point on the road—which is Home. You see it all, this epic of mankind, before your eyes; it is a limpid and awful truth, it has a naked and beautiful reality. You are now a man, little madman. When you left, four months ago, you were but a child—you with your high ideals and mad dreams. Now, I hope that you see everything, that you will from now on read it in the faces of the passengers of the world, the faces that comet across the surface of the Earth, forever searching for the destination. I hope, little madman, that you realize that the destination is really not a tape at the end of a straight-away racing course, but that it is a tape on an oval that you must break over and over again as you race madly around. And whether you give up the race after circumventing the swarming oval once, or whether you continue through the marathon alleys of life—whichever you do, little madman, you shall always return to the place where the road began.

For the place where the road began is composted of infantine hallucinations and youthful ambition, and these are deathless elements that remain within you forever.

This Home that I speak of, madmen, may be anywhere on earth. It is the soul of Man, I think, and it is a component, a mixture, a swarming vat-like concoction of all the ideals of Man, embodied upon one portion of the Earth's crusty integument, and thrust upwards in a gesture of terrible finality and beauty that shall forever beckon.

# New York Nite Club—

Outside, in the street, the sudden music which comes from the nitespot fills you with yearning for some intangible joy—and you feel that it can only be found within the smoky confines of the place. You leave the street and enter New York's night life—a sudden rush of festivity, not the wild dark festivity of Spain, but a cultured, toned festivity borne along by the nostalgic improvisations of a guitar, or the rich round moans of a Billie Holiday. There is the eternal smoke of cigarettes, the fine smell of bars ranged with colorful displays of bottles, gowned women, tuxedoed men, and those who reminisce, wrangle, and cry at the bar. You look down the bar—it is not like an ordinary bar, for there is something about the New York bars that no other bar can capture—and you see a gallery of faces, each as interesting as the other. Millions of dancing illusions cloud your eyes as you search into the eyes of these barflies—that one there looks a lot like a bookie, and the other much like an actor, and there is a high-priced harlot. Books and novels could be written about the lives of these rangy faces, these pouting velvet faces, these red lips, these dark mysterious faces, these jovial open-faced faces, these drunken dull-eyed faces. The bartender, looking a lot like a performer with the light of his brilliantly arrayed bar shining up to his face and softening it like footlights do, is mixing drinks. There is the hardness of the city in him—hardness, a certain look of hectic suspicion, a tinge of awed dismay, and an obviously false certainty that is helped along by the most mundane manipulation of a cigarette.

I remember once when I was quite childishly eating a hot fudge sundae at a fountain back home. It was raining, and I was as virile and masculine as anyone else in the place. But I was perched up on a stool and drooling in my fudge and cream like a child. I was self-conscious. Then in walked a fellow attired in soda pop clothes, a driver of the Coca-Cola trucks. He walked up to the cigarette counter with a preoccupied stride. The soda jerk recognized him:

"Howdy Joe. Just pull in?"

(Just pull in, I think. A truck driver, just pull in. Just pull in, the rain was slashing at his windshield. Just pull in, the hero. Wearing drivers' clothes, just pull in, and the rain.)

The truck driver looked carefully at his questioner, pulling out some money from his pocket and smoking knowingly on his cigarette. He answered, very curtly and with much competent authority, almost a scowl:

"Yeah."

(Oh boy, I sneer to myself. The great man, just pull in.)

I looked at him. He bought the pack of cigarettes, letting his last cigarette butt hang from his twisted mouth and spiral smoke up to his scowling eyes. He walked out, still preoccupied. A sort of false preoccupation designed to befuddle everyone with whom he communicated. Preoccupied with his paltry little truck universe, as if it were the only universe in the place. The big man, cigarette butt hanging from snarling mouth, Yeah, curtly scowling at the world, women and drink and trucks and the hell with anything and everything else.

Where is the naked unquestioning sincerity in this world today?

You buy yourself a Coke and take a table in an obscure corner. You light your cigarette and look around you. The music will soon begin—the little negro trumpeter is almost ready, but never quite begins. He holds the horn in his chubby black hands, with white fingernails, and he talks to friends and musicians around and below him. He smiles, and blows through his trumpet to emit a small round tone. Then he talks some more, jokes, maddeningly producing his horn to his mouth only to let it drop again in order to say something to the inevitable someone who is always around him. The music will never start, you say. And suddenly he starts playing on his trumpet.

Part Two

An Original Kicker
1941

# from Background

[. . .] In the Spring, I was back on the field working with the varsity backfield (Governali, Will, Wood, and I). There were glowing reports in the papers about me, but when the Fall of 1941 came, I did not return to Columbia. I had spent the entire summer writing and studying feverishly, and wanted to keep that up rather than return to a college education interrupted by dozens of immaterial activities, such as football, N.Y.A. jobs, meal jobs, typing agencies, ghost-writing and whatnot. I left Lowell and got a job in a gas station in Hartford, Conn., away from my disconsolate and reprimanding parents.

Curiously enough, I enjoyed my new status in life: it was peaceful to contemplate not being a Golden Boy of football, and to devote all my energies to writing. I wrote like a fiend, sending one radio script to Orson Welles which was never returned to me, even to this day. In the space of two months, I wrote about two hundred short stories. [. . .]

# There's Something About a Cigar

*This is one of several plays that Kerouac wrote at Colum-
bia in the spring of 1941. In a note to Sebastian Sampas
on March 5, 1941, Kerouac told him that he was hitchhiking home for a long weekend: "So that we can get
together and discuss over a banana split at Marion's, I
am bringing a one-act play I wrote this morning at 3 A.M."
Marion's was a small store with ice cream and a pool
table at 53 Martin Street in the Rosemont section of
Pawtucketville.*

A little play in several acts and scenes.

Date: March 23, 1941 Time: 1 A.M. (Date and time of writing.
This is mentioned because I feel that it will be illuminating to people to know that this thing was written at one o'clock in the morning
of March 23rd, 1941. Why, I don't know. It doesn't make any difference. As long as we get a little kick out of life, it's all right. There's
no harm done.)

Here in America last night, I saw an awful thing which people
call a play. It was awful. If that is what the theatre has come to, then
there is no hope for anyone except the cigar-smokers. Which brings
me to the issue.

Act One: Scene One: (Before the curtain is rung up, the audience
should be supplied with good fat five-cent cigars. The women
should at least light them and hold them in their hands; but the men
<u>must</u> smoke them. It is essential.

Because there's something about a cigar. As you shall
soon see.)

Ages ago, I used to lay down in the warm sun and close

my eyes. It was, of course wonderful. Like the time that I was naked, lying on my back in the grass, feeling the little insects run all over me and listening to the sound of the forest and the river. The forest and the river are just like a good cigar; they don't make any noise to speak of. A turbulent river and a forest in the morning make a lot of noise; so does a loaded cigar. But I'm talking about normal conditions, if there is such a thing.

The scene, then, is as of ages ago, where I used to be a fine poet. The sky is very blue, it is New England, there is a plowed field across the little stream, which slips by like beautiful blue-green oil. You can hear Time march on, not like in the movies, but like Time really does march on—a tremendous muffled roar. The doors in back of the stage should be open to let the sound of Time in on the customers. And it would be an outlet for the cigar smoke. Now we're all set. There is a young fellow in a bathing suit sitting in the grass, smoking a cigar. His hair is wet, and he just got out of the water. He is smoking this cigar and the first thing he says in the play is this:

Young Fellow: There's something about a cigar . . . .

(The sound of Time, the tremendous muffled roar of it all, is audible to all. If necessary, install a Time machine underneath the stage and let it reverberate in a restrained, powerful monotone. Also a few bird cheeps and lapping water. The sky is blue as hell. It is a New England sky. Blue as all hell. Now comes another young man in his swimming regalia. He is walking along the trail which follows the stream, and he approaches the cigar-smoking poet. He knows him. His name is Nick.

Nick: Where the hell did you get that stogie?

Young Fellow: At Joe's. I bought a dollar's worth—20 of them.

Nick: You did? Well, whaddaya say?

YF: Help yourself

(He does. He lights the cigar and sits down in the grass beside YF. He sighs and doesn't say a damned word. That's the wonderful thing about Nick.)

YF: That's the wonderful thing about you

<u>Nick:</u> What is?

<u>YF:</u> Nothing

(Now comes the third bather. He is <u>Walter.</u> His hair is all curled up in wet ringlets on his brow. He strides up to them with his cigarette. He has a white sweat shirt over his bathing suit. He sits down with a contented

<u>Walter:</u> Aaaah . . .

(Offstage we hear the sound of shouting swimmers. They come nearer. Now they are here, two young fellows racing. They are both naked, because they forgot their bathing suits. Anyway, nobody ever goes to this place much—that is, girls. They end their race and flop on the grass beside the three smokers.)

<u>YF:</u> Walter, throw that lousy butt away and have one of my cigars. There's nothing can beat a cigar.

<u>Walter:</u> Just as you say

(The two racers are PAUL and SEBASTIAN)

<u>Sebastian:</u> Zagg, you're not very polite. Don't you offer <u>us</u> a cigar?

<u>YF:</u> Of course I do. Help yourself. I bought a dollar's worth at Joe's

<u>Paul:</u> (Lights up his cigar; he is ringing wet.)
Broush—broush, burp . . . ahem . . . egad . . . kapf . . . kaff kaff . . . how does the stock stand today?

<u>Walter:</u> (Also assuming a business man pose):
Well, it's like this JP. Amalgamated rose two points today, but I'm afraid that Consolidated will go down (Walter does this very well, and he raises his leg to indicate a typical business man fart as he speaks. He is bursting with opulence, power, prestige, and importance. He again raises his leg.)

Nick spits calmly.

YF watches Walter and bursts out laughing. Everyone laughs, in his own way. Sebastian smiles wanly, YF laughs out loud, Paul has a pleasant high-pitched giggle that is not at all silly, and Nick slaps his thigh approvingly.

<u>YF:</u> You know, I used to smoke cigars and imitate burpers like Mouse just did. But now I've a new perspective. I

smoke cigars because there's something about them that gets me. For one thing, it's such a silly goddamn thing to do, that I have to laugh at myself. From there on, the coast is clear.

Sebastian: Laugh at yourself, and cry too. (He is getting into one of his moods, as he was in my last play. Now he springs to his full six feet and starts shouting at the top of his lungs:

Sunday in Moscow, gray gloomy Sunday in Moscow. Oh, ye bells of Moscow . . . ring . . . ring . . . I must see them. I am going there now. To Moscow . . . . (Sebastian runs off into the woods. In his youth, he read a lot about wood-nymphs and Pucks and stuff. So now he is going out to try it, naked. He is a wood-nymph too, because you can hear him all over the forest, reciting Poe's "Bells" . . . or should I say, shouting "Bells")

YF: Isn't that marvelous? And to think that the poor bastard has to get up in the morning every day and go to his business, sleepy, grouchy, exhausted, hungry, cold, sick, empty, bleak, disgusted . . .

Walter: It's a wicked world

YF: (Taking a luxurious drag from his cigar.)

But, there's something about cigars just the same. Like the time I walked out of a movie in New York and began to walk home along Broadway. I was cold, and shy of the world. Suddenly, I saw a cigar store. I said to myself, "Zagg, you're going to go in there and buy yourself a cigar. What for? I don't know. I'm glad I don't know. I don't want to know. I'll just buy one and smoke it." So I bought a cigar and lit it and walked out and went right along the street, a new man. I looked at every one with new interest, because the cigar gave me courage. It made me say: "Well, hello there. How the hell are you, you little pavement cipher, you little nameless, faceless cinder of Wolfe? I'm Zagg and I've got a cigar and I don't give a damn for anything, nor do I reject anything. I think that you've an ugly puss, but I like you because you inhabit this earth with me and we're both in the same boat." And there I was, striding along the street,

smoking my fucking stogie, laughing at the rich experience of it all. Nick farts, quietly and unassumingly.
There is a tremendous burst of laughter, which drowns
out the distant howls of Sebastian, the idealist.

Walter: (Smoking more appreciatively now)
Well I'll be damned if you're not right, Zagg. There is
something about a cigar!

YF: Well, what the hell do you think I'm telling you. I
said so, didn't I? What do you think I am, a scholar?
Or a diplomat? Or a bookkeeper? Brother, I say this
and I mean it, and I know I'm right. That's why I'm not
worried about world affairs. That's why I am worried
about the world. But I'm not the first one. As long as we
have forests and rivers and grass and cigars and human beings like you and the fellows, it's okay. There's
no harm done. World affairs go on and on and solve
themselves and then un-solve themselves; but the
world itself, she's something to worry about. She's the
only thing that we men have. And we can't have her if
we don't take time off once in a while to puff on a stogie, let's say, right in a spot like this.

Walter: I don't know what the hell you are talking about,
honest

YF: I don't myself. I'm trying to say something that's inside of me, that I'm dead sure about, but it doesn't
come out in order. Maybe someday I'll be able to do it.
That'll be my Big Day

Nick: Why did you spend a whole buck on these stogies?

YF: When I have money, it doesn't mean a thing to me.
The only time that money means anything to me is
when I have it. So I take this buck out of my choked
wallet and I buy this batch of cigars. (He takes them
out of his pocket, holding his pants up) Look at those
babies: 15 sweet little stogies, ready to be smoked.
Ready to spread good cheer, good will, and good smoke
here and there and everywhere. Poop poop. I'm going
in. It's a wicked world, so long babies, goombye, tweet-
tweet

(He rises to his feet and hurls the cigar into the water. He is very mad, because he has failed to express

himself. He dives into the water, and splashes around. We can still hear Sebastian shouting in the woods. The boys sit and smoke calmly. Suddenly, out of the blue sky, Nick speaks up:

Nick: You know what I feel like doing with this cigar? I feel like lying right back in the grass, like this (does so); looking up at the sky, smoking on it, like this (does so); laying a fart like this (does so at will); and just staying like this till I kick the goddamn bucket.

Walter: Yeah, but where does it get you?

Nick: I don't want to go nowhere

Walter: Well, brother, I don't want to rot in this little cheese town all my life. I want to go out and make dough and live right. I want to have power—tremendous power and money and property. With that, I can buy all the cigars in the world

Nick: Sure, but where are you going to smoke them?

Walter: Anyplace at all. Any place at all.

Nick: I like this place better. And I like Joe's cigars better than all the cigars in the world.

Walter: Why?

Nick: Don't ask me, kid. You know better than that. I don't know, I don't care. I just feel it in my bones. It's a wicked world, but right now it isn't.

(YF comes out of the water, dripping wet. He lights another cigar, puts back the 14 remaining stogies in his pocket, and sits down to smoke. He has given up. He no longer speaks. The play's over. The curtain comes down, this was the only act and the only scene; I'm sure that no one will like this play, but I do. Why? I don't know. I just feel it in my bones. It's a wicked world, but what the hell do I care. I can always light up a cigar and smoke it and say: "So what.")

As the audience files out of the theatre, Nick will step up to the stage for a few closing words: Nick: Don't worry. No harm done. It's okay.

# God

*Columbia freshman Kerouac lived in Livingston Hall,*
*which offered a view of the Butler Library.* Some of the
Dharma *includes a description that evokes the period:*
*"Evenings after supper in my collegeroom in Livingston*
*Dorm at Columbia, the fragrance of my old taped pipe,*
*the drowsy European momentous sad romance of Sibelius*
*or other classical musics on the scratchy QXR station, my*
*desk before me with its warm lights and studies, my*
*thoughts, self-confidences—[. . .]"*

It is I, speaking to you. I am seated here in my room, at two o'clock
in the morning. The page is long, blank, and full of truth. When I
am through with it, it shall probably be long, full, and empty with
words. It depends on God. He has endowed me with the power; my
performance depends upon the extent of his gift.

It is like this.

I am not trying to copy anyone. I am truthful to myself. I shall
write as if I had just been born, endowed with words.

As I began to say, it is like this.

Tonight, I wrote a short story for a fellow on this floor. I toiled
with it for an hour and a half. I had to make it exciting, fill it with
colorful and authentic descriptions, and pound it out into the conventional whole. That is, the wholeness of what is called the common short story. Beginning, middle, and end. It had to introduce,
enlarge, burst, and die down. So I plunged into it and finished it. It
would net me one dollar.

"With that dollar," I told myself, "I shall eat."

I was not proud of the story, called "Black Gold." The only things
about it that were worthy of pride were several descriptions. How
bullets "pinged" into iron pipes. How bullets spat into the earth,

throwing up little geysers of dirt. I am a very stinted writer. I know I shall have to correct it some day. Cliché is the word. But I had to eat, and I finished the story rapidly. I delivered the story, smoothed out the dollar into my wallet, folded it, thrust it into my back pocket, and went out to eat.

It was warm outside. The air was stifling and aggravating. I made a grimace and walked on, my shoes scuffling on the pavement. My head was slightly dizzy from the session with the typewriter.

"I have ten dollars in my desk," I said to myself in the street, "but to be frank with you, John, I wrote that story for one reason: with the dollar, I shall squander. I shall eat about 50¢ worth of food, then I shall go to a 50¢ movie. My ten dollars will be intact: it will be as if I had never spent any money, and yet I shall have eaten and seen a movie. It is great to squander, and to [be] able to walk in the street and feel free and easy. In this civilization of ours, money is a great thing."

Broadway was in a haze. The red lights were dim. There was no acute brightness. The haze of a warm day, at sunset. The air stuffy. From the Hudson, blasts of cooler air.

I entered the Cafeteria and went to the counter. I saw the food steaming in the aluminum platters.

A buxom blonde smiled at me over the food. She saw a young writer, unshaven. Open shirt, unpressed coat, unpressed pants. Young, though; and masculine.

"Meat loaf," I muttered shyly, forever in the act of trying to be as inconspicuous as possible. "Mashed potatoes. String beans. Thank you."

A glass of water, and buns and butter. The silverware. Sit down and eat, Brother. Partake. Be clever, and quote Homer: "They sat down to the good cheer spread before them."

I lunge the potato covered fork to my mouth. I lunge a piece of gravy-covered meat to my mouth. It waters for more. I butter the bread, and tear at it voraciously. Anybody watching? To hell with them, I'm hungry. String beans; potatoes; meat; sip some water, Kid, and wash it down. Cold and cool and fresh. The beverage of God. Ah, food!

I am walking out, contented. I buy a cigar at the counter. There's something about a cigar, the title of a recent story of mine.

Like a fool, I argue with myself on the way to the movie. Shall I smoke the cigar before or after the theater? I stop on the corner of the street to work out this momentous problem. If I smoke it now, I shall go into the movie a quarter hour late. And I want to see it right away, and come out early in time to make the sundae bar. The sundae bar closes at 12. All inconsequential to me and my life and you and God. And yet, standing on an American corner, in that moment of my life, I am seriously weighing the question. It is idiotic, yet sincere. I decide for the movie.

I won't describe the cinema. As usual, it stunk. One of the pictures had a lot of publicity to it—a young new Hollywood genius who injected his photoplays with hilarious humor—and yet I laughed only once: When someone fell down into a bed of flowers with an illogical crash. Can't say as I love Hollywood, you. It panders like an eager little shopkeeper. The situations are built around the time-honored ideas of woman bewitches man with curves and curls. Sure, I've been bewitched too, but we don't have to be animals all the time: every precious second, every conscious moment. But it seems to be the case most everywhere. So what am I to do, laugh at stuff like that? I sit in the theater and sneer. When the audience laughs, I turn my head slightly and say:

"Like that, boys and girls? You like that, huh?"

And boy, do they. Although, I have a confession to make for some other men. Those pseudo-masterminds who read the critic reviews and go to see the picture to laugh, because the critics said it was funny. Oh My!!!! And do they laugh!!!

"What a man that Sturges is!" they laugh. "What a man!"

Little shopkeeper, most of the time. Concession: He's better than most of them, which still isn't saying much. Do they need me up there? Of course not, I don't know how to pander. I don't want to know.

The other picture was good, until Hitler creeps in. The heroine, as is usual in these days, turns out to be a Jewish refugee from Germany. And when the hero kills a mewing little angora cat, it finished me. I walk out with my coat in my arms, completely pandered out. I love cats and hate propaganda.

I walked up Broadway and lit my cigar. There's something about a cigar. I must now come back to the beginning. I want to be candid, and truthful. I light the cigar and stroll along, smoking with relish. The world is good. I have squandered, and am plentiful with food and entertainment—neither of which was any too good—but both of which were there to take, without complaint. A dollar's worth of

New York, of America, of man's civilization. Give them the money, and they hand you the stuff. Take it, criticize it, taste it, and above all, get your fill of it. You can't be an artist unless you're a member of humanity. Hermits make awful poets, I think. You can't ruminate peacefully by a little stream in the woods unless you've just been liberated from the turmoil of civilization. Peace is a relative thing. And it always turns out to be short-lived.

I walk to Riverside Drive, talking to myself. I am feeling very truthful.

Nostalgia overpowers me as the broad Jersey coast looms across the river. I stroll along the walk, and stop to lean on the stone wall. I look down at the highway covered with whispering beetles. I see the lights on the water. I listen attentively and religiously to the all-engulfing roar of the earth and time. It's like a huge, eternal dynamo. Not a throb, but a steady breath of thunder—a gigantic sigh that never ends. The sigh of man, endless and everpresent. My cigar is wet at the stub. Warm, moist bit. The acrid bits of tobacco.

"Ah, Petit Jean," I say to myself in Canadian French. "How beautiful. How my memories return in full force."

It takes a little while, but soon I am no longer concerned with myself. The scene is too vast. The perspective is too wide. And different things occur which draw my mind wider and wider. God, Gents, is ready to walk in. And here is what happened:

I reached a huge conclusion. I reach conclusions very often, but this one is big. I have found God. It is the biggest conclusion in every man's life. And I am not hit like St. Augustine. It just comes to me calmly, with a bit of wide thinking. And here is how it came about.

First of all, a man came walking by slowly. One of his shoes creaked. His gait was steady. The creak was like clockwork. He came by, eyeing me curiously. I eyed him in my usual suspicious glare. I am very shy, you see. I am biased, like all of you. But not for long.

He goes on, the creak disappearing with him. Across the river, an incandescent sign says: "It is now . . . . . 11:38."

"Time," I say to myself out loud, puffing from the cigar. I look up at the sky. No stars: haze, darkness. A blanket over Manhattan. Time marches on like the rush of the falls: steady roar of milliseconds, one upon the other.

The time of man, I think, and the time of God. Time of man in numbers, time of God in the moment before a shooting star shoots, and after it fades. Time is there, no doubt. No philosopher can crap me about that. Advance of events, if that is what you want to call it. Advance of something, at any rate.

The sign: "Time is now . . . . . 11:40."

The creak is returning. The roaring hush goes on. The creak is nearer. I look up and see the flirtatious eyes of a homosexual, walking by with a steady creak of leather. Invariably, I start timing the creak with the cigar in my hand.

"Beat . . . . . beat . . . . beat . . . . . beat . . . just like clockwork."

I look at him with a disgusted glare. His eyes are wild and primitive. Lust.

The creak fades away again.

Title of a book, I think: He Shall Return Again.

I want to be truthful with you, men. In the beginning, always truth. Sometimes, my writing goes away from me and becomes succinct, sharp, too Joyce-like; I don't know if it is instinct. I am not trying to copy anyone. I am trying to say something. I am stinted. What the hell, Boys, I'm saying it, good or bad. I wish I had the flow of power that Wolfe possessed. But I don't want to copy anyone. I have too many things to say, lads.

I sat there, thinking. I just sat there on the bench, with a cigar, smoking peacefully, sniffing the cool river air, thinking. What about? About time, man, and God. My novel, which I plan to write in the coming summer. I think about those things.

Then, like the march of a dead man, the creak began to return. I listened with delight, beating my hand in steady rhythm. The delight in life's rich invention. I was amazed. The advance of the lost race of man: the homo. He is bearing down upon me, slowly, with lustful deliberation, flirtatious body, eyes glutting upon me. I looked up; he was an ordinary looking man, except for his eyes: they ate into me, and into my flesh. Greedy eyes, shining in the night. Hopeful eyes. A degenerated sag in his clothing. He went on, massing his points, marshalling his forces for the attack. He Shall Return Again.

I felt repugnant toward him. But then I knew that it was a sickness, deserving of pity. He cannot help it, I thought. And neither can I.

"It is now . . . . . 11:47."

The creak faded away, in regular squeaks.

A couple came by. A tall blonde, wearing a turban, striding delicately on long legs, heels clicking; a long serpentine body, rippling here and there. The man with his arm about her waist, his hand massaging the flaccid flesh, the silky skin underneath the cotton dress. To have and to hold, I thought. He must feel her flesh to know that she is with him, tangibly. He must have her, he must know of it, he must possess her. The flesh is so powerful, until one begins to go beyond it. The absolute. Look at that rock wall: granite, probably from Vermont, hewn into rectangular shapes and cemented together above the Hudson, to serve as a wall for mankind. Granite from Vermont hills, carried here in trucks. How wise that rock looks. Never says a word, can't be wrong. It has something that I haven't got; and I have something that it lacks. Who is the luckiest? The granite is forever truthful—it is in its nature. I cannot be forever truthful. Yet, on the other hand, the granite is part of this vast scene here on the shores of the Hudson; I, my fine young masters, am not only part of the scene, but am Master of the scene. I see it, smell it, feel it, and own it. The granite does none of those things. It merely is part of the scene. It is not conscious of the scene. I am. I may not be forever truthful, but I have a chance to try. The granite will never have a chance to own this scene.

The creak of leather shoes is returning through the night.

A man in limp clothes, felt hat with lowered brim. He is marching toward me, from the left flank. Creak . . . . . creak . . . . creak . . . . (the roar of Time seems to augment) . . . . creak . . . . creak.

"Poor demented bastard!" I say to myself.

The creak is upon me. He goes by, feeding upon me with his eyes. Hopeful eyes again. Hinting eyes, in the night. The laughter of a woman comes from a distance. The roar of a bus, starting. The creak goes by, and fades once more. March of death.

"Does he see this scene? Does he own this hazy heaven, that broad river, those New Jersey lights? No! He does not. He definitely does not. It is very pitiful, but he does not. I shall leave this cigar butt on the bench, and when he returns, he can use that."

And so I left, leaving the cigar butt on the bench. I left the granite stone, the scene I owned, and the creak of leather shoes. I walked on home.

And it was on the way home that I finally hit upon it. The consciousness of little children to the earth; the bias of grown men, struggling with the structures of modern civilization; the consequent and natural bias of the little children. Result? The dead men of today. God is the thing. God is consciousness. God is the perspective of the eye and ear and nose and mind. God is man; and man is God. Man lowers his head and lunges into civilization, forgetting the days of his infancy when he sought truth in a snowflake or a stick. Man forgets the wisdom of the child. The basic scheme of man has been neglected. But, my insane darlings, not with me around! God is the thing, theological, pagan, or real.

# If I Were Wealthy

*It would be six years before Kerouac saw the American in-*
*terior and West Coast, but in 1941 he dreamed about trav-*
*eling across country and around the world. He imagined*
*an ideal retreat in the Rockies. In late July 1947 the*
*twenty-five-year-old Kerouac went "on the road," heading*
*for Colorado. His first stop was Denver, where he joined*
*his friends Hal Chase, Ed White, Neal Cassady, and Allen*
*Ginsberg for a short while before pressing on to Califor-*
*nia. In* On the Road, *Kerouac's stand-in, Sal Paradise,*
*says: "And there in the blue air I saw for the first time, far*
*off, the great snowy tops of the Rocky Mountains. I took a*
*deep breath [. . . .] And here I am in Colorado! I kept*
*thinking gleefully. Damn! damn! damn! I'm making it!"*

If I were wealthy, here's what I'd do. Rather than to travel around
the world having porters lug my enormous baggage, sit wearily in
swaying rickshaws and look out with jaded senses at the Orient,
drape myself tiredly in deck-chairs and gaze out somnolently at the
surging surface of the sea . . . rather than that, I would work my way
on tramp steamers, I would drink with the crew in every port, I
would moil amid the reeking masses of the Orient, poking my nose
into mysterious doorways and antique shops; I'd mush to the Arctic,
I'd tramp through the jungles of Brazil and Africa, I'd have women
in Capetown, in Singapore, in Port Said, in Istanbul, in St. Peters-
burg, in San Francisco, in Havana, in Liverpool, in Shanghai, in
Morocco, in Sydney, in Sumatra . . . . I'd lope along on strawberry
roans through the stifling dried wastes of Arizona, I'd stride along
little roads in France, in England, and especially in Scotland (and I
don't know what the fascination of Scotland in me stems from, perhaps from Stevenson's "Kidnapped" or the motion picture "39

Steps" or "The Lady of the Lake."); I'd lie lolling among the green green hills of Ireland; I'd yawn whole afternoons away along the Mississippi, in New Orleans; I'd . . . but Oh this could go on all night.

The purpose of this story is not what I've already declared. The purpose was to indicate what I would do if I were wealthy, after all my years of traveling and living and being hungry, as regards to ending my days in peace. Here's what I'd do.

A little shack on the slope of a mountain in Colorado's Rockies; a beach wagon with which to procure provisions; two fine dogs; a fireplace inside, to surprise any visitors who might imagine from the exterior appearance of my shack that it was impoverished. Impoverished! Hah! Of course not! A shack with dirty grey clapboards covering expensive building materials, a shack with a rickety stovepipe chimney leading smoke out and up from a beautiful fireplace set in fine deepred brick; a shack with a huge and heavy library, all very rare and fine editions of classics throughout the ages; a somber brown library with a fireplace and deep-dyed leather chairs, worn from much meditation with one of many mellow old pipes; a shack with a beautiful cocktail cabinet; a shack with a bedroom overlooking the great projecting earth's grandest summits, snow-capped, sadly lost in clouds, towering mammoths of Colorado; a shack, gentlemen, in which I would end my days.

In the morning, I would awake and go out into the yard, where a cool deep pailful of cold water would stand beside the well. Into this I would thrust my head, following that with a vigorous application of a big towel. Then I would go about chopping wood for the fire, after which I would go back into the shack and prepare breakfast: And, gentlemen, when I say breakfast, I definitely do not mean bacon and eggs and coffee and the New York Times . . . . no, I would have the following: A plate of steaming, sauced beans; some toast plastered with melting butter; three cups of strong, strong coffee; and for dessert, a huge foaming glass of milk and a piece of apple pie—all this to the casual perusal of some Homer, or some Shakespeare, or some Wolfe.

Following this hearty breakfast, I would not pick up my guns and head out with the dogs . . . No gentlemen no! I cannot and will not kill animals. I would merely pick up a heavy staff and head out for a long walk with the dogs. In the afternoon I would study or write, or if I were tired of my loneliness, I would drive down to the airport nearby and fly to Los Angeles for a night at the Trocadero with the fashionable and lovely people of the time. But let me tell you that most of the time I would just sit outside of my shack and do things, build things with my hands, perhaps whittle sticks, or perhaps draw paintings, or perhaps describe the scene with pen, or read; or perhaps go in for a snifter of scotch and soda, or perhaps play my radio or phonograph or perhaps sleep underneath my big tree near the well.

In the evening, with the mountains steeped in absolute silence and blackness, I would make my fire roar and would sit before it smoking, my hands on the two dogs' noble and loyal heads, dreaming away the rest of my days.

# [One Sunday Afternoon in July]

*Until now perhaps the least-known influence on young
Kerouac was Albert Halper, whose prose Kerouac was
reading by early 1941. Halper (1904–84) was a short
story writer, novelist, playwright, and essayist whose work
often dealt with the lives of working-class ethnic people
in cities, especially his native Chicago and New York.
Halper's books include* Union Square, On the Shore, *and*
The Foundry. *In a notebook from October 1942, Kerouac
named "The Trinity" of Wolfe, Saroyan, and Halper as "3
Great American Writers" whose "words co-incide with
deed." He wrote that they (and Lin Yutang) "are concerned chiefly with the individual sensation of Life, with
its every-day mysteries and astounding 'commonplaces.'
They are the sensitive antennae who receive & impart Life
from the earth, and not from man's society alone."*

*In 1940 Halper wrote: "The first concern of a novelist is
to see life clearly, and as whole as it may be, and then
tell the truth about it." In "Young Writer Remembering
Chicago," from his short story collection* On the Shore,
*Halper says: "Folks, please listen. I would like to close
this little piece with a grand flourish, with a blare of bu-
gles, but I've got a locomotive in my chest, and that's a
fact . . . . When I was a kid, I went camping alone in
the pine woods of upper Michigan. [. . .] When I reached
the bottom of the hill, I struck an old railroad spur that
curved away, then straightened out into a direct line. The
shiny steel tracks, giving off a harsh glitter in the sun,
grew small and taut, meeting at the horizon; and as I began walking over the wooden ties I heard the faint sound
of a train. I didn't see the locomotive for a long time, but
heard it coming closer and closer. Finally it showed at the*

*end of the tracks, a small black beetle against the horizon.*
*I stepped off to one side to let it pass, hearing the sound*
*increase, seeing the far-off smoke. It whirled past me, shot*
*round the curve, and went out of sight, but I still heard it.*
*I can hear it yet.* Chug-chug-chug. Chug-chug-chug. *Lis-*
*ten to it.* " On the Shore *(1934), subtitled* Young Writer
Remembering Chicago, *may have given Kerouac the term*
young writer, *which he uses to describe himself in several*
*pieces written in the fall of 1941.*

One Sunday afternoon in July, I heard the music of a violin coming
over the radio in the kitchen. At the time, I was sitting in my room
staring at a window shade. The song was "To a Wild Rose," and the
moment I heard it, I knew where I was:

I was standing on the corner of 44th Street and Broadway in New
York on a Saturday afternoon, I should say, in the Spring. I was
standing near the curb, and everybody was rushing past me, their
eyes glued on themselves and not on life. My eyes were glued on
life, at that particular moment, because an old man with white hair
was standing on the sidewalk playing an old violin. It was "To a
Wild Rose." When he finished that, he played Brahms' "Cradle
Song." When he had finished that, he started again on "To a Wild
Rose," perhaps because those were the only songs he knew, or perhaps the fact that he was blind and would never see a wild rose
again accounted for it. At any rate, he played "To a Wild Rose," actually and literally.

My eyes were glued on life.

And they were full of tears.

I read something by Tess Slesinger, Albert Halper, and James T.
Farrell these past few hours. I was amazed by the fact that I was not
the only writer living, not the only young man "with a locomotive in
his chest, and that's a fact," not the only youth with a million
hungers and not one of them appeasable, not the only one who is
lonely among multitudes, and does not know why. Out of this
strange disease that made my brain reel with hope, and then despair, I thought I had something that would make me an original
writer—something apart from the Saturday Evening Post stories and
the clever New Yorker stories. But I find myself the brethren of
many other poets—and I must confess, what is my next move?

That, I believe, will work itself out in the same inextricably complicated and minute manner of Life itself.

Some of these poets?: Halper, Farrell, Slesinger, Thomas Wolfe the King, Saroyan, Marcus Goodrich, Joyce, T. S. Eliot, Langston Hughes, Whitman, Faulkner, and a million others including Homer, Virgil, Dante, Shakespeare, Coleridge, Hardy, Turgenev, Dostoevsky, Gide, Sandburg, and Kerouac. Ha ha ha ha ha ha ha ha.

The nice thing about Hollywood is its personalities, each one of which we can study at our own leisure and privacy in the movie houses: we sit there in the dark, while they cavort in the light of the silver screen—and we have ample opportunities to draw conclusions on them and perhaps dream up stories around them. I would like to write a story about a guy like Gary Cooper, and also Cary Grant, Charles Boyer, Joel McRea, Tyrone Power (he would be a dark brooding Romanoff), George Brent, Victor Mature, Melvyn Douglas, Burgess Meredith, and as for the women there are so many that I can't name them, but preferably Margaret Sullavan, Kay Francis, Garbo (all these have husky voices) and Hedy Lamarr, etc.

# The Birth of a Socialist

*As a companion to this short story, see Chapter Ten of Kerouac's novel* Pic *for the account of Slim working in the cookie factory. The real cookie and cracker factory in Lowell in the 1940s was the Megowen Educator Food Company at 27 Jackson Street.*

*Like other young people who had come of age in the Great Depression and were facing involvement in a horrific world war, Kerouac was wrapped up in the political and economic issues of the late 1930s and early 1940s. He imagined social and economic systems that might accommodate his own interest in working as a writer, an artist. He even devised a plan called Kerouac's Socialism in which he argued that shorter working hours would create more jobs. With a two- or three-hour limit per worker, there could be three working shifts in a day. He wrote, "Shorter hours will provide the laborer with a new desire to live, not to be a productive animal, but to have time to be a man, to have time to enjoy the rights of man in the use of his divine intellect, a gift of God that is overlooked by our overloads of the present Industrial Era."*

[This story is an attempt to bring to the readers the true meaning of slavery for others, in its most despised form. A man cannot impart the true feeling of things to others unless he himself has experienced what he is trying to tell of. I have experienced a day in a cookie factory, and in this story, I shall do my damnedest to show to the readers what it is like to do such a day's work, what a man thinks about in so doing, and what his conclusions should be if he has an ounce of brains.

Though this story may be brushed off as a piece of Communistic pamphleteering against the capitalists, I should like anyone inclined to do so to reflect for a moment. This story, I admit, and am proud to admit, is against the Capitalists. But it is also against the Communists. It is against any form of slavery, the Shavian concept of slavery. In a Communistic state, there can be slavery. The slavery of the masses . . . . better wages, shorter hours, more justified and more pleasant slavery—but still slavery.—Jack Kerouac, The Zagguth, The Zagg]

Did you ever stand on a street corner in America at five o'clock in the morning?

I did.

The sun wasn't even up yet, and the street was grey with the last sallow vestiges of brooding, disappearing night. I was standing on the corner smoking a cigarette. My eyes were still heavy, and in the cold morning air, my legs seemed to quiver with unnatural weakness.

I wasn't standing on this street corner in America at five o'clock in the morning because I wanted to see what it was like. No, I was waiting to be picked up by a car which was to take me to work in a factory. It was to be my first day of work in this factory, and for that matter, the first day of work in my whole life.

And there I was, standing on that corner and shivering inside my leather jacket. And in the East, the sun was just poking its top over the trees. There was vapor coming from my mouth, even though it was June. But an early morning in New England, Northeasternmost part of America, is pretty chilly, even in June.

While waiting, I lit up another cigarette.

Holy suffering cows, I say to myself, I wish I could have stayed in bed. Why did I ever get myself into this!

The street begins to assume a gilded glow, as the sun rises above the trees. The delicate little pipe of the birds rings through the dewy air. You feel immediately the hope of a new day, even though you are headed for a factory.

Across the street walks a mill-worker. He has been doing this for years, I say to myself, while this is only my first day. Look at him. He is middle-aged, and his face is resolute and tired in the early morning mists. He carries the lunchbox under his arm and trudges onward. He is on his way to the mill for another day of roaring heat.

He is not afraid. He has been told that man's natural duty is work. So he is not afraid, and hasn't been for fifteen years. But has he ever been uncertain? He turns around the corner and disappears from my gaze.

His natural habitat, after fifteen years, is the mill. It is too late.

The car arrives, and I jump in, slamming the door after me. The driver is a friend of mine. His eyes are puffed from the early hour, and he smokes a cigarette nervously as he wheels the car through the empty streets.

Empty streets!

Gentlemen, I retract that statement!

Going up the main street, we skirt a stream of people—at five o'clock in the morning—all heading for the maw of the mills. The Maw! Young girls, tired mothers, old men, kids fresh from High School who should be reading Tolstoi or Whitman. All of them are walking to the mill, and there now! The mill-whistle shrieks across the slumbering rooftops of the city, beckoning the millworkers with a tinge of irascibility, and with just enough smug tyranny to make my blood boil.

Yes, my blood boil.

For years, at five o'clock in the morning, my blood had always been peacefully coursing through my slumbering body. But on this morning, riding up the street and seeing the faces of those poor people of my own beloved city, my blood boiled for them.

And, gentlemen, my blood shall always boil for them . . . even though it may be too late for all of them.

Leo wheels the car into the driveway of our factory.

How the hell, he tells me, did you ever manage to get up at 4:30? I laugh.

I did it for the sake of science, I tell him.

We enter the factory. We leave the morning coolness and are suddenly hit full in the face by an unbearable, stuffy heat. This is a cracker factory—cookies, etc. The heat is saccharine, cloying, sweet. It is hot and specked with flour. The place vibrates madly with the machine lust of mighty motors.

Holy Hell, I say to myself.

We put on our white ducks and sweatshirts, in the locker rooms, and light up a cigarette.

Leo says: You'll get used to the smell in here after a while. I don't smell anything myself after two years.

[ 87 ]

I take a drag on the cigarette and say: Well, I won't mind the smell. It's pretty nice.

I look around. The other employees are seated about, smoking and listening to the little radio that is propped up on a shelf. The announcer is telling us about a big German drive into vast, mysterious, Asiatic Russia.

Napoleon—Borodino—Burnt Moscow: These words flash in my mind, but I'm not very aware of them. The thing at hand is this factory in America, for $20 a week. It is my first day.

There is a whistle. They all get up and go to work.

I walk toward my machine, and note its mad tangle of belts and screws and wheels and cranks and shafts and brakes and iron plates. There is a huge tubful of sticky substance waiting beside this machine.

Shovel this dough, says the foreman, like this.

He digs into the thick paste with a shovel, forming a square. He picks up this 70-pound lump of substance and puts it onto an apron on the machine. He spreads out this substance with his hands till it is now in small lumps, ready to go through the rollers and emerge on the other side a neatly cut ribbon of hot, steaming dough. With curiosity, I follow the machine and see what happens to the ribbon. It is a wide ribbon, and it reached a part of the machine where it is punctured by a down-coming cutter, forming small cookie shapes. The residue goes back above the machine, returning to my apron. The little ovals continue along the machine into the terrific heat of a long oven. I imagine that it emerged at the other end of the factory a full-fledged cookie, where it was ready to be packed into boxes by a host of young ladies who should be home planting the beans in the garden.

But what can I do about it? All I can do is pick up the shovel and proceed to feed this factory with dough. Otherwise, it will stop functioning.

And so begins my day's work.

In fifteen minutes, I am exhausted. For fifteen straight minutes, I have been pressing down into the stubborn dough with all my strength; for fifteen minutes I have been pulling out these prodigious wads of stuff out of the hot tub and casting them into the maw of the machine with tired, greasy arms. My shirt is already soaked. My eyes are burning from the perspiration which runs down my brow. My hands look small and weak in the buttery light above the machine.

And every time that I have fed the machine, I must return to the tub for more, because the machine is hungry, and the apron keeps turning and the factory is on full-time schedule, and we must hurry and produce for America. Whether or not my body is aching and crying for a short rest, whether or not my head reels from the awful reek of this hot paste which I have to hug to my breast and spread with my sticky hands on the apron, whether or not my stomach is on the point of upheaving all the guts in my system, whether or not my ears buzz from the painful machine inexhaustibility of this thing, whether or not my human mechanism is on the point of collapse in the roaring heat of this madman's asylum for unquestioning fools—whether or not I can go on keeping up with this devouring machine, I must keep up my work. I must go on digging into the disgusting vatful of humid fudge, irregardless of my own feeling, because the machines must [be] fed, the factory must go on functioning, and any halt would mean a loss of profits for the gentlemen who are at present far away from the deafening racket of this fool's paradise!

I must quit, I say to myself. It becomes a chant. I must quit. I must quit. I quit. I quit. I quit. And the machines roar and roar and roar, all [to] the tune of a few gasping words from a dry, dying mouth: I quit. I quit. I quit. I quit. I quit. I quit.

An hour has gone by, and I have swallowed my desire to vomit. My stomach is heavy and aching. My shirt is a soggy rag. My face is streaked with the filth of the capitalists. I am wallowing in the mire of other people.

I, a human being, a young man, groveling through the mire and filth and dirt of others.

Should I stand it?

A tremendous laugh resounds through the factory. A huge, happy belly-laugh. The toilers stop for a moment, and stare at me with agony.

HO HO HO HO HO HO HO HO HO HO HO!!!!!!!!

What a joke, I say to myself. If I should stay in here, I would just as soon get rid of my brains and transfer them to a plow-horse on the farm.

HO HO HO HO HO HO HO HO HO HO HO !!!!

[ 89 ]

I go on working, because I realize that the fellows will call me a quitter. I will do anything in order not to be called a quitter. I will work till my fifteen minutes rest at 8 o'clock and then I'll go home and go to bed and sleep.

I dig into the tub, and my arm muscles contract painfully. My arm stiffens, but I loosen it and proceed to press into the dough. I form a square, bend toward it, my abdomen pressing against the high edge of the vat, and pull up the hot hunk. It weighs a lot, and my arms ache. But with a mighty grunt of sweat, I swing this armful of capitalist mire into the machine and gambol in it with my arms, spreading it out into small lumps.

It seems to me that I have eaten every bite of this hot fudge—every ton of it. My stomach protests.

I dig once more, without a rest. The machine goes on, and I must go on too. The machine is a machine, and so is Zagguth. Yes, Zagguth the human being is a machine. If you don't believe it, you should have been there that day in June.

Again my muscles stiffen. The one in my right arm stiffens swiftly, and my hand is drawn upwards in a curious, paralytic state of inactivity. I have to use my left hand to release my right hand from its prison of contracted muscles.

I go back to work, dropping large beads of sweat into the dough. The people of America, I say to myself, will eat these cookies, and in them will be the sweat of Zagguth. That is the way America is supposed to be . . . built on the sweat and blood of our people, and all that sort of stuff. All right then, if that is the case, have some more sweat. And two huge drops fall into the vat of fudge.

HO HO HO HO HO HO!!!!. I laugh, and the agonized looks of the other dead men return to me. Such agony! Why the agony! Agony and sweat and heat. Blood and sweat of America?

O, thou great propagandists, I have discovered thee!

At eight o'clock, I am relieved. I go to the lockers and stretch out on a bench. The bench vibrates madly with the lunacy of our age. I start thinking about the way cookies used to be made.

An old lady, kindly. She is whipping a batter of cookies in a clean little dish. She cuts the cookies delicately, and serves them proudly to her happy family—small, heart-woven little cookies for her loved ones.

But today?

Hundreds of unquestioning fools who get up at five in the morning and rush to a huge, vibrating asylum. In there, they toil in agony and they become old and calloused and unhappy with the era. The cookies are concocted in huge furnaces and tremendous, sickening tubs. They are carried to a young man with a shovel, who proceeds to feed the factory without rest. He dies all day, but the factory must go on. The cookies rush to the ovens by the billions, and rush out of the ovens into a million boxes. They are hurried out of the factory, into a hundred waiting trucks and rushed and scurried out upon a thousand roads.

Jesus Christ, I say to myself as I figure those things out. It can't be right. Somebody is deluding somebody, and by the Holy Cow, it won't be me!!!

I lay on the bench and it jumps and vibrates like mad.

I start to laugh at the idiocy of it all. What else do you expect anybody with an ounce of intelligence in him to do? Do you expect him to take this all in with a moribund mug, a serious puff on the cigarette (like those others are doing right now as they listen to the little radio on the shelf), a quietly efficient word or two, [child's] in the nuthouse and they don't want to believe it, because THIS my friends is the ERA!!

Again I laugh out loud, and they stare at me in agony.

I can still see those agonized looks. What's the matter with him, they say, is he crazy? What a nutty bastard! What the hell is he laughing at?

Which makes me laugh even more, not with contempt, but with genuine compassion and pity. And so, goodbye my factory friends. I am leaving you forever, and I am sorry that George Bernard Shaw was never divulged to you. Nor Saroyan nor Joyce nor Walt Whitman nor O'Casey.

Goodbye, boys.

I walked out of there, after sticking it out for eight hours so that the mill wouldn't be held up. I did it out of pure politeness, and a desire not to make any one inconvenienced. All throughout the day, I laughed and laughed at the silliness of it all. I wore a paper hat and the hot steaming dough got into my skin, and down into my tormented stomach. I worked and worked like a dog. Huge calluses came up, but the machine had to be fed. My arms contracted painfully, yet production had to keep up. A huge factory, operated by throbbing and terrible machinery, was depending on the weary muscles of one young writer.

After the day was over, I took a shower and told one of the workers that I was quitting.

Can't take it? he asks, smiling.

Perhaps I could if I had to, I replied. But I don't have to. I wouldn't want to have to. I'm a man—with brains—and not a dumb animal.

To myself I concluded: It is not right for me to give eight hours of my precious life to anyone at such a gory task every day. I should rather keep those eight hours to myself, meditating in the grass, let's say; or walking thru the woods.

That afternoon, I went swimming. I brought a book of American poetry. I sat down on a rock in the cool water up to my neck, and I sat there reading William Cullen Bryant's "Thanatopsis." People stopped and laughed at me. But I was engrossed in the book, the water was cool, the sky was gorgeous, there was a caressing breeze, and the world was again fit for a man.

I went to a show that night, saw how badly one picture was written, and decided that I would write scenario for a living rather than shovel dough in a blasting-furnace factory.

# No Connection: A Novel That I Don't Intend to Finish

Well, here I go, spouting off some dribbling words in saliva ribbons like the faces in the Book Review supplement of the *Times* or *Tribune*. It's a curious thing, this writing business. This "No Connection" thing here is a novel. Why the hell am I writing a novel? Who's going to read it? And why read it? Whatever I have to say will undoubtedly be of no use when a pair of stockinged limbs go clicking by on seductive heels. And when a guy finds himself in the path of an onrushing army of soldiers brandishing bayonets, what does all my writing or the writing of anybody else matter?

One Goddamn thing is clear to me. We are all animals. Jack London's "Gnat-swarm." Tom Wolfe's "Man-swarm." A swarm of heaving, pulsating organisms; an ocean of sensateness, composed of pastel pink tissue and sickly gray entrails, swelling and breathing in one grand mass, making noise and erecting bridges, wearing clothing and exhuming odors of fresh blood, perspiration, and flesh. That's the word: Flesh. That big word. It means a lot. It glows and ripples and stretches and bleeds and pierces. We are all animals, and we all cease pulsating and oscillating as soon as we are dead. After that, we rot and fall apart and absolve into dust.

On one fine Spring morn in 2948, Teodor Alexandar, the erudite professor of Anthropology at Eunuch College, goes strutting along over my dust, singing the latest song-hit.

Hell, my fine brothers, let's see what this novel is about. A novel is usually written by novelists. I am a human being, with a soul, a vanity, an ego, and a suitcase. I am a poet and a writer. I am not a novelist. I live on this earth, and if you don't mind my saying so, the other man-creatures that exist with me are damned difficult to get along with. And I don't doubt that they find me difficult also. I'm speaking in general terms.

General terms. Words of man. "Words of ages."

Did you ever read Walt Whitman or Barbellion? They are two

guys, both dead now, that I admire because of their keen sensitivity to life. They know they are made of flesh, they accept it, and die.

That's nice.

It's a short, short story: and it's got a tremendous kick. Not a O. Henry kick at the end. A Thomas Wolfe kick. A Thomas Wolfe kick is like the kick of a mule. O. Henry kicks are like a scotch and soda with too much soda.

Let's get on the ball, as they say in America, a country with broad plains in the middle, flanked by mountains and wild sea-coasts. The man-swarm managed to dot the sea-coasts with resorts, etc. But when you get up high enough, you don't see them anymore; just the jagged outlines of the continent, jutting into the sea and retreating into the land. Also, brothers under the skin, when you get high up there, you can't see the universe of a rose anymore. So stick to your size.

Like all other poets, I am kicking. I want to kick, you might say. You say, all poets like to kick. And this one here, Jack Kerouac, wants to kick in an original manner, but damned if he can find something original. He wants to be an original kicker, so that people will look at him and say: That fellow is a poet with an original bone to pick. They'll bury his hatchet with him.

The Question Before the House is this: Who is this poet Jack Kerouac, and what's he kicking about, not that there isn't anything to kick about . .

Who?

He's a nineteen-year-old youngster made of painful sensateness that keeps aggravating the gray matter in his skull. Enough of this biology, you say, and who is he? I'm not a physiologist. I'm a working man, and I haven't time to dub around. I've got to get back to work. Make it snappy. Who is he, and no funny stuff.

(Listen to that Twentieth Century man-creature blow his lungs out: Ho, what a tragic little thing it is.)

Jack Kerouac is a little man-creature, standing so high and weighing just about enough to crack some thin ice. He's a hell of a punk, not because he wants to devote his life to talking to his fellow men and telling them some helpful things, but because he insists on being an unusual man-creature, rather than a mediocre man-creature.

Unusual or mediocre, he is still a man-creature.

Valuable untruth or invaluable untruth: still untruth, non?

And this little bit of a punk wants to be looked up to, girls and all. He does things to enhance his man-swarm prestige, and then he basks in the warmth of it all. Sometimes, he pulls a beautiful boner. When that happens, he is angry as hell, but he is still proud. Next time, he says.

Let me say something, little man-creature called Jack Kerouac: Don't delude yourself. You're just a little punk. When you pull a boner, you have all the right in the world to be sore at yourself. But don't forget that boners are relative things, like everything else in society, or man-swarm. Gnat-swarm. Ha ha.

Don't kid yourself, you tiny globule of greasy lard. Drip down the basin, and run down the crapper, and keep your mouth shut. You were given sensateness to die, and reason to be fearful. Whoever gave it to you went fifty-fifty with you: It's up to you to make the best of it. Some people have died happy, others haven't. Fifty-fifty, you little piece of whipped cream. It's up to you. Therefore, whoever gave it to you was not entirely a hell of a heel. He was the Compromiser.

Don't delude yourself, insignificant itch. Pin-point punk. Live and vegetate and run around on your little tentacles. Breathe thunder. Tell your fellow gnats to smarten up, and if they don't tell them again. If you don't smarten up yourself, hang up your spikes.

American language. Smarten up, or hang up your spikes. One word for it: Beautiful.

How to smarten up? That's the point of poets and poetry. They keep dawdling about, trying to find the way. They never do, but they improve. Sometimes they come damned close to it. Some have hit it on the head.

Be a proud man-creature. Dignity and pride and kindness. That's why Jack Kerouac is a poet. He figures it's the most man-like thing to do. If Kerouac were a pigeon, he would do the most pigeon-like thing. He is a man, so he does the most man-like thing and writes for his fellow men. He assumes from the beginning that most of them can read.

This has been a hell of a novel.

What is sex? Sex is rigid bone, covered with velvet skin, pounding and ripping into fleshy cavity with heart-pounding passion and blood-red lust. Sex is bang! Bang! That's sex, brother, and don't kid yourself. Bang! Pound! Bang! And them comes a rush of luscious fever, an ocean of pin-prick sensation, and a shuddering climax of gushing hot blood. Pow! And then to hell with sex. That's sex, kid.

A novel is a story of man's development, I think. Development is the soul of Fate. My first novel will be a novel. Everything develops, and then dies. That's a novel. This novel is now ended.

# On the Porch, Remembering

If you're on a porch in the middle of Summer, under a night-sky rich in stars and vague nebulae, and you have your head thrown back for a good view of everything up there, you are bound to remember a lot of things. There is all about you the sound of a Saturday night in a mill city of New England, and if you are on my street, you can hear the river whispering over to the left. You can hear music coming from open windows, and up the street there is the exciting light and music of a traffic intersection. People are wearing their best, men with straw hats and white shoes, women with light summer dresses, and wide-brimmed hats, young men on the store corner wearing new suits and smoking out of full cigarette packs and impatiently leaning against the wall as they try to decide what everything is all about.

And oftentimes some little children go by underneath your piazza, and they are so innocently absorbed within their little ego-universes that you realize that they are safe for a while at least. And the sky! On the particular night that I remember, the sky was thick with huge chunkfuls of nodding light, and they were all packed together to form a beautiful spectacle of light and darkness. Right off at the start, if you have your chair tipped back against the railing of the porch and look in upwelling awe at the night-sky you will become a poet for a night at least. The stars seem to be close, just above you and watching you with intense patience. But, on that night when they seemed so, I wasn't fooled one bit. I knew they were indifferent.

And as I sat there, the mystery of the universe began to augment before me until after a while I had to tear my gaze away from the sky lest I should go mad with the eternal of it all. Instead, I fixed my eyes upon the Men's Club across the street from my house, and inside I could see them shooting pool. Through the screened windows I could hear them talk and laugh, some of them rubbing blue chalk on the tip of their pool cues, some of them leaning over the tables intent on their play. I knew there were spittoons somewhere on the floor, because one man spat every half-minute. The roof of this club sagged, and the fire escape which led up to the screened door hung in its skeleton grating by the light of the moon.

And then I began to remember.

I remembered one day out of all the myriad thousands of my life, one day back in my childhood during the seemingly dull, dark, and dismal '20's. I suppose the fact that I was a morbid child must account for my saying that the 1920–1930 era was a dismal one, but at least, to me the tone of that era will forever remain colorless and tasteless, for it was not until the '30's that I began to grow up and learn to appreciate the world about me.

I remember myself seated in the parlor, on That Day. Outside there is one grand vision of Gray Time—a vast tedium that seemed to envelop and encompass every pore of the world. The sky is exceedingly tasteless, its pallid solemnity hanging over the roofs of the city with a heavy gloom. The parlor is dark and dull, and in the corner and behind the chairs and sofas broods a sombre black color. I am seated on the sofa, listening to the clock ticking in the kitchen, equally gray and listless, and to the sink with its song of the dripping faucet. I am all alone in the house (I suppose my mother had gone out to the store) and I stare languidly at the roofs of the city, disconsolately feeding upon the overwhelming drabness of the cloudy sky like vultures at lean fare.

I am about six years old, and am dying a thousand prosaic deaths.

What is there to life, little boy seated in the parlor? Whatever the future holds in store for you, will it not be rendered gray and barren and stupid by this enormous Gray Time? Does not life, at this moment, narrow down to one little gray ball of Time, stuffed down your throat and choking you? Is there nothing but death to assuage this?

Here, then, is something that I cannot overcome: A cloudy day. Perhaps if I were to be distracted from these idle thoughts by some calamity, I wouldn't give a cloudy day, the Great Gray Time a second thought. But yet I can still remember vividly myself at the age of six, sitting in a parlor, listening to the eternal sigh of the Gray Time, and wondering whether it wouldn't have been better not [to] be born.

# The Sandbank Sage

*On the first page of this typescript Kerouac notes: "SOC = stream of consciousness." At the bottom of the second page he writes: "stream of consciousness is too intelligent to come from the mouths of children; I use it in elaborate English to imply their drifting thoughts." He adds: "This is quite raw, my novel shall be more compact & smooth." The sandbank in Kerouac's area of Pawtucketville overlooked Riverside Street, just beyond the campus of what was then the Lowell Textile Institute and is now the University of Massachusetts Lowell. The former Kerouac family homes on Sarah and Phebe avenues are nearby.*

Back in the days of my boyhood, there was a youngster in the neighborhood who used to be the laziest child imaginable. The women talked about him all the time, at the supper table. He was the casual talk of the town. He couldn't be the main talk of the town, because he himself was too insignificant and inconspicuous.

"That boy is no good. He will never be any good. He is too lazy."

Yes, he was too lazy. Every day, he would sit down on the top of the sandbank and gaze at the hills.

"One day," he told me on a cloudy morning, "I shall go into those forests and explore them."

"You're nuts," I told him. "They have already been explored. They are full of houses and roads and barking dogs and rubbish."

"They are not," he said, biting a twig. "They are wilderness. I shall explore them some day."

And so he would sit there all day, gazing. From down on the street, we could see him up there, a speck straddling a cliff. The sandbanks were dusty in those sunny summer days. We could see him up there; sitting quietly, looking into the distance, the eddies of dust swirling about him.

One sunny day, I was climbing the sandbank with my staff, talking to the trees and telling them that the prophet had arrived. I the prophet, I was shouting. I, the new prophet. Look at me, trees, and weep. I have come to save you, branch by branch. Bend before the winds, but break before me.

He was up there, sitting on the jutting cliff, gazing quietly. I came to him.

"Alcide," I roared in his ear. "I am the new prophet."

"You," he said. "Have been reading the Bible."

"Hell, I have not. I saw a movie of the life of Christ. He got nailed to a cross by a bunch of cannibals. I dream of him every night. I wish my mother would let me wear a long robe. I would really look like a prophet."

I stood beside him and looked at the New England hills. They were curved delicately on the horizon, veiled beneath a lovely pall. Pale, wan ghosts. A colossal cyclorama, circumventing the landscape.

"Prophet," he said profoundly, "let me alone."

I walked away.

A few weeks later I was a World War soldier. I came by, carrying my rifle, crawling in the dust, begrimed and alert.

"You Hun!" I shouted from behind a bush. "Yell Kamarade, or I'll shoot you."

The boy shifted his position from the top of the hill, and turned his head to look at me.

"You bore me," he said. "Go away."

"I'll shoot you nevertheless," I said. And I did.

The next day it rained in torrents. I had forgotten my sweater there, and when my mother found out, she commanded me to get it before it became completely destroyed. I found it, a crumpled mess of soggy clay and wool. Poor lost little thing, I roared to myself. Alone in the rain, glistening wet and limp and covered with pieces of sand. Little pieces of sand on a sweater in the rain, rivulets running through its valleys and mountains, carrying grains of sand. Little sodden mountain of forgotten mush. Musty mud.

The boy was on top of the sandbank standing and looking away.

He wore a raincoat and a little Gloucester fishermen rain-cap. He stood and looked. I disarranged my little mountain of lead-heavy wool, and shouted through the rain:

"You're nuts."

He said nothing.

The next day, it was warm and sunny. I was walking to the store, dragging my feet through the hot sand, the lost Foreign Legion hero.

"Water," I muttered. "Water."

He was on top of the bank, sitting down this time. It was not raining; he was sitting down, munching on a blade of grass, like Whitman. What is the grass? asked the man carrying it to the child with full hands.

"Hell," he said, when I reached him. "Look at those hills. How long have they been?"

"Been where?"

"Just been," he said.

"I guess since the beginning of the world," I said.

"Of course."

The sun beat down on both of us: shimmering radiations—the distant hills are dancing, Father. They are dancing the Rhumba, the Tango, and the Jive.

"Hell," said the lazy child. "I'm going into those forests some day."

"When," I asked.

"When the time comes," he said.

I went to the store. I walked into the grocery shop, sweating. I was uncomfortable, waiting. The fresh apples, smelling off cool waves. Flies buzzing about, annoying. Sticking paper, hanging down. China, I roared to myself. Hanging mandarins, hung by the neck for throwing knives. Knives flash in the dark Shanghai alleys. Hang, you mandarin, and love it. Flies love it.

"Twelve cents, Johnny," said the grocer.

To hell with you, I roared to myself. I walked home, handed the package to my sister. I went back to the swirling sands of the bank. No longer a hero of the French desert forces.

"Alcide," I said. "May I sit with you?"

He shifted his position on top of the sandbank to turn his neck.

"No!" he said. "Go away. You bore me!"

I went away, and in the yard, Tarzan came by on an elephant and I roared, To hell with you.

The next day, I went back to the sandbank. Alcide was not there. He is gone into the forest at last, I cried to myself. He has gone at last. All afternoon, I sat on his spot and gazed at the far-off woods, smiling.

Alcide's family moved away. They roared away from our street the next day, the truck tottering with beds and chairs. Alcide was sitting on the top of the pile, his legs folded like an Arab's, quietly riding along and swaying with the truck. His brothers were yelling with joy. Alcide was thunderously quiet. His brown little eyes stared down at me as the truck grunted sway, its chassis low slung and smoking and stumbling up the street like a giant frog that is hurt and cannot leap.

I have not seen Alcide for years. I don't know what happened to him. He went away from us, but not from himself, I assure you. Alas for him? Hell!

Hell! I roared as the truck teetered around the corner and disappeared.

Today, the sandbank is slowly swirling itself away. The distant hills are still there, with more houses.

I don't know; apparently, we're losing something. We must not let it go. Any more of this stuff, and we shall all die. If I was a millionaire, I would search for Alcide until I found him or his grave. Then I would carefully prop him up on the top of the sandbank, tear down the houses in the distant hills, grow some trees there, and then throw a cordon around the sandbank.

"Stand back, you pack of howling dogs. Let this boy muse. Find your own Goddamned sandbanks!"

In New Jersey today, while looking over the mass production in the Ford motor plant, I took a moment off to smoke a cigarette, and in so doing, I looked out of the window. Behind me roared Ford's Ford-makers; in front of me, through the turbid window pane, stood a cliff, on the other side of the street. On top of it sat a speck, looking over the whole blooming scene with the wisdom of altitude and perspective and silence.

Hell, I roared to myself in the plant. As long as the women of America keep turning out Alcides in mass production, we're all set. There's a new one up there now. Hell, I thundered, as five Ford-makers bumped into each other, trying to beat the assembly track to the deadline.

Alas, Hell!! I boomed to myself. Not for the little speck, at least. One at a time, Gents, one at a time. Let the prophet come by with his staff. Get out of the way. You'll get a staff on the head.

# Farewell Song, Sweet from My Trees

*Attached to the typescript of this story is a slip from the office of Arnold Gingrich, editor of* Esquire, The Magazine for Men, *with written comments from three readers: "This doesn't quite make it I'm afraid," "Doesn't jell to me—," and "Good—tho not for Esky" (the last note initialed "AG"). The slip is not dated, but in a diary entry from December 1941 Kerouac writes: "Worked on 'Farewell Song, Sweet from My Trees' today. Will finish job tomorrow and mail it to* Atlantic Monthly. *Also wrote 'Story of a Touchdown' a somewhat paced, hysterical psychological study of a paced, hysterical football player's mind—will send that to* Esquire. *I <u>must</u> sell my stuff—it is the only thing that will justify my exhaustive plan for full-time study in 1942." In October 1941 Kerouac wrote in a letter to Sebastian Sampas that he had submitted the story to* Harper's *magazine. Writing about his family leaving Lowell in August 1941, Kerouac alludes to the "farewell song" of the trees in both* The Town and the City *and the 1968 version of* Vanity of Duluoz.

*It is not surprising that Kerouac would have been writing and attempting to publish short stories around 1940. Between the two world wars America saw a revival of the short story, with some of the prime examples of the form being produced by Ernest Hemingway, Thomas Wolfe, William Saroyan, Willa Cather, Eudora Welty, and Richard Wright. In 1940 more than sixty magazines in the United States and Canada were publishing stories regularly, and the same year forty-eight story collections were published. The arrival of the annual* Best Short Stories *became a publishing event.*

The Song?

. . . . . . . . . . . Listen to the song of the trees, the swishing song, the swishing song! Oh listen to the song of the trees, the swishing song, the swishing song . . . . .

My trees have stood there for generations, I think, but I myself have been listening to them for ten years. It was ten years ago that we moved into this neighborhood, the furniture van groaning with the stacked weight of our belongings, and that was when I first began to hear those trees sing. In the summer night I used to sleep in the hammock on the screened porch, and there stood my trees tall and black and singing. One night I lay awake right straight through till dawn, listening, and then I rose and passed the milkman as I headed out for the forest in back of our neighborhood. When I returned at sunrise, spent and sated with the glory of it all, I went back to my blankets.

"Get up, you lazy child!" scolded my mother, coming down to do the breakfast and yawning.

Ah, mother, mother.

Those were the rich tumbling days, golden indeed. As I make these observations, sitting on my old porch, it is exactly 2:37 A.M. The night is black. The star-packed sky is drawn right down to the treetops, and shadows loom huge and spectre-like. It is a man's night, I tell you, with Substance and Form. The kind of night that Goudt liked to achieve in his biblical engravings. The kind of night that brings nodding chunkfuls of starsparkle clear down to rooftops in thrilling immanence. My pipe spirals off its fragrant fume, I shift in my seat on the steps, my hat rests on the back of my head, and I am very sad.

You see, I have to pull up my stakes and roll. Tomorrow morning, when the swift and clean dawn appears, a big van will rumble up my little old street, will puff and roar laboriously into position, and release a band of men who will immediately begin to load on our furniture and other household objects. My family is moving away from this neighborhood, from this city and state, and migrating to a strange city, many miles away. This is the last chance I'll have to sit on my porch, looking at the lumpy little dirt street, the three street lamps, tall singing trees, and the drowsy bungalow. It is all over.

I am only a boy, but I know a few things. I know, for instance, the hidden legend of my old neighborhood. We have all lived here for years, our lives plied in casual proximity, garage-door slamming mornings, mother-calling noons, hammer-banging afternoons, child-screaming sunsets, radio-blaring evenings, and finally, river-hushed and tree-swished nights . . . I have seen these things, and never mentioned it to anyone. I have taken it all in with a silent, vague joy. And now, suddenly, I must leave. I must leave the song of my trees forever, and the grief that is in me, the pressure against my shirt-pocket, is unbearable . . . . Time, damned and cursed Time must persist, and does. New Time advances, destroying old Time. Time advances in its maddening amble, unstopping. All things persist and will not delay for one meagre second. Why? Why? Why?

Stop! Go back! Go back, damn you, go back!!!

"Hush, child . . ." moan my trees. "Farewell, child . . . . farewell . . . . farewell . . . ."

Ah, well . . . . this, then, has been my home and my land. That, there, the leaning fence that I knew. And over there, the lean melancholy telephone pole that I knew. These things I knew in my boyhood, and now I must leave. Why couldn't I just simply turn back Time and begin all over again? Why? Why the advance of Time? Why? A slow mounting rage, and then: Stop, Time, stop! Go back! Go back, damn you, go back!!! I hurl my pipe into the little front yard, scattering a furious shower of orange embers.

"What is the grass?" asked the man, fetching it to the child with full hands. And the child saith unto him: Go thou unto thine Host, for he hath spread a sumptuous board; avail thyself of his good cheer, and in partaking, question not.

"Okay, okay," I say, American-wise. "All right."

"But now wait!"

Listen!

The breeze just came, a rather cool August breeze, and it is going through my trees. A sound advances . . . .

Listen to the song of the trees, the swishing song, the swishing song! Oh listen to the song of the trees, the swishing song, the swishing song . . . .

Listen to that lullaby! Have you ever heard such lovely music, sir?!!! A million little green leaves in the summer night, trembling together tenderly and all joining in the chorus. Hush . . hush . . wush . . hush . . hush . . wush . . . shhhhhhhh . . . . .

The haunting tug at my shirt-pocket grows heavier. In the middle of the night, while people sleep, I sit silently sad.

And suddenly, in a luscious flood, memories come up to me from the beauty and mystery of the night . . . . millions of memories, tumbling in my hat. Ha ha ha, I say. Ha ha ha.

Memories . . . . I have plenty of those, sir. Those were the rich leaping days, golden indeed. The first kid I met was Fouch. He was Greek, lived just across the street, and the first time I saw him he was sitting on his porch steps, if you please, like William Saroyan used to do in Fresno, California. I was pouting at him with silent, outraged interest, hidden behind my mother's parlor curtains. Fouch and I got to know each other well, and since I was the more dominating brat, I took over the reins of our prosperity. We negotiated many a trade with Pete, who lived on the corner, and came out of it with fabulous cargoes of dime novels, including The Shadow, Eerie Tales, Masked Detective, The Spider, and Secret Agent X. Yes, sir, that was back there in those good golden days . . . . hush . . hush . . wush . . hush . . hush . . wush . . shhhhhhhhh . . . . . . Here I am on my porch, remembering.

Those dime novels . . . . it wasn't so much the killing in these stories that we used to feed upon, it was rather the dark and mysterious labyrinthal movement of our heroes, the sibilant hiss of their secret sanctumed laugh, the fall of rain on Fifth Avenue mansion at night, the slow creeping menace of masked justice along Manhattan depths, and above all, our hero unmasked and posing before the dull eye of the world as he sits lounged in brown-hushed gentlemen's club, comfortably below Moosehead and cigar smoke, facing fireplace and chessboard with intelligent opulence, while outside the grand window skims a yellow taxi over the rain-sleeked Manhattan street. Ah, but we loved these stories, and how the image of New York grew deeply and slowly into our boy minds!

. . . hush . . hush . . wush . . . I'm on my porch, remembering . . .

Into the neighborhood roared Bill, bringing with him his nervous chatter, his boast, his large heart. Bill also was a dominating brat, and there developed between us a tremendous feud, while flitting in the background like a wise Ghost was smiling Hellenic Fouch, calmly inheriting the Golden Mean. Bill and I ranted and raged and roared, and Fouch was right behind us, borne along and smiling. We were kids, we did everything.

Once I ran a newspaper, the Daily Owl. I printed it by hand with a pencil, and pasted pictures at the appropriate spots, using my own delectable hand-wrought captions. Bill was my star reporter. One Sunday my family went riding in the old Plymouth and while we were away, Bill broke into the house and deposited a terrific scoop on my work-desk: LOCAL HOME-MADE WAGONS DISAPPEAR! (Bill failed to mention that these "homemade wagons" of ours were so noisy that in all probability a delegation of neighbors had commissioned someone to eliminate the rickety nuisances from the local scene.) Anyway, it was quite a paper. My Hollywood correspondent was a melancholy little Greek boy named Sebastian; he came from another neighborhood, but had heard from afar of my publication. He used to submit his daily column with a sad smile, and I would print it laboriously into my paper. The subscriber was Fouch's older brother, who was an ill man, and who used to read it from cover to cover. He died some years later. I shall never forget it.

Bill used to draw cartoons, and after a while I closed down the paper and took up cartooning with Bill. Every Sunday afternoon we would sit in my living room, turning out strip after strip of adventure serials, while my mother cooked some caramel pudding for us and while my father sat in the parlor listening to the negro singers with tears in his eyes. Oh, those were the bounding days, rich indeed. We went to school together, and bragged all the way, every day. Once, Bill and I got mad at each other and didn't speak for about six weeks . . . . until one evening we met in the street, both of us carrying a copy of those precious dime novels. I hadn't intended to speak to him, but as I neared him a sudden pang of regret coursed through my boy-heart, and I realized that I liked this fool braggart, that all those six weeks had been wasted weeks.

"Whatchyou got there?" I asked casually.

"The Shadow," said Bill, thumbing through the exciting pages.

"I've got Secret Agent X," I said. "Swap?"

"Okay," said Bill.

We swapped. I felt wonderful, and so did Bill. The world was good . . . . . . . . I'm doing some mighty fine remembering . . .

This fellow Pete I was telling you about . . . . . he used to take us down to his cellar and let us feast our eyes upon his rich store of dime novels. Then he would load our arms generously, jesting continually, large-hearted Pete. "Here you be, Tsi-Gene!" he would say to me drawling. "Cast yore orbs on that fer a while . . . . an' now if you gen'l'men will excuse me, I'm goin' on upstairs for my vittles . . . ." He had all kinds of magazines down there, but 80% of them were Westerns. He loved them—and I'm sure that the thing he liked about them was the drawl of the thin-lipped cowhands, their smoke-blue eyes, their long lean rawhide walk.

"Shore," Pete would say. "Shore as yore standin' here . . . . an' now I reckon I'll lope on to the shack and rustle me some grub . . . . Adios . . . . ."

Pete had a brother named Mike, who never said anything. He used to walk around with his long arms swinging regularly, his short legs straddling amazingly out of proportion, a huge noiseless stride that seemed forever going uphill. It has never been recorded or proven that Pete and Mike ever spoke to each other, although they were normal and friendly brothers. It's just that they never thought of talking to each other . . . . it was merely a matter-of-fact thing that required no particular attention on the part of either one. However, we used to play basketball in the park with the two of them. Mike was always on one team, Pete on the other. It was a tremendous spectacle to watch them give each other the old hip . . . . . whack! . . . . . . whap! . . . . each silent and red-faced with a comical, wordless anger. It was, however, their way of communicating to each other . . . . . . whack! . . . . . . whap! . . . . the old hip, a deft insinuation of the buttock at the right moment . . . . . whack! . . . . . whap! . . .

In this little old neighborhood of mine lived a bunch of younger kids who used to fill the sunset hours with the uproar of their gun-fights . . . . . . taaah! . . . . taaah! . . . . taah! . . . . you could see them dart from barrels and dash heroically through a hail of bullets, blazing at both toy muzzles with Buck Jones abandon. One of these kids was Salvey.

One summer, he suddenly disappeared from these nightly battles, and two weeks later we discovered him, to our amazement, standing on the corner of the Variety Store with the "big guys," smoking and spitting calmly.

Salvey used to go swimming with us to the Brook, and when he did the jack-knife dive off the grassy bank he looked like something you might call flapping fins. That's how slender and how flexible he was. He was so loose that when he stood relaxed, his abdomen hung dejectedly . . . . . we named him "Cave-in."

And then there was Mel, a brute of a boy with the power and

roar of a gorilla. He was our hero, but it took Fouch to control his mind. Fouch used to get Mel all excited by doing a grotesque, half-squatting dance, adding to that several choice phrases and popping out his big almond eyes in a hypnotic stupefaction that swayed and maddened the boy bull. We were afraid to commit any foul deeds on Fouch, for fear he would unleash his monster and send him after us.

Mel, Fouch, and I used to go to the wrestling matches every week. It was great to sit there and watch the big hams grunt and groan in the throes of their enormous farce. The roped-in square was lost in a sea of cigarette smoke, and sometimes the wrestlers would throw the referee out of the ring.

However, Mel was a fine boy. He was a strict Catholic, and anyone that should show any signs of deviation was certain to incur his bull wrath. We kept our blooming metaphysics to ourselves.

There was still another neighborhood celebrity, back there in those gushing days. We called him Wattaguy, and he used to walk down the street with a ridiculous zeal that flung him along like a bobbing cork. Once when I had been playing alone with my imaginary horse-races in my room, I had heard him enter downstairs and ask my mother for me.

She was following instructions. "He's out," she said.

"I'll take a look anyway," he beamed, rubbing his hands vigorously. I put out my light and crawled under the bed. Wattaguy came into the room, turned on the light, and dragged me from under my hiding-place.

"What the hell are you doin' there? Come on out. We're playing chess!" And we did. Wattaguy was a swell kid, just the same.

And then there was the time we had a horse. A wealthy friend of my father's had given it, a six-year-old mare, to myself and my sister. My chum Mike, who lived clear across the city, was nuts about horses. He practically boarded with us while we had it. One day, the horse broke loose from my yard and ran wild-eyed through the entire section. Mike and I chased it with a lasso, up the sandbank, down the street, along the river, up the street, and up the sandbank again. We finally lured the frightened beast with stable food and haltered him. It was a great day in the history of our neighborhood.

And Oh we did a million other things! We were kids, and we did everything . . . .

And these are but memories. The little neighborhood sleeps, three melancholy lamps shed their light, the cottages are squatted squarely on the familiar ground, shadows loom black and ghoul-like, starwealthy sky touches singing treetop, Augustcool I sit.

Hush ... hush ... wush ... hush ... hush ... wush ... shhhhhhhhhhhhhh .....

I sit here remembering, and the trees sing me their farewell song.

I remember a lot of things. I remember exactly how the sun shone on Bill's sandy hair one afternoon on the sandbank in the long-ago Summer gold; I remember also the shimmering rooftops in the heat, the distant sounds of afternoon—a woodsaw, someone hammering, a child's shout, slamming door—I remember all this and how the sun burned down in yellow fire-shafts, how the sand under my "sneakered" foot was redhot . . . . . . . Oh Hell! I defy any man to refuse me! Look at that afternoon light, sometime back in the summer of 1933; look at the dry pebbled street, the crazy blaze-dance that melted its sparse tar, do not refuse me but look! look! look! . . . . . for here is a moment transpiring on the earth, at one place, at one time, a precious drop from Time's ancient waterfall, and now it is long-ago and gone, forgotten and dead. The moment is over, has been over for eight years, yet I want it to return blazing! Yes, where is Bill today? Where?

Bill is in the Philippines, at the army base in Manila. He is all the way around the side of the world, and although the world turns, we never meet. Yes, Bill is in the Philippines, and today the sun-blaze is yet upon his sandy hair. I sit here on a porch step in Massachusetts, in the middle of the night, August 1941. The sunblaze is yet upon his hair, but is it precisely the same sun of eight years ago in New England? Is it? Is it? And there is the irrefragable damnation of the whole brutal fact, there is the curse of Time, there is the song of the trees and the tear that surges at the burning gates!! . . . . . because it is not precisely the same sun of eight years ago in New England, it is not! it is not! and I cannot get to understand it!!

What is this thing Time?

Fouch is still living across the street, and tonight he is sleeping while the trees, high and dark and magnificent in the night, bend sadly and sing softly and Fouch hears them long through the night. Time! Fouch is not a young man, and he smokes cigarettes with an exasperated scowl. He sits in his kitchen at night and stares angrily at the green walls. His mother reads the Greek Bible, her lips silently mouthing the beautiful words. Yes Thalatta! Always Thalatta!

Why Time?

And tomorrow morning, with the swift and clean dawn, the truck will come and be loaded. Then, I shall sit in the back and watch the neighborhood as we roll away forever. My home and my land . . . .

Ah well. Remember the child: In partaking, question not. Question not, you fool.

Hush . . . hush . . . wush . . . . shhhhhh . . . . cool breeze and tree song . . . It is all over, it is all over . . . .

But I have been rich in days. Oh yes, I have been rich in days. They have tumbled down upon me, one upon the other, and are still tumbling today. It is true that I have to pull up my stakes and roll along, that I have to tear up my heartroots, but it is also true that I have been very very rich, and shall be very very rich, for the days do tumble, one upon the other.

And whatever is to come, I am content, for I have been rich in days, and shall be rich in days. I guess it is the same way with my country . . . . America too is rich. America is rich in years, ripe with generations. Whatever is to come, she too will be content, for she has been rich and will be rich. In her great wealth she will thrive. In my great wealth I shall thrive. The days have been golden because gold has been put into them. The days will be golden because gold will be put into them. This is Manifesto, simple and priceless. It is good to be rich. It is invincible to be rich.

And now, from the farmyards in back of my neighborhood comes the scrawny-throated fanfare of a rooster, clear and clean. Dawn cometh. The first bird blurts his tiny twit. In the East appears the dirty grey vanguard of a new day. Wavy blankets of ghost mist cling to the still dark ground. I feel the chill of dew. And with all that, there is the serenade of my trees, tall dark trees singing way up there in the breeze, looking down at me sadly, farewell, farewell. A million tender rustlings, a vast soft song from my boyhood trees.

I look up at the trees, staring into their sorrowful profusion of night-green: "So long trees. I've got to move along," I whisper to them. "So long . . . . . . so long . . . . . oh so long . . . ."

And now I tell you I am weeping, quietly and without tears . . .

That old swishing song.

# [I Have to Pull Up
My Stakes and Roll, Man]

*This is a later and longer version of an extended riff in the
original manuscript of "Farewell Song, Sweet from My
Trees," from August 1941. The passage is the narrator's
answer to the Merrimack River's question "Hey, who the
hell are you?" as he prepares to leave his neighborhood of
many years. The first version concludes: "I am of the
American temperament, the American temper, the American tempo, river. And I tell you I am not Socrates wearing
a robe, nor Shakespeare in breeches, but I am a poet in
trousers, hat, shirt, coat, shoes, socks and my hair is
combed, parted on the left side, I can jive a little bit, I
play football and baseball, I go out with dames and I love
America. That's who I am."*

I have to pull up my stakes and roll, Man. I'll tell you what I am,
first. I am part of the American temper, the American temperament,
the American tempo. I wear trousers, (and with the latest trend) I
wear long suit-coats, I try to get hold of the looser collars, the trick-
ier ties; I aim to be a dapper man. That's what I look like; and
maybe sometime you'll catch me with a turned up hat, Joe College
himself, in the flesh.

I don't wear robes, cloaks, nor breeches. I'm not Socrates, I'm not
Shakespeare, I'm not Goethe. I'm Kerouac. And I'm in the 20th
Century, 1941 A.D., right now. I am a poet, a philosopher, and I base
my theories on science, of which I am quite ignorant, if not stupid.
But I am no jerk, I assure you. I don't write verse, I write poetry.
And I am no jerk, because I know that I am part of the American
temperament, I love swing bands with a terrific bucket man (drummer), and I love to have these bands dish out life and bite and beat
(a steady beat, like Krupa's, that rocks the dance floor with soul and

precision) and I love to see those jitterbugs and their subtle bounce with the rhythm, their women who step quick and jerkily and spin with their jitterbug gams showing up to the garters, I love America and I love to look at those jitterbugs who let their hair grow long and sleek, with a knockout dazzling wave; their wide-brimmed, low-crowned hats (3 1/4 inchers); their pegged trousers with high belts; their swaggering walk, the way they smoke, the way they sensation-alize, show off, the way they let you know about it, the way they click their shoe heels, the way they look around with a broad sweep and take in everything, pedestal themselves, talk good and audibly, expose themselves and turn the world into the blare of bands, the jive, the women-drink-smokes-debauchery-you thick bastard-Ho Ho-Make me know it, Dorsey, Make me know it!!!!!

Yes, I have to pull up my stakes and roll, and I told you about one part of the American temper because I am part of all of it.

I love a retired Yale professor; I love the jig bands (colored); I love André Kostelanetz and his sobbing string section; I love a street in Vermont, dusty and lined with discolored shacks; I love Boston's Back Bay; I love the Daily Mirror; I love the C.C.C. camps in Colo-rado; I love Miami and all the chiselers down there; I love Saratoga's race track, the Travers stakes, the Cup, (I remember Discovery vs. Granville, I remember Whirlaway, I also remember Aristides and the Derby, and after him Domino, Old Rosebud, Regret, Clyde Van Dusen, Johnstown.) Oh, yes, Man, I'm no jerk; I know my country, my onions, I know I'm part of the temper. I love Joe DiMaggio and the song about him, Les Brown's arrangement; I love the cyclotrons at Columbia and Notre Dame; I love William Randolph Hearst; I love Broadway, and Beacon Street in Boston, Philadelphia in an Oc-tober twilight and the flash and excitement of an intersection; I love Carnegie Hall; I love Brooklyn, 293 State Street and the Flatbush, Bainbridge Avenue, the Bridge, Coney Island; I love New England, I tell you I do; I love the dopes who argue on Times Square, Boston Common, on street corners in 'Frisco, WallaWalla, Denver, Waco Texas; I love America; I love its tempo; I love the Navy Yard in Portsmouth, the Marine Base in Virginia; I love Hollywood (don't get me wrong) and its Walter Pidgeon, its Brenda Marshall, its Boyer and Garbo and Gary Cooper and Edmund O'Brien, directors Ford, Sturges, Welles, Rita Hayworth (o man), I love its movies its people its personalities its Technicolor; I love New York, the New Yorker, Esquire for Men, Life, Time, the Atlantic Monthly, published in Concord, N.H.; I love New Haven, Yale, Hotel Taft, the trolleys and the beaches and the air-cooled theatres, the distinguished elms singing over houses austere; I love Estes Park, Colorado, the dirt street and wooden sidewalks and mountains; I love Arizona, the dude ranches; I love Chicago, the suburbs, Albert Halper—"kernels, pop, pop, pop for dear old Chicago . . . . . . my arms are heavy, I've got the blues; there's a locomotive in my chest and that's a fact." ; and I love Asheville, N.C. with the people sitting on the porches in the summer nights listening to the trains shriek in the valleys, and little Tom Wolfe sitting on his porch steps, listening, seething, "a locomotive in his chest."; yes I love Saroyan and Fresno (the ditches in the fields, the vines, the Assyrian barbers, the flying young men on the trapeze, the Uncles Melik, Jorgi, etc. the Beautiful People); I love America, yes I do. I love the White Sox, the Dodgers, Ted Williams and Pete Reiser; I love America, I tell you I do.

# Odyssey (Continued)

A series of short uneventful rides, and I find myself standing by the side of the road just over the Connecticut border. I am shaded by a natural wall which has been cut to make way for the road. Across the street are grass and trees, and up to the right, a nice little house. The sky is very blue.

It is so nice here that I feel like staying here forever, or at least for the night. But I must carry on in order to get home. Home spells comfort and security. This place spells poetry, ants in your clothes, and hunger.

To be exact about this writing game, now, let's face it: A writer wants to cut a slab out of the whole conglomerate mass-symphony of nature and life and present it to his readers. Why? Because, Art is a readjustment of perception, from physical actuality to a perception expressed by the artist. This trip of mine occurred during the vast ant-rush of that day in May; it was a sequence, and ran from New York to Lowell, and took 12 hours. But now I am presenting it to my readers in the form of Art, so that their cognizance of this sequence is readjusted from reality to art. Why does the human being insist on presenting reality through an artistic and expressive medium? Why doesn't he let well enough alone? Why should he express Life, through Art? Since the cavemen did it themselves, carving crude images of animals on stone, I am concluding that man is making an attempt to intensify consciousness, which is a very religious thing to do. Art, therefore, is in one measure religion. That may be why the Catholics like to call Art the language of God, or the such. But I say that Man, seeing Life about him, desires to express himself about this phenomena, and in so doing, exercises what is probably the only differentiating faculty between human and brute: That of Art, the act of readjusting perception, from reality to a new objectifica-tion and revaluation, thus exhibiting a religious desire to worship what we have about us, which is Life.

This settled, the writer now sets forth to document reality.

Well, I got a ride from a man who loved books and music. He recited William Cullen Bryant and praised Sir Walter Scott and Stevenson and Reid. He drove slowly and talked about himself. It was amazing, riding in a sleek car with a tender soul who loved the romance of Scott through streets strewn with realism—filling stations, stores, hydrants, straw hats, window fronts, no sign of Ivanhoe nor Rebecca.

# [At 18, I Suddenly Discovered the Delight of Rebellion]

*Kerouac revisited this handwritten piece in 1945 and added the last four lines, beginning with "at 19."*

At 18, I suddenly discovered the
delight of rebellion—and was
drunk with it 1 ½ years, not
knowing how to wield this mad
thing, being more or less wielded
by it. Saroyan sparked it—
indolent, arrogant Saroyan. It
ruined my first College year.
But after the drunken stage,
I shortly gathered up my reins
and began to direct those daring
white steeds of rebellion into
a more constructive direction—
into a direction that was
bound to be the beginning of
ultimate, complete development
& integration.—at 19 1941
    at 23, in 1945, what can
    I add?
    Or, perhaps, at 74 in 1996?

# Observations

What more do I want but a meal when I am hungry, or a
   bed when I am weary,
or a rose when I am sad?
What more does one need in this world but the few joys
   that are afforded
him by this earth, this rich bursting earth, that flushes
   with bloom each
Spring, and leases its luxury of wet warmth to us for a
   glorious summer?
What more do I want but a woman when I am in passion,
   or a glass of water
when I am thirsty, or music when I am lonely?
Why, I need not your sumptuous sitting room, nor your
   full-vistaed garden!
Nor your wainscotted bedroom with overhanging canopy
   and oils! All I need
is my little den, with a window to let the sun shine in,
   and a shelf of
books, and a desk, and something to write with, and
   paper, and my soul:
   Where can I find my soul?
   In solitude said my friend, in solitude.
   Yes. I have found my soul in solitude.
No, I don't want riches! This has been said so many
   times before. And
when I say the world is bursting with plenty, I know the
   starved millions
will laugh: but I shall laugh with them and overthrow: I
   know whereof I
speak: I am not a prophet, I am, like Whitman, a lover.
   Whitman, that

glorious American! Barbellion, who will go with you,
    anywhere, any time,
any fashion, for nothing, for everything. Come, I will go
    with thee,
said Whitman: Whitman, the underrated, the forgotten,
    the laughed-at,
the homosexual, the lover of life.
    How shall I sing?
    I shall sing: I shall record the misery, observe on it,
        and point
out how to abolish it. Blah.

# Definition of a Poet

In 1941 Kerouac wrote: "You say, all poets like to kick. And this one here, Jack Kerouac, wants to kick in an original manner [. . . .]" Over and over in his early writings he refers to himself as a poet. To Kerouac, the poet was the ideal, the highest form of a writer, the artist-writer, of whom he wrote: "Their use lies in being able to erect structures of thought for mankind." He admired Walt Whitman, whom he credited with shaping "a living philosophy for his fellow countrymen." He described Whitman as his "first real influence" and the reason he decided to hit the American road.

Young Kerouac experimented with poetry in all forms, but traditional verse forms did not suit him. In 1940 he explained why: "I feel that the words are put backwards. I'd rather have simple prose-poetry, to the point, concise, and more digestible. Outside of that, poetry is sublime. Poets are happy people, because they too are sublime." He later added a few original forms to the array of poetic forms, including the "pop," a three-line American or Western haiku without syllable restrictions, and the "blues," which he defined as "a complete poem filling in one notebook page, of small or medium size, usually in 15-to-25 lines, known as a Chorus, i.e., 223rd Chorus of Mexico City Blues in the Book of Blues." Kerouac connected the blues and poetry, as does contemporary American poet Charles Simic, who writes: "The reason people make lyric poems and blues songs is because our life is short, sweet, and fleeting. The blues bears witness to the strangeness of each individual's fate."

A poet is a fellow who
spends his time thinking
about what it is that's
wrong, and although he
knows he can never quite
find out what this wrong
is, he goes right on
thinking it out and writing
it down.
A poet is a blind optimist.
The world is against him for
many reasons. But the
poet persists. He believes
that he is on the right track,
no matter what any of his
fellow men say. In his
eternal search for truth, the
poet is alone.
He tries to be timeless in a
society built on time.

# America in the Night

## —1—

Listen!
Kroooaaooo! Krrooooaaooooo!
'Tis the train whistle, now, in the night,
Kroooooo!
I'm on a train, and I've got to whistle too. . . .
The real, the true America,
Is America in the night.

The guileful sleep, guile-less;
The egotists sleep, ego-less;
The timid sleep, fear-less.
Across the midnight face of America—
They sleep. . .

## —2—

The real, the true America,
Is America in the night.

## —3—

What is a youth?
I see one now—he is the youth of ages.
Frowning silently, he smokes—
A soldier in Alexander's legions?
Quietly, he adjusts his regalia.
A young driver of Arabian caravans?
He yawns in the night, then listens:—
Krooooaaoooo. . . . !!

Of the fleet of Nelson?
A Tatar? A young soldier of Kublai Khan's?
A crusader? The young Iroquois warrior?
A black defender of Khartoum?
Yank in France?
No matter—they are one, all are one.
And the same—the youth of ages.
An American sailor.
With me he plies the black waters of night,
Aboard the good ship S.S. America.


—4—

Red, white and blue they say?
America?
Don't kid me, I say to they:—
America is blue
Right through—
Blue!
Improvise, black saxist, improvise!
Tell them with your black soul
That America is blue,
That America is the blues.
Play that throbbing tremolo—
Let me stand beside you, approving.
Bring him a soap box,
Let him stand up and play the blues.
Kroooaaaooooo!


—5—

Sibelius, tell us about Nature!
And you brave Waldo—
And thou also Thoreau.
Tell us about the dark forest in the night—
Patient, untelling, and wise.
And you Gershwin, and you Runyon—
Tell us about New York town . . .
In the night, in the night.
They tell me God made night to sleep—

Zounds! My dawn is in the West!
The darkness is over the land,
And the melancholy lamps glimmer,
And the train thunders through . . .
In the night.
Krooooaaooo!


—6—


Sandburg, Wolfe, Whitman, and Joe—
They all work for the railroad.
Sandburg, Wolfe, and Whitman sing—
While Joe pulls that old whistle string:—
Krooooaaoooo! Krooooaaooo!!
Lordy but they're blue—
—Those lovers of the blues!

# Woman Going to Hartford

I see the burnished
tenderness of the
countryside. Summer
is over, and that great
thrill I missed; next
summer, then.
Meanwhile, the tender
char in the sky.
        Old earth, old old
earth. In the city,
leaves, air, sad people,
something old & lost.
        Soon—winter,
        My child—in the
park, tawny grass,
        fiery tree, wind,
        cold wind about his
        little scarf. Does
        he wonder too?
What, Oh what is
        it?
Something old & lost,
Madam. Old earth, old.

# Old Love-Light

*October was a time of year packed with meaning for Ker-*
*ouac, even as a young man, as is illustrated in the two fol-*
*lowing pieces. "I Tell You It Is October" calls to mind*
*Thomas Wolfe's October rhapsody that opens Book III in*
Of Time and the River, *with Eugene Gant back home af-*
*ter his father's death. Kerouac later wrote in* On the Road:
*"In inky night we crossed New Mexico; at gray dawn it*
*was Dalhart, Texas; in the bleak Sunday afternoon we*
*rode through one Oklahoma flat-town after another; at*
*nightfall it was Kansas. The bus roared on. I was going*
*home in October. Everybody goes home in October."*

The railroad buildings, dingied
by scores of soot-years,
thrusting their ugly rears
at your train window, are
a sign of man's decay.
Once, I took a train
instead of a bus. A bus
takes you on a highway
lined with filling stations
& lunchcarts. A train
runs smack through the
forest. I wanted to
study the forest in October
and I took a train.
    It was astonishing to read
what I read about October
the following day. I thought
I had it all figured out—

I thought the lonely little
houses, lost in the middle
of great tawny grass,
shaggy copper skies and
mottled orange forests, were
full of fine humanity that
I was missing. Instead, the
writer informed me that
it was chlorophyll that
colored the leaves. I
thought I had all the
significance of October
under my hat & pasted.
I thought that October
was a tangible being,
with a voice. The
writer insisted it was
the growth of corky cells
around the stem of the
leaf. The writer also
said that to consider
October sad is to be
a melancholy Tennysonian.
October is not sad, he
said. October is falling
leaves. October comes
between Sept. & Nov. I
was amazed by these facts,
especially about the
Tennysonian melancholia. I
always thought October was
a kind old Love-light.

# I Tell You It Is October!

There's something olden and golden and lost
  In the strange ancestral light;
There's something tender and loving and sad
  In October's copper might.

End of something, old, old, old . . .
Always missing, sad, sad, sad . . .
Saying something . . . love, love, love . . .

Akh! I tell you it is October,
  And I defy you now and always
To deny there is not love

Staring foolishly at skies
Whose beauty but God defies.

For in October's ancient glow
  A little after dusk
Love strides through the meadow
  Dropping her burnished husk.

It may be that I am mad, sir:
  Or perhaps hope in vain . . .
But Oh! October is sad, sir,
  As mournful as midnight rain.

The melancholy frowse of harvest stacks,
The tender char of morning skies,
The advance of Emperor October,
Father! Father!
Father November of the sombre silver,
Oh I tell you it is October!

# [Here I Am at Last
# with a Typewriter]

*Written on October 13, 1941. In the Saroyan story "Myself upon the Earth" from the 1930s, the narrator longs for his typewriter, which is tied up in a pawnshop: "After a month I got to be very sober and I began to want my typewriter. I began to want to put words on paper again. To make another beginning. To say something and see if it was the right thing. But I had no money. Day after day I had this longing for my typewriter."*

Here I am at last with a typewriter, a little more the hungrier, a little less the hungrier. There are some kinds of hunger, and there are other kinds of hunger.

As I write the first paragraph, it occurs to me that the print of this typewriter is similar to the print of a typewriter which I used in College, exactly one year ago. This is a thing which astonishes me no end, but affects you not. But the fact remains, here I am, one year later in life, with the same kind of typewriter, only the letters I put down are different, with more truth, sanity, health, background, and backbone than the old ones. When I was in college, I used to write for the fun of it. Now I'm in dead seriousness.

I see by the papers, and by Thomas Wolfe, that America is sick. This is a bad state of affairs, and it is being covered up by a lot of talk about hopeless Europe. Because Europe is hopeless at the moment doesn't mean that America is to overlook her own defects. The National Defense move, a huge gesture on the part of a great nation for the benefit of a huge war, brings to my mind one amazing fact: Why didn't we ever make such a tremendous drive for the sake of good things, rather than war? Why do huge movements such as this National Defense emergency have to be huge simply because they are propelled by greed? Why did our movement for American

reconstruction measure up to this movement for war like a Lilliput-
ian flea to a Brobdignagian dinosaur? (I'm talking about the W.P.A.
and the National Defense?) It certainly makes you feel like vomiting, sometimes, in true Woollcott contempt. America is sick as a
dog, I tell you. That's why, with my new typewriter and a lot of yellow paper, I am grown dead serious about my letters, my work, my
stuff, my writing here in an American city (Hartford). I will talk all
about life in the 20th Century, and about America's awful sickness
and about some individual sickness I see in men and about good
things in this life, namely, books, October skies, other varied weathers, women, Johnny Barleycorn, the Love of Man, a warm roof. I am
alone in this boomtown, you see, but I am not silly. I am not going to
rent a cheap room and starve. I'm going to rent a nice little half-
cheap room, and starve halfways. That's because I have a good job,
and those silly guys didn't, the suckers. (The lovely, the poor, the
great suckers who in their solitary suffering and complaint, have
added a jot of truth to America's small pile of the stuff.)

Oh, yes, I am about to see life whole . . . . man's travails, man ply-
ing his self-made civilization, man's decay, man's dignified despair
and nobility. I am about to see it and smell it and eat it. It is going to
be fine for me, I tell you. Fine for me, either way.

I am a writer, and thus it will prove valuable for me to study this
place. However, before I start writing in dead seriousness, I want
to add one thing. One of the remedies for American sickness is
humour—there isn't enough of it to go around—and I think it ought
to be fed to the people. This kind of humour, for instance:

You are sitting on a stone wall in the city, watching the people go
by. It is midafternoon, and two little kids come up and ask you if you
work in a filling station. After you say yes, you look back to the
street, and everything has turned comical. The answer is the kids.
Kids are not hankerers, they are just happy living men. Perhaps this
may sound childish, but the children themselves will vouch for me.
I know a guy who sees something comical in everything, but he also
goes too far. I just thought I'd let you know. Remember humour.

Ha ha ha.

It's a great thing. . . . it's irony, and add to it pity. Pity and irony,
America, pity and irony. Stuff as old as the Bible.

# [Atop an Underwood: Introduction]

*Immediately following this typed introduction to* Atop an Underwood, *on the same sheet of paper, is Kerouac's short story "The Good Jobs." He later recorded the introduction as "1941, October, Hartford," without the specific day noted. It is likely that he wrote the introduction soon after establishing himself in Hartford with a job at an automobile service station, a room, and a rented Underwood typewriter. He worked the clay of that real-life experience as he wrote the 1968 version of* Vanity of Duluoz: *". . .when I came home at night tired from work, after eating my nightly cheap steak in a tavern on Main Street, came in and started to write two or three fresh stories each night: the whole collection of short stories called 'Atop an Underwood,' not worth reading nowadays, or repeating here, but a great little beginning effort. [. . .]"*

*Kerouac describes himself "writing little terse short stories" in the mold of Saroyan and Hemingway. However, the stories composed in Hartford, and he claims to have written two hundred in about eight weeks, were rarely stories in the conventional sense, with a setting, plot, characters, and dialogue. Reading Saroyan and Hemingway would have given Kerouac a sense of flexibility with the form of a story. For example, Saroyan writes: "Do you know that I do not believe there is really such a thing as a poem-form, a story-form or a novel-form. I believe there is man only. The rest is trickery." The bursts of prose poetry also bring to mind Whitman's Civil War writings in his* Specimen Days. *Whitman drew on "impromptu jottings" in notebooks for those accounts.*

*The term* story *better suits the Hartford work if we think of Kerouac's using it as a journalist might have, in a newspaper or magazine story, the product of a reporter. Most of the time he was reporting on his own life, filing dispatches to the world desk from his personal cultural front. He was an old-time "newsie" with his bulletins, columns, and stories. He would give himself an assignment, then spin a piece of yellow paper into the Underwood, and start chewing up the blank sheet like a man devouring an ear of native corn. He often filled the sheet of paper top to bottom and margin to margin. There was barely enough space to contain his overflowing mind, so he wrapped up the thought and punched in the final jk on the last line—and you imagine him reaching for another piece of paper to start a new line of talk. He uses the page as a compositional field in the same way he turned the American dime store pocket notebook page into the ultimate pragmatic poetic form: end of the page, end of the blues chorus.*

## ATOP AN UNDERWOOD
by Jack Kerouac
F.P.
—Sixty Little Old Stories—
\*\*\*
## INTRODUCTION

Hello, this is Jack Kerouac F.P., a new writer.

F.P. stands for furious poet.

Here are sixty little old stories for you to study at your leisure. I have made them short in order to augment their dignity as regards to fullness and completeness. Also, you will most likely go a little more slowly in your reading of them, due to the fact that you will feel 59 stories ahead of you the moment you start reading the first, and 58 stories ahead of you the moment you start reading the second, and all that. There is a kind of mute sanctity to a story, and if you have to read enough of them, you will no doubt take it a bit slow and not try to gobble everything up in one night, idiotically, like Clifton Fadiman, who I maintain has never read a book in his life.

I am making a drive for slower and finer reading.

Try it. You will find that it pays more, fills you with respect for the world of letters, which is another department of my drive.

Try it now. Read this slowly and religiously. I am making a drive toward slower and more religious reading. You will find, as you go along, that I am also making a drive toward a whole mess of other things.

Jack Kerouac F.P.

Harcourt, Brace & Co. New York (!)

# The Good Jobs

*This story follows the introduction to Kerouac's* Atop an Underwood *and springs from a Hartford tradition, door-to-door sales. The city's nineteenth-century publishers introduced the concept of subscriptions, pitched house to house by traveling salesmen. This is where America's first Fuller brush man took to the streets too.*

To talk like Albert Halper once did, I've held down a lot of good jobs in my day.

The best job I ever had was in Connecticut. As you will presently know, I do not like to work, or to be nearer the truth, I do not like to surrender the hours and minutes of my life to anyone, let alone a fogy old employer. I rather like the idea of having all my hours to myself: eating a fudge sundae, watching a movie, sleeping on my couch, singing in the bathroom, studying the woods, kidding around with a girl, playing cards lazily, writing, etc. All kinds of stuff that America brands "shiftless," at one time or another.

I am a shiftless fellow myself, you know. I am rather proud of that. Perhaps I might even lay a claim, in all seriousness and in due gravity, to being the most shiftless man in the world. This is because I have been bungling things up all my life, happily, and my conscience is clear. I am a thorough bungler.

Now, this job I held down in Connecticut was ideal. It called for about six hours of work per day, but the way I did it, it called for only an hour a day. I was a salesman, and instead of soliciting these people with white fences around their little homes, I preferred to stuff their mailboxes with leaflets, quietly tip-toeing so that I might not disturb them. It is against my inner principles to go up to a beautiful little home and harbor any solicitation in my heart.

I absolutely refuse to bother these housewives, and therefore I took great pains not to disturb them, hoping inside that the company would tolerate my incapability to actually sell for a least another two weeks. So I went from door to door, as they say, stuffing mailboxes with leaflets and creeping down the steps. Once I got caught. A housewife espied me sneaking off and captured me.

"Yes?"

"Oh, nothing," I smiled. "I'm just distributing samples and stuff." I had the interests of the company well at heart, I assure you sincerely, but I also had the interests of these private lives at heart. However, this was one grand exception.

"Come here," she said, "and tell me all about it."

I spent a whole hour listening to her tell of her son, who was lazy, and her daughter, who was very athletic and played basketball. I liked the part about her son. He sounded like a swell guy, and undoubtedly this house contained much fine humanity that I was missing. But the woman talked about a lot of other things, and I got bored fast. I left, and was so exhausted with the morning's work, that I retired to the forest.

That was the nice part about this Connecticut job. After my daily hour's work, I used to retire to my nook in the forest, and would lie there for hours, studying the woods and watching the sky. It was a stone's throw from an airport, but whenever an airplane roared across the sky above me, obstructing my view of the clouds, etc. I ignored it and passed it off as a bad job by man. I also studied the fallen leaves, and watched them sail off from the trees one by one. You see, it was October, and the ground was warm, dry, almost choking. It was an emotional experience for me of great consequence. That is so, because I will never forget it. It was a swell job.

One afternoon, I wasn't alone studying the forest. There was a girl with me, and she was all mixed up about the stuff I was saying. It was nothing; I was only trying to teach her to see, with her eyes. She watched the airplanes, but I ignored them completely. I am not used to them yet, but I suppose I will have to soon.

It was a swell job. It contained just the right amount of forest-studying time for me. . . . . almost all day. As you see, the girl was part of my curriculum. I will even go as far as to say that I am quite a lover of girls, and am vexed plenty of times by the problem which they offer me, and all mankind. But I will overcome that, too.

Anyway, that was my job, and a good one too. It was the greatest job I ever held down, because I got a lot out of it, which is the utilitarian way of judging things, no? My conscience, is it necessary to repeat, was clear, and is still clear. As a bell. I am the world champ bungler, except when it comes to Pity and Love.

But we'll go into that later. Pity and Love have nothing to do with this, the greatest job I ever had, and even perhaps, the greatest job of all time in all the world itself.

# From Radio City to the Crown

Everybody knows about Radio City, with its beautiful stage shows, its tremendous organ music, its fine moving pictures, the immense sweep of its interior architecture, the deep lushness of its lobbies, the magnificent oil paintings hanging from majestic walls, the tall trim ushers, the luxuriously plushed seats with plenty of arm space, the efficient air cooling system, and above all that odor, the odor and savor of abundance, wealth, opulence—that odor of luxury, "the best that money can buy," the smells that come radiating from large, ample, and luxuriant things, the faint suggestions of massive squat comfort that things of wealth will create in the mind.

Well, the Crown is also a theatre, and it is located on Middlesex Street in Lowell, Mass., my old home town. The Crown, in my day, was infested with rats upstairs, but we used to ignore them and concentrate on the movies. It was cheaper to sit upstairs, and we went up there rats or no rats.

Well, just a few years ago when my gang and myself were just about growing up to be men, we used to go to the Crown every Sunday afternoon to see the double feature. Henry used to put on his green suit and ring, and that's when he would flash his gold teeth. It was then we called him Kid Faro. The rest of the gang would also attire itself nattily; there was Kid Faro, myself, Fouch, Freddie, and Salvey.

Before we went in for the afternoon's performance in the Crown theatre, we used to buy a Mr. Goodbar in the store across the street, or perhaps go to the White Tower just down a block for a nickel box of ice cream. Kid Faro used to buy a bar of candy, the aforementioned Mr. Goodbar, and when I had my ice cream finished in the movie, I would usually ask him for some of his sweetmeat. Kid Faro used to proffer me a chocolate-covered peanut, or at best, a small corner of the bar. Kid Faro knew his onions.

Well, the show always bored us, naturally. We were all about

17 years old. We would watch the horses ride across the scene, and the cowboys turn in their saddles to shoot. It was always the same thing. But somehow or other, every Sunday afternoon, the five of us would dress up nattily and stroll down to the Crown for a double feature, ten cents. I guess, way down deep, that we all knew that this was the thing. This was it, and we should not lose it. We all dressed up and moseyed down to the Crown, five American boys walking down the street beneath the telephone-wires, past the package stores and second-hand stores and laundries and variety stores and closed barrooms and drugstores and restaurants. Five American young men, walking down the street on a Sunday afternoon, talking, walking past the houses and things of the city, of the state, of the country; walking along toward the Crown. It sure was the thing.

Sometimes we would raise hell in there, on the second floor where the rats used to be when we were only so high. We would yell out as loud as we could. Fouch had a specialty of his own. He would yell out this word with his resounding voice: "Aaah-ooh-way-braasshh!!" It was supposed to indicate the flatulence of a huge fat Wall Street financier, but only the five of us knew that. The rest of the people in the Crown just laughed because it sounded whacky anyway. But we laughed even louder. I pulled it a couple of times myself, and let me tell you, it was great, sitting up there on the second floor of the Crown and shouting: "Aah-ooh-way-braasshh!" and hearing girls snicker, fellows laugh, and the cop come running up the steps as best he could. The cop was about 70 years old, so we didn't have much to fear from his tottering quarter. The thing is, we never abused him. We just went to the Crown and sat down upstairs, sometimes watching the western badmen shoot it out, sometimes raising hell for the Americanism of it all.

It was the thing that got us . . . the thing . . .

# ... The Little Cottage by the Sea ....

My folks once lived in a little cottage by the sea, about 150 years ago in Brittany, and just a few months ago in West Haven, Conn. The first day we moved into that little cottage by the sea, it was raining very heavily, greyly. My dad and myself were helping the movers rush the furniture into the house from the truck, which was parked in the mud in front of the cottage, the motor facing a lashing gale from the Sound, facing the great menace of monstrous rolling waves of grey water and spray. My mother stood in the parlor, huddled, watching us bring the things in, and looking out across the mud at the massive grey heave of the sea, listening to the boom and smack of the big waves against the seawall. "My," I'll bet she said to herself, "what am I getting myself into?"

But it was all right. When the movers left to go get the second load of furniture, I put on my bathing trunks and walked across the mud, picking my feet tenderly among the pebbles, heading for the great menace of grey sea, unafraid, thrilled, furious with power, mad with the glory of the elements. I walked into the water and began to swim, rising high up with the crest of the waves, and then sinking way down into their greyblack valleys of water and foam; testing the salty spray, smashing my face and eyes onward into the great sea, swimming out and laughing aloud. I ploughed on, bobbing up and down in the play of the mighty waves, getting dizzy with the rise and fall of it, seeing the horizon in the grey rainy distance and then losing it in the face of a monster wave.

I put out for a boat which was anchored; a small rowboat, with the words "We're Here" painted on the bow. Well, I was there all right, and I scrambled aboard with some difficulty, because the little boat was heaving crazily, side to side, stern to stern, rolling motions, thrusts forward and back, then rolling again . . . . but I made it, and sat myself on the bow, facing the sea, facing the tremendous wind and rain which cut my face until I thought it would bleed.

I turned, and saw my mother back there on the porch of the little cottage by the sea; she was looking at me, waving with anxiety and fear. I gestured that everything was all right, made a motion which said: "Boy, this is fun!" But it was more than that, more than that.

Suddenly, looking at my mother back there on shore, looking out to sea at her son, looking out to sea where her son was afloat in the savage rage and roar of the tempest, a speck in the ocean's huge fury, it came to me that this had happened before in the lives of my people. It occurred to me that many a Kerouac mother had stood on the steps of a little thatched cottage in Brittany, over there on the cold Northwest coast of France, standing there and looking out to sea for her son, her son, her son lost in the tempest, her son lost in the storm of the sea. Oh, but it was strong, strong! The thought came to me and I gloried in it . . . . . I sat there and faced the smash of the gale, laughing, and thinking about the ancient Breton fishermen, of whom I was a descendant, who had been out to sea in a storm while their mothers stood on the porches of little cottages and looked out to sea for them, praying and waving their handkerchiefs and griev-ing, grieving. Man, but I was a Breton that day! Man but I was pow-erful. Man but my mother looked heroic, ancient, great and mighty, standing there in the rain and looking out to sea at her son.

Well, I weathered the storm. I sat there in that little bit of a boat and saw the horizon dance crazily, roll drunkenly, heave savagely. I let the rain blast at my face; I bailed out with my hands, rolled with the boat, laughed like a lunatic.

Then I knew that this moment was a great moment in my life, and therefore I decided to swim back [to] shore and begin remembering it. I slipped off and made for the beach, stroking madly, hugely; ac-tually striding in the ocean's breast, lavishing in its enormous full-ness, pulling at it with wet arms, kicking feet widely, eating up yardage in the water. I got to shore and went in to the little cottage by the sea, dripping wet, walking solidly on the ground like the an-cient Bretons used to do.

# The Juke-Box Is Saving America

I was sitting at the table, eating. The soldier went up to the bar and ordered a beer. He had on his winter issue, belt and buttons and all. He adjusted his little cap carefully, jauntily, and paid for the beer. He was a clean looking soldier, and as far as I can see, he looked like a real soldier.

Drinking his beer, he noticed the juke-box in the corner. Walking up to it, he inserted a dime and asked the telephone hostess to play "Pack Up Your Troubles in the Old Kit Bag." She played it, and the soldier returned to the bar for another beer. One of the drunks in the tavern got up from his table and began to dance to the lively, gay tune. The soldier watched him, quietly pleased. When it was through, he went back to the juke-box and asked the hostess for the same number again. The tune returned, and the drunk resumed his dancing.

I was astonished, inwardly. I ate my steak with great delight. The juke-box, I said to my steak, is saving America.

For the third time, the soldier played the tune. This time, the drunk began to march around the tavern, swinging his arms in a military manner, left-flanking around chairs and about-facing at the walls; left-obliquing at the booths, and column-lefting at the wait-ress who hurried around him. The soldier adjusted his cap carefully, stood up straight, and watched, quietly pleased.

I began to think about the words of that song. They implied, I concluded, the best war philosophy of them all: Which is, go ahead to the war and forget it; it's nothing, and have fun. But the main point is that the soldier paid out his money for music, which is a good sign for America.

# ... Hartford After Work ....

I just got back to my room from work, ostensibly speaking, and I must tell you about the song, the symphony, the clash of light and hurtle of dance that is Hartford after work. Bob drives me home in his car and plays some torrid jive on his radio; and the hotter the music gets, the wilder Bob gets, until after a while he is tearing along at the rate of sixty miles per hour, dodging people, swinging around corners with a rhythmic flourish of his arms, hurtling over little lumps on the street floors with a beautiful and hot knee action, whisking and whipping along to the hot music, beating his hands on the wheel with the rhythm, tearing around the city in his car with the music blaring, tooting rhythmically at all the nice looking chicks that walk on the sidewalks with slender stockinged legs, and finally coming to a screeching stop in front of my cheap rooming house, yelling out rhythmically: "Seeya later!" And then he is off in a blur of jazz and speed, going home from work, to a supper, a nap, and then some girls in the evening; he is tearing around to beat hell, the music is hot, and Bob is all rhythm, all wound up American-wise, redhot Bob in his redhot orgy of speed and jazz and sex. Zoooom! Whacko! Step on the gas, toot the horn, whip through that intersection, you don't give a damn Hartford, you've money, women, drinks, you've got everything, you've a supper, a nap, a date; Zoooom! Whisssk! Dart around that pedestrian and turn up the radio; let's swerve in this old street while the jazz, the jive, the swing gets hotter, hotter, hotter, swifter, hotter, hotter!!! Through the streets we fly with rhythm, little old Hartford of the Aircraft, little old Hartford of lights and dance and blur of jazz and wings of song and Swooop! Swooop! Swooop on, swooooop on. Faster . . . . . faster! Blare, Jazz, blare! Whoooops! Look at those legs . . . Hey! Honneeeeeee! Yow! Looka them legs, willya? Jazz, blur, sex, speed! Zoooom! Man alive, Bob gets redhot, redhot! He's all rhythm, all grace, all sex, all speed! He's all wound-up American-wise, as redhot as the sun that sinks beyond West Hartford, sadly silent. Bob is on the loose, he's all there, he's on his way, he's roaring around, he's all rhythm, I tell you, all rhythm . . .

Well, that's the way it is. That's the way it is when you live in Hartford, work in Hartford, and at night you come home from work with a guy like Bob. It's all Hartford, all rhythm; strictly Hartford, strictly rhythm. It is what is Hartford, all this talk. It is nothing else.

Then you go to your room and find it steeped in darkness; when you raise the shade, you find the dark red gloom of brickwalls at dusk. You open the window and let the November air come in, carrying with it the odors of alley, of tenement, of garbage pail, of backyard fence and skinny tree. Then you turn on the light and find that your wallpaper is a dull stained brown; that your bed is lumpy, the blanket as old as Job, and as poor; you find your typewriter, and suddenly, beneath its majestic keys, beneath the rows of word-makers, book-makers, letter-makers, beneath these owlish little keys of passion you discover to your sudden horror a brown cockroach, and it discovers you, it runs out from beneath the ancient sanctity of your keys, it speeds along the surface of your working desk with a horrible swiftness, as of death, it blurs its many legs and floats to the edge of your desk, it starts down the side of the desk, flying swiftly with small blurring horror, its brown back hard and shell-wise in the light. When you kill it, you do it with loathing, revulsion, with a desire to vomit. But you know that war is war, and that the enemy must be taken.

Hartford after work is terrific. You go out on the street and head for the restaurant of your choice glancing at all the lights that flicker on Main Street, thinking about which place to eat. The Black & Silver, the Cardinal Grille, the Parkview, Friar's, Juddy's, John's, the Brass Rail—all of these places where a man may eat in the midst of warm gushing humanity, men and women eating, drinking, shouting, Hartford after work is terrific. In the place right across from this cheap hole of a room there are checkered table cloths, and a telephone nickelodeon with a hostess at the other end who will play any number for you, and too there is a fine beefstew, some pinball machines, and ceiling fans. And suddenly you find that the people in these places are full of rhythm, that all of Hartford is full of rhythm, that it is rhythm, it is a Boomtown in rhythm.

# ... Legends and Legends ....

*Given the language, diction, and rhythm of this composi-*
*tion, it is likely that Kerouac translated into English the*
*real or imagined voice of a Canadian French–speaking*
*storyteller, perhaps his mother or a character standing*
*in for her. Kerouac's parents, Leo A. and Gabrielle (Le-*
*vesque) Kerouac, both immigrants from Quebec, Canada,*
*were raised among the Franco-Americans of Nashua, New*
*Hampshire. Married in 1915, they settled in Lowell, where*
*Leo worked for the French-language newspaper L'Étoile.*
*Kerouac's ancestors on his father's side were Bretons from*
*Brittany, France, and his mother's people had Norman*
*roots. The French Kerouacs once held two castles in*
*Brittany; the one near the city of Brest is called Château*
*de Kerouartz. He also claimed to have Native American*
*bloodlines on both sides. The Kerouac family traced their*
*Canadian roots to the community of Rivière du Loup in*
*Quebec.*

"The Kerouacs have always been the same; get them in a one room, and they will gab and gab and gab, until there is such a noise that you can hear it up the street. Oh, they're an awful bunch, your father's people, Little Dear. They have always been; from the time way back in Canada, way way back in Canada, they've always been known to be the most foolish, the most stubborn, the most inhuman people around."

"Inhuman?"

"Well, yes, in a different sort of a way. They will not be brutal, physically, they will not hurt a fly; but Son they have no feelings! no feelings! they will see the awful suffering of their own blood and will not bat an eyelash, will not raise a finger to help. Why your own father, Little Dear, has lived some five hundred yards or so away from his brother for years, and has never paid him a visit! Brothers! mind you, Brothers! Six years within a stone's throw from each other, yet they never set eyes on each other. I tell you, the Kerouacs are and always were the most foolish and inhuman of all people I have ever known. You take your father's mother; she was a fine old woman, working her finger to the bone trying to keep the family going, and yet she never got an ounce of help from any of her sons or daughters. Oh, let me tell you, your dear father is an angel compared to some of your uncles; your father, Little Dear, is absolutely an angel when compared to some of those brothers of his. Oh My, but they were a cruel lot, a stubborn lot, a foolish lot. Your father will admit it, you know he will, you've heard him say often that his family had been hard! hard! on his poor mother. And the old man! My Goodness, everyone in the town knew that your father's father was crazy! Absolutely crazy! a nut! And cruel! Oh my but how could such a man exist! He drank and drank and drank, killed his wife and himself with his drinking, leaving behind a snarling pack of cubs that were Kerouacs. Oh, your father's father! My how such a man could exist! Here! Let me tell you . . . . he used to stand on the porch of his home in the midst of thunderstorms and shout up to the heavens, to God, daring him to strike! Daring God to kill him, and there's your father's poor old mother kneeling in the kitchen and praying while her husband stands there bareheaded in the rain, howling and roaring up to the heavens, drunk as a dog. And he used to almost drive her to her grave by juggling oil lamps—you know the big tall oil lamps we had in those old days . . . . . and daring God to blow himself and his home right up to hell and heaven. My Goodness, Little Dear, if ever the kerosene should have touched the flame there would have been a horrible explosion, and you wouldn't be here, nor would your father. My Goodness, he used to stand there in the kitchen, tossing the oil-lamp up and down, daring God to strike! and his family all coiled up together in a corner, whimpering like dogs. Crazy! I tell you, the man was crazy! And your father's brother who stole all that money from his own brothers and sisters, took your grandfather's insurance after death and kept it for himself, all of it, every cent for himself. Oh, let me tell you, your father is awful, but he is an angel compared to the rest of those Kerouacs. Ah! the Kerouacs. Don't talk to me about them . . . . it was my family, the Levesques, that was the family. Kind, quiet, generous people; simple people. Look at your Aunt Alice, a woman in her fifties, and she has the most beautiful white hair in the whole world, . . . why, up there in Montreal today, men still turn when she passes along the street, a beautiful stately woman with white hair, white white flaxen hair. She was my father's sister . . . my father. Oh Little Dear if you had only known my father. He was the kindest man that ever lived. He was a tall handsome man with white hair; he was very handsome, and so loving, so understanding. He had unhappy marriages; his first wife died, that was my mother, and his second wife left him, that's your Step-grandmother in Brooklyn. Oh Little Dear, what you don't know about my family, my own people, and about your father's awful race of madmen . . . what you don't know won't hurt you . . . . Oh Little Dear, those Kerouacs . . . . of course mine was a simple folk, we had no booklearning, no culture as they call it, but we were the fine people, the gentle people; your father's people were devils, they were wolves, they were a mad mad lot . . . . a mad mad lot, your father's people . . . ."

# ... A Kerouac That Turned Out Sublime ....

A lot has been said about my father and his people, a lot has been said about them and they have said quite a bit themselves about others. Look at me, shooting off my mouth with a typewriter, writing the sort of prose that scholars would not even consider spitting upon. Ah, the scholars . . . . essays on the sociological significance of the New Order in Europe; essays on the psychological basis of Hitler; essays on the Lost Generation and its influence on the new generation; essays on Bolshevism and its effects on World Peace . . . . all those things that have no relation whatsoever with life, here in this world, life from day to day, the struggle to exist, the problems which arise from family living, community living; no treatment of these things with any ounce of sense, only with a lot of scholastic conceit, academic egotism, something to make you want to give up reading for good. If a scholar will give you an exhaustive theory on the Lost Generation, I would prefer Thomas Wolfe's remark that there is no such thing; or Will Durant's theory that the most important thing about the world is the family, that progress comes from the family itself; and my own inexhaustive theory that the Lost Generation is nothing but a body of men who were born during a certain World Crisis (superficially speaking), and who grew up reading books, calling themselves the Lost Generation, not knowing that there have been and will be millions of Generations and that all there is to this word Generation is that it implies the force, the impulse of life, and that with each succeeding Generation, there is that little bit of progress added on, so little that it takes centuries for Generations to differ from one another. In other words, or from another corner of the gallery, I would say that the family is the thing, that all the families of one generation make up the personality of that particular generation, and not the children themselves. For I know that to be a man is one thing, and to be the member of a family is a man plus responsibilities, which implies

[ 148 ]

that there is more to life than theories on the lunacy of Hitler and his New Order, or essays on the Modern Trend to romantic realism in literature, etc.

But I have been neglecting my story. What I have just said is the result of an hour spent in the Public Library, poring over current periodicals, finding no spark of human worth in any of them, only a lot of oratory about the American Dream, freedom for all peoples at all places at all times, (let me tell you, Sir, freedom is an inner thing, and do not underestimate that remark, by all means); a lot of Rooseveltian (excuse me) blarney about the immense ideal of freedom which the world seeks today, the great shadow of death floating in the heavens, and movies in which you see the heroine looking up to heaven as the picture nears a close, looking up to heaven as the light gets brighter and the oratory is poured on, or ladled on, in great eloquent quantities, and the music mounts in fury, until you begin to imagine that there will be such a burst of light in the heavens, such a tremendous quantity of Utopian nectar, so many Gods floating around, so much oratorical heaven that you will die from the shock of it. (To think that they want to convert my beloved back-alleys, garbage pail and old redbrick wall and empty whiskey bottle, into a cloud, pink color, with oratorical angels basking in it, flapping their wings of empty eloquence.)

Well, again I have deviated. It is a tough time, folks, believe me; it is a time when a young writer knows he is wasting his time, for people have become insane, blind, foolish, they have gone off in a foolish tangent, you lose faith in them, you realize that the world of letters is no more, you wish you were an Athenian Greek, or something, so that your life's passion would not go in vain, in vain . . . but you remember Wolfe, Saroyan, and Halper, and you figure what the hell nothing is going to stop you if nothing stopped them . . .

This Kerouac I speak of who became sublime was my father's sister. Folks, she became a nun, and let me tell you that when she writes letters to my father, writes to him from the serene gloom of her religion, there is warmth! human warmth! there is no empty eloquence, there is only the kind of love that I know must still reside in the hearts of men, the kind of love that we are losing, the kind of love that I am trying to cling to, and let me tell you that my father's sister is a sublime and a great woman.

# The Father of My Father

*In her Lowell-based study* Franco-American Folk Tradi-
tions and Popular Culture in a Former Milltown, *Brigitte
Lane discusses the "languagey language" used by the
Kerouacs and others in Lowell and New England: "Franco-
American French is indeed a language of its own: an
incredibly direct, concrete and flexible language whose
linguistic features are frequently discussed with passion by
the more educated Franco-Americans. [. . .] Derived from
joual (French-Canadian French), it is definitely a dialect
of its own." Lane explains that the regional French features "extreme modernisms (acquired through the borrow-
ing and reshaping of American linguistic forms)" and
"ancient" terms. In naming the language of his household, Kerouac used the terms* Canadian French, New England French-Canadian, patois, *and even "Canuckian
Child Patois Probably Medieval" (from the note to his
poem "On Waking from a Dream of Robert Fournier").*

This is a very important story because it deals with a man who was
also named Jack Kerouac, and who was the father of my father. This
strong personage died when my father was fifteen years old, and in a
very tragic manner. He died melodramatically, indicating perhaps
that someday a poet would stem from his blood. And I'll be damned
if it didn't happen that way.

This is a very important story. I must treat it carefully, reverently,
and tragically.

Honest Jack, they called him in his home town, which was a
small New Hampshire city on the banks of the Merrimac River.
Honest Jack, the best carpenter in town, and the father of eight children; Honest Jack, who like the poet of his posterity, stood about

five feet ten inches tall and was built like an oak, and whose footsteps my father can still hear, coming down the streets of Nashua, echoing through the lanes of sleeping houses, a firm powerful step of a firm powerful man.

Honest Jack was a staunch Catholic, and one night a whore accosted him as he was crossing the railroad tracks.

"Ma putain!" he roared in French. "Go home and go to your father and allow him to spank you. You whore! You should be ashamed of yourself. Go home!" He roared and roared, and the whore ran home.

Honest Jack was a Breton. He had the blue eyes and black hair which predominates these hardy Channel fishermen. Brittany on the Northwestern coast of France. The hardy Celts of France, blue eyes and black hair, the sea, women standing on the shore waving at departing ships, like "Riders to the Sea," the Celts of the Sea. Honest Jack stemmed from this people. Somewhere in his blood was the aristocratic blood of a woman who had married one of his seaman ancestors, and then the Revolution, and the flight to Canada; the land grant in Quebec, and the loss of it through English scheming, and again the Kerouacs are of the land, and still are today. Honest Jack the carpenter in Nashua, N.H., in 1895. This amazes me no end.

Honest Jack was fearless. He dared God to strike him with a thunderbolt. Whenever there was a thunderstorm, he would stand on the large porch of his home and roar at the heavens, waving his bony fist at the lashing tempest.

"Frappes!" he would cry. "Varges! Varges, si tu est pour! Varges!"

He would use this enormous language against the storm. It meant this: "Strike me! Blast me, if you will! Blast me!" The language called Canadian French is the strongest in the world when it comes to words of power, such as blast and strike, and others. It is too bad that one cannot study it in college, for it is one of the most languagey languages in the world. It is unwritten; it is the language of the tongue, and not of the pen. It grew from the lives of French people come to America. It is a terrific, a huge language.

At other times, Honest and Fearless Jack would take an oil lamp and juggle it, all the time daring God to blow him up right then and there. His wife (and my father's dear mother), who was named Clementine, used to stand by with fear in her heart, watching her magnificent husband do the strong things that he did, wondering why he wasn't weak like other men, not knowing that only real men are considered mentally amiss. My father's father was a magnificent man.

One day, he suddenly grew tired of life. He began to drink each night, rising early in the morning to go to his work, always on time, but every night he would get drunk again, and come back home early in the morning, muttering. On Sundays, he would not drink, but would stalk around the kitchen humming church hymns. After a year of this, his son (my father's brother) denounced him for his actions, and he died that night. My father's brother is brooding over it today. It was tragic.

# Credo

Remember above all things, Kid, that to write is not
difficult, not painful, that it comes out of you
with ease, that you can whip up a little tale in no
time, that when you are sincere about it, that when
you want to impress a truth, it is not difficult,
not painful, but easy, graceful, full of smooth
power, as if you were a writing machine with a store
of literature that is boundless, enormous, endless,
and rich. For it is true; this is so. Do not forget
it in your gloomier moments. Make your stuff warm,
drive it home American-wise, don't mind critics, don't
mind the stuffy academic theses of scholars, they
don't know what they're talking about, they're way
off the track, they're cold; you're warm, you're
redhot, you can write all day, you know what you
know, like Halper; you remember that, Kid, and when
you feel as if you cannot write, as if it is no
use, as if life is no good, read this over and
realize that you can do a lot of good in this
world by turning out truths like these, by spreading
warmth, by trying to preach living for life's sake,

not the intellectual way, but the warm way, the way
of love, the way which says: Brothers, I greet you
with open arms, I accept your frailties, I offer you
my frailties, let us gather and run the gamut of
rich human existence. Remember, Kid, the ease, the
grace, the glory, the greatness of your art; remember
it, never forget. Remember passion. Do not forget,
do not forsake, do not neglect. It is there, the
order and the purpose; there is chaos, but not in
you, not way down deep in your heart, no chaos,
only ease, grace, beauty, love, greatness . . . . . Kid,
you can whip a little tale, a little truth, you can
mop up the floor with a little tale in no time; it is
a cinch, you are the flow of smooth thrumming power,
you are a writer, and you can turn out some mean
stuff, and you will turn out tons of it, because it
is you, and do not forget it, Kid, do not forget it;
please, please Kid, do not forget yourself; save
that, save that, preserve yourself; turn out those
mean little old tales by the dozens, it is easy,
it is grace, do it American-wise, drive it home,
sell truth, for it needs to be sold. Remember, Kid,
what I say to you tonight; never forget it, read
this over in your gloomier moments and never, never
forget . . . . . never, never, never forget . . . . . please,
please, Kid please . . .

# ... Hungry Young Writer's Notebook ....

*This homage to food prefigures ravenously descriptive passages about food in Kerouac's books. A brilliant example is the scene of Hector's cafeteria in New York City in* Visions of Cody.

How about a thick mushroom soup to begin with? Let us place it in a rather heavy bowl, white, stained, cracked at the edges, well eaten-in; let us dip into this with a large wooden ladle the steaming sauce, spotted here and there by a piece of cooked mushroom. You find it next in the heavy white bowl, ready to eat, to slurp, to swallow in ecstatic frenzy, to completely render invisible—and to do this, our quiet host hands us a large silver spoon with a black wooden handle. You grasp it rudely, with your whole fist, and dip the silver into the depths of the thick saucy substance. Before you extract the first large spoonful, you bend down to smell the soup. Oh, it is pungent; a scandalous sprinkling of pepper and salt, and a cute little sprinkling of paprika. You finger a small piece of brown mushroom, extract it from its hot tempting bed of glut and smell it careful: Ah, let's call our shot:—it is the smell of the Subtle Pungency and the savor, the odor, the piquancy of sublime ravishment. Ah, let us eat. You dip the large spoon in, lift it to your mouth, and insert it to your mouth. You swallow the first mouthful, and it is like the nectarous drug of heaven. A small mushroom is discovered in the midst of your palate . . . you chew it carefully with your fore-teeth, and find that its timbre is delicate, that its body is tender, succulent, dainty, spicy; and with it all is the thick creamy sauce, the savory soup, oozing down your throat, the molten lava of heaven.

Let us proceed to the steak. A thick tenderloin, Mein Host, and I'll have yet some mushroom on it; mashed potatoes covered with parsley; a side dish of saucy yellow corn, glistening in the light of this heaven; some fine fresh French-Belgian bread, with large thick crusts and yielding white dough; large crinkly crusts, the kind of crusts that you tug at, and when you tear it apart, there follows a stream of warm white dough, and with all this generous gobs of thick yellow butter . . . . Oh, I must tell you more, and I don't care how it sounds, or what defects there are, for sir this is hunger! hunger! hunger! and there is no other appeasement but the word . . . . the steak has arrived, and Mein Host fades back into the shadows, eager to serve me . . . . I begin to eat. The steak is huge, about two feet long and one foot wide, with a thickness of two inches. Through it runs a great bone, protruding at one end like the mighty hock of a beast. I grasp this bone and snarl into the steak, thrusting my mouth into the warm brown side of the meat, gnashing bestially with my savageful teeth and tearing off huge brown folds of meat, great flaccid flabs of bloody meat, chewing with a carnal fury never before equaled in time. O My God, but I eat. I chew with tremendous passion, swiftly, swallowing the meat in massive mouthfuls. I wash this down with a huge potful of nectarous coffee, well flavored with cream and sugar . . . it is a special pot that I drink out of, created for the occasion—it is one foot high, and looks like a tankard of ale; the coffee is in this pot, brown and deep and sluggishly steaming stained smells. I dart my spoon into the golden corn and take a bite, swallowing the mashy sauce of its yellow munificence; I carry a mountain of mashed potatoes to my mouth on a fork and let the whorly masses turn slowly in my mouth, creating tastegland secretions, and then slipping slowly down my throat in warm full piles. Then I swipe down another magnificent slug of coffee from my tankard, and return voraciously to the slab of succulent dripping steak, sinking my teeth into the juicing mountain of meat and pulling off penchant stringings of sweating rare beef, covered by a delicate crunchly hide of browned loveliness.

Well, sirs, for dessert I had a hot fudge sundae with chocolate ice cream; I'll tell you about that some other time. At this time, I must go to bed and forget hunger.

# A Young Writer's Notebook

*The ending of this piece points in the direction of two of
Kerouac's later works: "Home at Christmas," a memory of
pre–World War II Christmastime in Lowell, which appeared in* Glamour *in 1961 and is included in* The Portable Jack Kerouac, *and the teenage love story* Maggie
Cassidy, *published in 1959. The novel's opening scene has
Jack Duluoz and his pals singing "Jack O Diamonds" on
their way to a New Year's Eve dance at the Rex Ballroom
in snowy downtown Lowell. In early 1953 Kerouac wrote a
one-page "preamble" to the novel in which he explains
that he wants to tell Neal Cassady how he fell in love:
"How beautiful can a woman be?—that when . . . after I
met Mary Carney on New Year's Eve, at a dance, dance in
the Rex . . dancing hall, it was snowing and GJ was sin-
gin Jack O Diamonds, and we walked by Lucksy Smith's
house out in Pawtucketville, [. . . .]"*

How a poor little guy like Shorty has to throw up a barricade of
gruffness in order to survive, altho he is in himself a gentle young
man, altho he never washes his face . . . . . about your Randy Shep-
perton, the way he smiles and then wipes it off like lightning, leaving a worried face, haggard in the light; how he laughs hollowly, to
make politeness, bores you because he is always making politeness;
and above all, how he swallowed slowly when you told him the bad
news, instead of seeming worried, he just stared blankly, poor kid,
haggardly swallowing slowly in order to conceal all the fine things
that I wish he'd broadcast in sincere swoops of the hand . . . . Tell
about Fabe, and the way he throws up a front of dignity in front of
his kid, little father and little son; how he loves to orate with a flourish, with a driving point . . . . . Tell about work-happy N., his

[ 157 ]

nervous look, his bitchiness at times, his goodness at times . . . a little bit of everything in everything . . . . tell about how a piece of
work mellows if you let it alone to study later . . . . . tell how it feels
to go to bed hungry, how it feels to want a woman and not have one
(Ho! they all know that!) . . . . tell, tell, tell . . . . . how a cheap whore
can think she is better than you . . . . how a little slip of a skirt
thinks she can change the entire weather, tissue, and color of your
thought by the wiles of her scrawny self . . . . . my goodness . . . . tell
of the hostess juke-boxes, and the dedications . . . a man walking
into a tavern, saying hello Joe, everything fine and you begin to
think that men are decent after all, but when he leaves, the others
begin to talk about him, behind his back, and you realize that the
Brotherhood of Mankind is dead, damn it . . . . tell, tell, tell . . . . tell
also the sombre silver of November . . . . the smell of cordy raw-
nesses in doorways and the way the cold wind goes down your jersey, freezing your chest . . . . . tell of Halloween in your mouth, the
wild black orange gibberings and the screeching fury and horror of
the harvest frowse, the witch, the pumpkin lit by candle and dripping, the night is black and it is Halloween, rattle the window and
rattle the knee . . . . . the legend of your progenitors . . . . . . . tell,
tell, tell . . . . about the N.Y. Times book review, how trite it is in the
main, how unimportant and smug it is, how disgusting it is in
the end . . . how a young writer can go to town, but not forever . . . .
tell of Xmas at home in Lowell, the snow falling in the street,
padding feet, the lights in the window, blue, green, red; the smell of
candies and nuts inside, the bitter gum smell of the tree, the gifts,
sitting in the plush sofa of the parlor with a glass of dark port wine,
watching the tree and thinking things over, looking at the tree with
silent melancholia, thinking happily about Xmas at home and snow
drifting down past the arc-light on the corner . . . . . . Halper standing in a Manhattan doorway, cold, laughing in the snowfall . . . .
Wolfe walking by the Boston Harbor, smelling the warehouse and
the wharves, feeling food, voyage, thrill, clangor of the heart, Faust
is back . . . . . tell of Saroyan waking up in the night across the Para-
mount, his hair freezing on his head, laughing at the walls, the snow
falls in Manhattan . . . . . and above all tell of Kerouac walking in
the streets of Lowell in the winter's night, looking up alleys illuminated by the round cold disc of the moon, knowing the clear
screaming glint of star in winter, knowing the black black outline of
squalid wooden porches in Lowell, Mass., dirty alleys, grimy back-

porches black against the white moon of winter, narrow little alleys with solitary ashbarrels throwing a shadow on the frozen ground, walking up the long street, empty echo of steps on the frozen sidewalk, knowing the silence and beauty of winter midnight in Lowell slums . . . . . . . . remember, Kerouac, to notice the thing that is New England in the winter, men riding by in a dirty grey '30 Essex, three of them in front on a very cold grey day, cords of wood on the back seat, the old car puffing and steaming in the dead cold New England winter afternoon . . . . that's it, the dead cold winter afternoon of New England . . . . dead cold greyness . . . . snow falling on Moody St., and the light from Rochette's diner, and the New Year's Eve 1939, Jack O' Diamonds, the Rex, Freddy, the snow, remember? Above all, Zaggie my child, remember the thing that counts, the great big thing that stands up alone and predominates shaggily, like a dead cold winter afternoon in grey raw New England, grey raw, raw . . .

# [I Am Going to Stress
a New Set of Values]

I am going to stress a new set of values, which people have been minimizing in importance up to now on account of their apparent unimportance as compared to the lofty ideas of economists, historians, scholars, etc. In actuality, I am going to show that this scale of values surpasses the supposedly magnanimous one; that it is actually the one which builds up the world and man to meet all the vicissitudes and trials which make up the day and age.

Dear Reader,
What you are about to read is nothing more than
exercise. I believe that form has been stressed too
much. The following stuff is not written with an eye to
form; it is written with an eye to complete expression.
A novel form has the most complete expression, except
that it is boring to see straight prose staring at you
in the face every time you turn a page. Also, my system
has more vitality, what with the dialogue, the comments,
and the dramatic action. Do you know what I am talking
about? I don't either. That is the soul of imagination,
and imagination is the soul of literature.
    So long and take it easy, because if you start
taking things seriously, it is the end of you.
                Jack Kerouac,
                    American casual poet of
                    no renown whatsoever,
                    but equipped with a
                    complete inner con-
                    fidence that would
                    stagger Saroyan.

P.S. Whenever you get tired of everything, go down

to a saloon, or a pin-ball machine house, or
jump in the river. However, if you do it every
day like I do, you don't get anywhere. But who
wants, as Nick says, to go anywhere? And furthermore, you can get sick of everything every day like
I do and be one thing:—A casual poet with no
regrets, no excess baggage, and humour and intelligence
and goodnight my old mad masters, so long and
forget it. It is no harm. That's the idea of
it all. How many times do I have to tell you.
Sleep it off in bed, and when you wake up, work
yourself up to a lather, world it all day, then
go back to sleep it off at night, unless you
have a woman with you in bed. In that case,
don't sleep right away, but be sure to do so
after you've spent. Good night, boys.
The Grim Reaper isn't grim at all; he's a
life-saver. He isn't grim because he isn't
anything. . . . he is nothing. And nothing is
a hell of a lot better than anything. So long, boys.

# [I Am My Mother's Son]

I am my mother's son. All other identities
are artificial and recent. Naked, basic, actually,
I am my mother's son. I emerged from her womb
and set out into the earth. The earth gave me
another identity, that of name, personality,
appearance, character, and spirit. The earth
is my grandmother: I am the earth's grandson.
The way I comb my hair today has nothing to do
with myself, who am my mother's son and the
earth's grandson. I am put on this earth to
prove that I am my mother's son. I am also
on this earth, my grandmother, to be her
spokesman, in my chosen and natural way. The
earth owns the lease to myself: she shall take
me back, and my mother too. We have proven
the earth's truth and meaning, which is, simply
life and death.

  "I woke up in the middle of the night
  and realized to my horror that I did
  not remember who I was. I knew not
  my name nor my appearance. When I
  went to the mirror, I failed to recognize my image. That is why I am
  my mother's son and the earth's grandson, and nothing else. I am here to
  prove that fact, and in so doing, I
  am also the earth's spokesman: that is
  so because I wish to prove it twice,
  once for the earth, and again for my

brothers, so that we may live together
in beauty."

Say, fellow, you know who I
am? I'm Jack Kerouac, the
writer: husky, handsome,
intellectual Jack Kerouac.
Notice how I comb my hair
and see my handsome gar-
ments. I'm the boy from
Brazil. I love jazz, I
love North Carolina, I
love Socialism. I'm sel-
fish, I'm irresponsible,
I'm weak, I'm afraid. I'm
Jack Kerouac the poet, the
seaman, the scholar, the
laborer, the newspaperman,
the lover, the athlete,
the flyer, the Lowellian?    (I am my mother's son.)

# [Howdy!]

Howdy!

This is Jack Kerouac, speaking to you.

I have just returned to my little cheap room from a day's work, ostensibly speaking, and find things in great shape. The radiator is working, and outside it's cold and raw; the room untouched, for I have the only key and am completely the master of this certain portion of the earth, $4.50 per week. Only thing wrong with the whole affair is nights: there are bugs in the bed, and I have to scratch and rant and fever quite a bit. But I hope to get the bedbugs fed up with my blood, so that they will leave me alone some time. Then everything will be perfect, because I have my typewriter, paper, and plenty of good books in this room, plus my radio and the light bulb hanging down lighting up the whole place clearly, with the precision, might I venture, of cubic realism. Above all, there is myself in this room, wearing a red football sweatshirt, great brown crepe-soled shoes, white football socks, green gabardine pants, ring on the right hand's small finger (10¢ ring); wallet with no money in it, some loose change, a half a bread and some slices of cheese; keys to the kingdom; paper, manuscripts, notes, books, typewriter, cigarette butts, toothpaste, towels, radiator heating well, and hidden behind my desk an old gas stove slimy with black grease, lards, and fat. On the wall, spots of grease. On the floor, old cigarette butts; on my bed, the oldest blanket in the world, in America at least; a face cloth hanging from the bureau drawer; my filling station suits piled against the bottom of the writing desk; the top of my writing desk a bit greasy, but not enough to disconcert; the smell of urine predominant, I believe; and outside my window, an alley grate covered with discarded boxes, wrapped-up swill, apple cores, various refuse; opposite that, a massive bleak red-brick wall rising to a small aperture of the Hartford sky at dusk, the windows sadly and luminously gray, shabbily drear, facing the ending day with phosphorescently haggard weariness; and then I pull down the old brown shade to hide this scene, as I turn to ply my life within this dreaded four-walled prison, the kingdom of the slave.

## 2

I will tell you what this is—my life at this moment. Just now, I was reading Halper on the bed, engrossed, hungry, eager, happy, very alone. I had a mirror beside me, in order to catch glimpses of any fleas that I suspected were playing about my hair, jumping from the filth of the room into myself, intruding into the private cleanliness of a clean young man from a clean home; I wanted to see them and kill them, but it turned out to be my imagination, and I wound up just looking at my face in the mirror. It was not at all handsome, I thought; it was wild, old—my hair horrifying and crazy, lines running down my face, and with my head on the pillow, it looked to me like the portrait of a dying man; a stubble of beard, and bright shining eyes, lines down the side of the face. There were no fleas, just my old face and old wild hair.

Then, let us finish this up. What is this life? What is Hartford? Hartford is cold now, November 11, 1941; sombre silver November, the old father of October, older than time itself; cold on the streets, raw and wooden-like odors in the hallway of this cheap dive; but once you are inside the barrooms with their spittoons and booths with people in them, music from the juke-box, men playing pinball machines, all the fine rich heat of humanity under one roof laughing and laughing, and the smell of beer and food; now the music grows louder, my typewriter resounds through the flimsy walls, and they bring me a plate of hot powerful food and I water at the mouth. That, then, is Hartford; raw wooden-like doorways, biting wind in the streets, clear precise lights on Main Street, people hurrying by red-nosed and on the way to a real palpitating destination; the entrance to the taverns, and then the taverns themselves, the food steaming and glistening in the tavern light, music streaming love through your heart, blame it on the heart, because this is my life at this moment.

Then back to the room, slowly it begins to befriend me, too slowly, but slowly by all means; the silent eloquence of its objects and a lonely young man sits and thinks and smokes, and then turns to read Tolstoi and Halper and Lin Yutang and Wolfe and Saroyan, and then turns to his typewriter and goes on, the locomotive in his chest chugging faster and faster and getting heavier and heavier every moment.

# Today

Today is November 12th, 1941. It is my last day with this typewriter, and tomorrow I shall have to return it to the agency, because I have no money with which to renew the rental of the machine for another month.

Hell, they're taking away everything. Even myself.

You see, first I go hungry, and I am writing this at nine o'clock in the evening without having had any supper except some old bread and cheese. Secondly, I have no cigarettes, and my lungs are crying out for the strong body of smoke. (Will one or two of you readers slip me a spare butt on the sly?) Thirdly, they're going to take away the typewriter, and then I will be left alone in this room with nothing. You see, my heart resides in a typewriter, and I don't have a heart unless there's a typewriter somewhere nearby, with a chair in front of it and some blank sheets of paper.

They took my food, my drug, and my heart away. There is no man left to speak of except 180 pounds of bone and flesh. But I'll manage. Now this here is a simple story. This morning, I had four cents in my pocket, and was walking around South Hartford, freezing; and not having had any breakfast, I decided to chisel a penny from someone. I saw some workmen digging a ditch, but I kept on walking, ignoring them. I went into a drugstore, thinking up a clever sentence: "How about a four cent cup of coffee?" I knew what the reaction would be to that—the counterman would laugh heartily at the predicament of being one cent shy, and proceed to draw me a cup of steaming hot java. A good joke, this guy happened to be just one cent shy, but he had his wits about him. Ho ho.

Ha ha ha, I said to myself. This will work.

But all I did was stand around and stare idiotically at the magazine display. Then I walked out into the cold again. I went up along the street, and being alone, I began to talk to myself, jangling my last four pennies in my pockets. "Food!" I said, "Food!" I began to imagine myself sitting in an old English tavern, back in 1669, in November, with a huge tankard of brown ale on my right and a tremendous meat-covered bone in my left hand, ripping off prodigious stringing slabs of juicy beef with my enraged teeth, letting the savory drip of blood play around my palate, make it water painfully for many more, many more great attacks on the food! food! food! "Scrouch," I said, imagining myself ripping off another big piece of viand. "Scludge . . . squidge . . . munch . . . emgupp . . gulp." What a feast! I walked along the road like a madman, striding hugely.

Well, in this way, I managed to hold on for a while. This was today. In the evening, my comrade came up to my room to visit me. He sat on the bed, offered me a cigarette, and started to read some of my work. I hovered about eagerly, feeding him manuscript upon manuscript. I talked excitedly, stumbled over my words, grew hoarse and passionate in voice as I always do when I get strong, good and strong. He read on, and then offered me another cigarette. It was fine, very fine. Then he left; we made plans for a trip. He and I are going to sit in a car and drive right out to California, in about three weeks. We mapped out the journey, figuring on going through the south where it is warm and where there are weeping willow trees with moss and old houses with ground level porches. I told him I wanted to spend a whole hot sunny afternoon lying beside the Mississippi River, in New Orleans, sunning, yawning, slapping off the flies, dozing, yawning some more. Okay, he said. He and I are going to sit down in his car and drive right out to California, in about three weeks.

Well, that's the story. I told you it would be simple. It was today. Now, as I write, it is night and tomorrow they are going to take away my typewriter and my heart. So I just thought I'd write a few words down on paper, just for the hell of it. It was nothing much, just a little legend about myself and my hunger and my heart and the trip to California and the loneliness of this small room in Hartford.

# This I Do Know—

That I shall be influenced by
Wolfe, Saroyan, Halper, Whitman,
and Joyce in my writings.
That Keats was right: It is
not Life that counts, but
the courage that you bring to it.
(2) That the earth is groaning
with plenty—enough to
kill any young Faustian.
(3) That utter sincerity & honesty
is all my writings need
in credo—such as: I do
not despise riches, I see that
they enable a man to sit
aloof, content, missing the
filth & untruth, in part.
(4) That life is good, moment
to moment, & bad, on
the whole, for lack of
design. We must make
(always have) our own design—
relate ourselves with ourselves,
each other, society, & universe.
Love only is design (only is consistent)

# Search by Night

*Set on Pearl Harbor Day, December 7, 1941, this is Ker-
ouac's first extended use of Canadian French dialogue
and his most raw, naturalistic presentation of ethnic characters to date. In later books, such as* Doctor Sax *and Visions of* Gerard, *he used this language to great effect as
he rendered the speech of Duluoz family members.*

*After hurtling through the city on a quick visit in Sep-
tember 1962, Kerouac sent a letter full of Lowell memories
to* Lowell Sun *reporter Mary Sampas, wife of the Lowell
newspaperman Charles G. Sampas. She quoted from the
letter in one of her columns. He wrote: "[. . .] on the night
of Pearl Harbor, after I had seen* Citizen Kane, *I walked
home from the movies watching the wash stiffly waving in
the cold moonlight snow wash lines of Moody and Cheever
and cried [. . .]" In Book Six of* Vanity of Duluoz (1968),
*Kerouac also revisits this Pearl Harbor Day episode.*

From the low-lit fastnesses of my study I looked solemnly at the
newspaper headlines. On my work desk, its brown pigeon-holes
stuffed with ledger, manuscript, sheet, inkwell, sentimental
token . . . . on this old desk of mine I lay the screaming visage of a
Hearst tabloid—it said: JAPAN DECLARES WAR ON U.S.A.; PEARL HAR-
BOR BOMBED!

Outside the window, in the yard between my house and my neighbors, there glowed the cold crater silver of a December moon in
New England . . . . and there was silence as of death, upon the cold
hard ground. Frost decorated the window, Dickens-like. I looked
out upon the winter night, was silent in the presence of a stupen-
dous hush, listening for the sigh of our slumbering hearts.

"Poet," said the cradled moon, "go to sleep with your brothers.

[ 170 ]

Go to sleep, for it is night in Massachusetts, and our brothers are reposing in stillness."

I sat there, unstunned, mildly thrilled by the great tidings of War—for in all of us, hidden, lies the glory and folly of the Achaean heart, the Trojan breast, the clangorous song and shout of Homer.

"War!"

Deep mumbling movements in the foundations of the chest, stirrings in the belly, the eye is kindled.

"War!"

I rose from my chair and stared at the headlines on the paper, standing and smoking a cigarette. Surely this was not the night for slumber!

In a silent and fiendish glee, I stole illicitly from the warmth of my home, clad in the American garb of topcoat, scarf, trousers, clicking-heel shoes, sweatshirt with Prep School insignia, and white woolen socks. In the clear deadcold of New England winter, I stood bare-headed in the night, listening to the immense soundlessness of my slumbering city. Cold crater moon, how you glared in deathly silver! How you were luminous, how you splashed your icy lead-white upon crude New England! How you screamed noiselessly in your high piercing solitary gleam!

I went through the streets of the city, making the dry sound of footsteps, creating a rhythmic click of the shorn foot, advancing in strides among sleeping homes.

It was wonderful! And I was not alone; and too my mind was not content. For it was a search, and though it really was fruitless, almost boundless in its stupid aspiration, yet it was a search—by night.

I was not alone. Walking down the street, seeing barren crater-glow along the shabby length of its bedded route, I suddenly perceive the bobbing figure of another human being. Another footstep, quicker than mine, most fretful. It is a millworker returning from the "night-shift." We pass each other in the night, moving along gracefully in opposite directions. My brother, yet I do not know him, I do not speak to him. We only exchange quick suspicious glances, mine is almost belligerent in its nocturnal frown and scowl. (Ah yes, I am a fool!)

Now my search is resumed. I stride on along the silence of the street, looking for the War.

But in New England, when the rapier-keen air pings your ears, when the dry razored blue of December night advances to freeze your thighs, to numb your toes and soles of your feet; when the keen point of Winter, the bluecold blade begins to tingle your skin, there is little of the War to be seen. (Oh I am not being silly here, I know what my words say.) When you hear brown husked leaves crackle among the frozen boughs, when you watch the stars tremble coldly in their virginal altitudes, when you see how shadows between houses and tenements and blocks can be so black! so black!—and when, standing near a canal running through a tenemented slum district, you see how street lamps throw gold on the water, how the moon throws cold cold silver on the water, how the ripple-visaged water lies in a silent and slumbering world—in New England, when you are witness of all this, there is little of the War to be seen.

But the War is there, raging in remote distances, the thunder yet unheard, the fire yet unspread. You know that the War is there and that your search is really fruitful.

I entered a lunch-cart, rubbing my pinged and pinched eartips with warm palms. The overwhelming odor of greasy hamburg was everywhere in the warm little confines of the place. Several men sat hunched on stools, munching. I moved along, toward the great sleek "nickelodeon," a beautiful and large music-box, which for the cost of a nickel, could fill the little restaurant with the soothing thrum of American dance music—or, if you preferred, with the precise and lifting beat! beat! beat! beat! and accompanying brass blare of American "swing" music. I chose a tender love ballad—sat before the lovely colored music-case and listened to a baritone croon loving phrases, accompanied by the dreamy spiral and spin of reeds, the deep and steady resonance of a rhythm section subdued. The mood was created. The whole bawdy structure and atmosphere of the tiny "hamburg" emporium changed instantly as the music started—from ordinary clock-ticked, arm-scratching moments to lovely and glorious moments of female Love, romance, and strength, sudden added strength!

And as always, the balladry affected me, the incredibly tender caress of the saxophone section affected me, and tears strained at my dried, restrained ducts. In a rush of tenderness, I was transplanted. The music had created the mood, had created a new "myself" for the instant—I was sentimental, full of love—a grand vision of America swept in triumph before me, and an imaginary girl, with dark meditative eyes and frowning brow seemed to be stroking my face with tender searching fingertips . . . . I sat moodily, overcome with nostalgia for everything I'd ever hoped & wished for yet hardly knowing the sum of these aspirations, hardly understanding the fundamental construction of these dreams, hardly touching them, suddenly clutching them all in one huge & exciting second, only to lose them, to rise and fall in foolish meditation, and to emerge, as the music ceased, smiling grimly and for the moment understanding Faust, for the moment having seen the shape of the War, for a moment having succeeded in my search. But so brief! so brief! so very brief! . . . .

"Here's your hamburger!" barks the counter man, his gray greasy face glistening at you in the buttery light. "Coffee wid' it?"

"No, thank you."

In America, you sink your teeth into the lovely confusion of meat, soft white bread, onion, butter, grease, and ketchup called the "hamburger," and in so doing, satisfy a hunger in yourself which is exclusively and completely American. I did so, greedily letting the juicy mess lavish in my palate, feeling the cordy body of raw onion, smelling and relishing the sandwich, the smell of the place, the smoke and the talk. The great window at the end of the counter was frosted, looking out upon a clear cold cratered night. Men came in, banged the door, lusty with the vigor of our grand & glorious weathers. Men with pinged ears and cold thighs, and eyes that have seen New England wooden tenements, crude and new and of raw outline in the bleak black night and silver-strewn mooncold, with noses that have frozen drily in the sworded blue-black of New England December, in the cold night, in the clear cold silver night. And men, too, who know of the War, who hear its remote rumble.

"Ernest, Calvert, 'tara pas chris' de chance—! Ha ha ha!" . . . lustily they greet each other in a vulgar & ugly jargon called New England French-Canadian. "Héh Batêge!"—"Ha! ha ha ha!" In great bursts of tormented, twisted, severed French, they pick and puckle each other, prattling incoherently, half of the time in coarse & obscene N.E. French-Canadian, half of the time in rowdy, faulty English.

This, Gentlemen, is the language of the New England French-Canadian, who is the rarest animal in the various N.E. mill cities, who is the bawdy, rowdy, gustful, and obscene inhabitor of crude wooden tenements, infestor of smelly barrooms along infamous slum streets, crude-handed laborer of factory, ditch, and field.

"Tu connas-tu Georges Rousseau?"

"Oua, oua . . ." hastily, hurrying the other along.

"Eh ben, Calvert . . . . . y'ava une bonne job . . . . (changing quickly, effortlessly) . . . in the local Silk Mills . . . you know, de fella wid de new Cad'lac . . . (spoken in Brutal Canuck, heavily, ponderously accented, almost idiotic) . . . well, he'll 'ave to be goin' back to Devens now . . . . Ha ha ha—(harsh & brutish laughter) . . . his 'e sore!! his 'e sore! six dam' years in de army, already to get marry . . . an' den, back in de dam' army . . . . ha ha ha . . ."

"Well," observes the dour-colored counterman, his Canadian blue eyes steady and persevering. "Hi guess we're all goin' to expect 'tings like dat from now on . . ."

"Yah—pretty serious . . ."

"Pas mal, pas mal, Calvert . . ."

"Ha ha ha— . . ." nervously harsh, almost animal-like in its crudeness and lack of genuine humor.

And so these men know of the war and its far-away flames. They know, and the search is not entirely in vain. Now back into the cold hard whitened street. Now resume the crunchy beat of footsteps, advance through the sleeping city, search on for the form, the character, the body, the eye of the War.

At the bridge, a tall red-nosed policeman stands in the deadcold of night, a cigarette butt hanging from his grim and lonely mouth— he is guarding the bridge. (You have learned about this previously— an officer of the law has been placed at each of the four bridges of the river city; to guard, day and night, from possible Axis sabotage—rather remote possibility, we all realize, but still a good idea, a safe and sound move.) This, then, the eye of the War? This, then, the reward of a nocturnal search through frozen sleeping streets?

No! The policeman ignores you, he seems to be infuriated at the prospect of standing all night in the cold—(as I sit now in my warm study, writing with quiet pen, he still stands there alone in the cold night, alone, alone)—No! That is not the eye of the War. That has something to do with it, but your hunger is far from appeased. Your hunger is more searching, of larger and deeper scope. The eye of the War is something else, somewhere else—somehow different from the ordinary.

Search on!

You walk alone through the streets, feeling the cold of the stones & cement, and begin to wonder . . .

[ 174 ]

Presently, I approached another lunch-cart, another typical New England milltown hamburger house. Again the smell of frying beef, of butter . . . . a large pan with pats of ground red meat drowned in a puddle of boiling grease.

I sat down to eat, searching for the eye of the War, eating and smoking and searching. A whore came in from the cold, her very French features blue from the icy air. Hawk-faced, with long-lashed and coquettish brown eyes, heavy-breasted, she went up to the counter & spoke confidentially with the short order cook.

"Did you ever 'ear such a 'ting, Hah?"

"You mean Pearl Harbor— . . . ?"

"Oua, oua!" she affirmed, sternly.

"Ah oua!" said the counterman with a sad Gallic wistfulness. "Ah oua!"

They both ruminated slowly with genuine sadness & compassion. She shrugged her fine shoulders.

"Ah ben, quesqu'on peut faire!"

"Oua . . ." he echoed. "Oua . . ."

"Deux hamburgers, héh Joe?" she finally asked, addressing him familiarly.

He prepared them sadly, still thinking about Pearl Harbor. It was very casual, as persons would be with a lively and vital topic which had no personal color in it. And I suddenly began to see something, but before I could formulate anything, a shabby person stamped in from the cold and gave the woman a meaningful look. Obviously, she knew him slightly . . . . invited him to sit with her—and in a flash, the thing was accomplished, the thing was arranged & ready, here within the flimsy wooden walls of a little New England mill-town eatery on a cold dark slum street. (I tried to contrast this with the way it might have been done in New York City perhaps in one of those orange-juice, white-tiled, brightly lit sandwich counters where sallow, sagging-jowled New Yorkers gobble up hamburgers in resentful, scowling silence, and exit without a word—in such a place, the acquisition of a street-walker would have been a long and foolish thing, first the secret, stolen stares of black glut, then the casual and ratlike character of the approach, which would be unsuccessful in the lunch-cart because of New York's lack of human warmth; and thirdly the savage, prowling and lustful pursuit into the streets, terminating successfully in some illicit doorway away from the empty red & blue glow of street lights, and even in the success of the acquisition there would be nothing but filthy sneakiness, false casualness, and a shaming feeling of naked fear, dark-eyed, winking terror and lust.) Ah not so in my home-town not so! There, an acquisition is a quick, warm, human thing. There is no lustful string, no prowling pursuit, no shame-faced hinting. That is one large difference between New York City & my home-town . . . . . and thus, I might have begun to draw contrasts on the preceding illustrations, at that moment, had I not suddenly realized that the eye of the War was not there, that I had gone out into the streets at 2 A.M. in the morning to search for something that did not exist.

For the eye of the War had changed nothing, not even the people, and this brought me to the thrilling realization that the American people are really strong, that though we lack grace, we do possess certain unfinished grace; that though we are trying to cover up with false virility, false coarseness, underneath us there is a great current of courage, even daring, and a blessed love of casualness & calmness that shows itself only in times of great emergency.

Nothing was changed. There was the cold crater glow of moon, the crude upthrust of wooden tenement, the brutish French-Canadian gabble in greasy lunch-cart, the dream-giving American music, the graceful interplay of sex with social ease, the genuine American heart of Love which lay hidden beneath a false armor . . . . . all these remained, the war rumbled remote, and the eye of the War was not there. The American people had taken it in their stride, . . and it was, I tell you and always will, a huge, earth-devouring stride that could conquer the Universe.

And so it is.

My search by night for the eye of the War had been unsuccessful . . . . and yet, of course, it was so very successful.

# Part Three

## To Portray Life Accurately
## 1942–1943

# from Background

[. . .] In December of 1941, I returned to Lowell and was hired by the Lowell Sun as a reporter. The Sports Editor said: "Now, Jack, you'll have to start up from the bottom, writing small articles here and there, and keeping your eyes and ears open. The newspaper game is a tough game!" Three days later, I was writing 90% of the sports page while the Sports Editor and his two other "sports reporters" were down around the corner conducting a hot-stove league over a glass of beer.

The situation amused me one day, and angered me the other. I began to write a novel right in the City Room about Lowell and the three attendant ills of most middle-sized cities: provincialism, bigotry, and materialism. After hours were spent in the Library studying, where I learned more in three months than I could have learned in three years at college. I delved into everything: history, sociology, psychology, the classics, philosophy, evolution, and even psychoanalysis. Nights at home, I ate up Joyce's "Ulysses" and Thoreau and Wolfe and Dostoevsky and a dozen other favorites. I still have the novel I spoke of, and intend to touch it up in a few years.

Spring returned again, and, armed with a letter of introduction to James Hogan of Republic from a Boston columnist, I started off on the road for California. I wound up in the South, working on construction jobs and lunchcarts, hopping freights from city to city, casually enjoying myself in the warm sun, a young and languorous tramp. After three months of that, I went back home and joined the Merchant Marine. We went to Arctic Greenland and Iceland, a torpedo missing our bow by ten yards on the way back to Boston. Arriving safely in October, with a wad of money in my wallet and an Eskimo harpoon under my arm, I was surprised and pleased to find a telegram from Lou Little waiting for me. He offered to make arrangements for my return to Columbia. Back I went, signing up in the Officers' Training program and finding myself in a Baker Field scrimmage no less than 48 hours after debarking the S.S. Dorchester (sunk five months later off Iceland.)

That Saturday, I played a few minutes in the Army game and decided to drop the sport for good. After my stint at sea, I felt it was too much physically. I again turned my attention to my studies.

It was then I made fast friends with Prof. Mark van Doren, who encouraged me to keep on writing and particularly liked my interpretations of Shakespeare. I got an "A" in Advanced Composition from another encouraging and friendly instructor. I renewed my typing agency and tutored more French, wrote once more for the Columbia Spectator and Jester, and was enjoying myself thoroughly until I ran out of money in December. I transferred to Naval Flying, flunked out there, and went back to the Merchant Marine.

In the Merchant Marine, I began work on a novel entitled "The Sea is My Brother," did informal research on the subconscious mind and dreams, and traveled to Casablanca, London, Liverpool, Belfast, and Glasgow. After writing 80,000 words on the novel, I decided to remake an entirely new version of it and title it "Two Worlds for a New One." I am working on this at the present. As well, I have two stories pending at the New Yorker, [. . . .] So much for the past and present.

# Sadness at Six

*Kerouac signed this piece "Jack Kerouac, CP," meaning
"casual poet." As for the special designation, consider
this: in the short story "The Three Swimmers and the Grocer from Yale," from his collection* My Name Is Aram
*(1940), William Saroyan writes: "He was sure some man.
Twenty years later, I decided he had been a poet and had
run that grocery store in that little run-down village just
for the casual poetry in it instead of the paltry cash." In*
Some of the Dharma, *Kerouac writes from his perspective
in the early 1950s: "In 1941 when I was 19, two writers
pulled me out of my natural interest in the 'Casual Poet of
Lin Yutang and Saroyan' as I fancied myself then, purely
in fields idealizing nature and the blue sky. The two writers were nothing but Western Faustian Space-Time tension
writers—Joyce and Dostoevsky. 'Much knowledge is a
curse.' But Dostoevsky had the compassion of a great Or-
thodox Saint underneath his Western City Decadence.
Joyce is really trivial except for his involuntary uncon-
scious visions of the truth elicited through a style. And so
is the Jean-Louis of Modern Prose."*

*Centralville is an expansive, mostly residential section
of Lowell on the north bank of the Merrimack River, opposite the "mile of mills," where Kerouac lived until he was
ten years old. Here he vividly recalls his second birth—an
awakening to the universe. Writing to Neal Cassady on
December 28, 1950, Kerouac explained that he remembered being born and added: "Six years later, on a similar
red afternoon, but in dead of frozen winter, I discovered
my soul; that is to say, I looked about for the first time
and realized I was in a world and not just myself."*

The day I was born, there was snow on the ground and the light from the descending sun made the windows in Centralville glow with strange and lovely melancholia.

I was six years old, walking home with my sled.

Suddenly, I was born: I began to wonder, genuine mature wondering. I was wondering about this: Why is everything sad now, as I go home to my supper. Why?

I was born, therefore, in 1929, about seven months before the great stock market crash in Wall St. In Centralville, I didn't hear a damned thing, and for all that, I was busy wondering anyway. I had no time to dawdle with worldly affairs; in the newspaper, I looked at the big headlines telling of the stock market crash, but I didn't care much, apparently, since today all I can remember is Popeye & the Thimble Theatre, by Segar, Co. 1929, King Features Syndicate, and so forth. Nothing about the stock market crash, only Popeye in the funny page.

The day I was born, on my way to supper with my sled, hands feeling red-hot with energy, myself steaming into the winter air from underneath the warm scarf, I stopped to look at the sad windows of the houses.

Why, why? I asked myself, aged six. Pourquoi, I might of said, because I was French. At any rate, I wanted to know, and I couldn't quite make it out, and I still cannot make it out, which is in a nutshell the story of inward war, raging inside of me, Science vs. Poetry, Bazarov vs. Wolfe, and all that sort of thing. (Tennysonian sentimentality vs. the Gallup Poll, or better, Shelley vs. Eleanor Roosevelt.) It is an astounding question, and needs to be solved.

I came very close to solving it, the first day I was born. Since then, I have been getting further and further away from the answer, until today, I am ignorant. At six, I was wise. Even Oil-Coordinator Ickes was wise at six, and Walter Winchell also. We were all wise at the age of six.

But today, we are more or less insane. There are exceptions, but I don't want to start anything. Not at the moment. I am busy writing a story called "Sadness at Six."

I was walking along, dead, and suddenly I saw the windows of Centralville gleaming redly, quietly; I heard a dog barking, and the children who were still coasting on the hill were making plenty of swell noise; it was February, I shall presume, and the sun was getting redder and redder all over the whole neighborhood there was a strange old color as of dream and I was born, amid radiant glowings, born into this world to get in line with the boys, the good boys or the bad boys, either which way, and with a sweep of wonderment, I began to live—a man on the earth, his relation to all things, to himself, to his fellow man, to his society, and to the universe. I was born in February 1929, which makes me 13 years old as I write. Not bad for a kid, hey? Yes, I was born, and the music began to filter into my being, and the colors accentuated deeply, and the weird flutings as of Joyce could be heard emanating from my lips, and I was a man on the earth at last, age two minutes five seconds. I went home and ate my first meal. That's all I remember, and there is not much else to say. I was born suddenly, at the age of six, and I am thanking whoever did it for me—be it Bazarov's God, or Wolfe's, or Aquinas'.

# The Joy of Duluoz

*The following is an excerpt from an unfinished work that was the third book in a trilogy of novels Kerouac imagined writing contemporaneously with his experiences in 1942. He had already completed Part I of the trilogy,* The Vanity of Duluoz, *which follows the adventures of a young man and his friends in Galloway, a city like Kerouac's Lowell. After a stint as a reporter at the* Galloway Star, *Robert Duluoz is ready to leave home, "anxiously seeking to become a bitter and desperate exile."*

*In Part II,* The Vexation of Duluoz, *Kerouac planned to treat Bob Duluoz's travels and the intensifying war's impact on him. Here is how Kerouac imagined the third book, to be called* The Joy of Duluoz, *which concludes with Duluoz fully engaged in the war: "[. . .] the* Joy *is not the crowning glory of the Duluozian saga. Your author is attempting to portray life accurately, and in so doing refuses to bring things to a definite terminus.* Joy *is more of a period of stolen happiness, happiness ripened by the fruit of Duluoz's brooding, suffering, and wandering; it is a happiness that we shall realize, at the close of* Joy, *is only tentative."*

*Kerouac takes the titles of the books in the Duluoz cycle from* Ecclesiastes; or, The Preacher, *Chapter 1, the same section of the Bible that Ernest Hemingway mined for the title and epigraph of his novel* The Sun Also Rises. *Verse 14 relates to Kerouac's vision: "I have seen all the works that are done under the sun; and behold, all is vanity and vexation of spirit." Kerouac recycled his 1942 title, and* Vanity of Duluoz *came full circle in 1968, with art shadowing life, as the soured writer-narrator tells his wife at the close of the story: "[. . .] I did it all [. . . .] But nothing ever came of it. No 'generation' is 'new.' There's 'nothing new under the sun.' 'All is vanity.'"*

*In Satori in Paris, published in 1966, Kerouac explains that "Duluoz" is "a variation on the Breton name Daoulas," which he "invented just for fun in [his] writerly youth. . . ." A Satori in Paris notebook entry reads: "Duluoz is fictitious, Daoulas true." He had come across the name while working at the Lowell Sun. Daoulas was a recognized Greek family name in Greater Lowell; there also was a New England Franco-American poet named Charles-Roger Daoust. A careful listener can hear the Franco sounds of Kerouac's middle name Louis, his boyhood parish, St. Louis, and his ancestral Canadian home of Rivière du Loup in the fictional name. Kerouac linked Joyce's Stephen Dedalus and his Jack Duluoz as sound-alikes and related character types. As Kerouac worked on the Duluoz saga, starting in 1942, he tried various character names, including Michael Daoulas, Michael Dalouas, Jack St. Louis, and Jacques le brice de Daoulas de St. Louis.*

\*\*\*\*\*\*
**1**
\*\*\*\*\*\*

Bob Duluoz stepped out of the sleek new car turning to make a pretense of politeness to Diana. She stepped out with her long legs and smiled with blank swiftness. They were parked at the front of the Iridium Room, West side, fashionable New York. Kenneth Barton-Bascome slammed shut the front door of his racy auto. His companion, Vera, stood impatiently preening with a preoccupied woman's smile.

"I'll park it across the street," said the doorman in the golden light of the foyer front. Kenneth Barton-Bascome handed over the keys and then opened the door of the Iridium Room before the imperious footman had a chance to dart forward his eager services.

The four of them marched in. Vera turned fullbody toward a mirror and fawned approvingly, preoccupied. Diana strode loosely, chattering in her child's voice:

"Oh I really adore this place, it's so . . it's so . . . restrained!"

Sardonically, Duluoz tilted his head and said to himself: "Yes!"

Kenneth Barton-Bascome toddled along beside Vera, his blond hair waved and clean, his white collar prominently correct over the broad back of his fine gray topcoat. Kenneth never walked; he toddled. He was unofficious.

As they reached the well-lit entrance to the Iridium Room itself, Duluoz remembered the Frontiersman Club in Galloway, Mass.

"Bored! Bored! Bored!"

When they made their entrance, it was most likely Duluoz who attracted the larger portion of attention. Vera strode statuesquely with her high hair-do. Kenneth toddled unobtrusively. Diana floated and her eyes shone. Duluoz glided in, bored, wearing an expression of indulgence and indifference. He realized, halfway to their table, that he had walked into the fashionable Iridium Room with blasé suaveness. With the worldliness of a John Milton!

Ha!

Restrained music bubbled about the room in burgundy measures. The electric organ soared about like falling veils of silk. Restrained faces glanced up from tables. What restraint! Hanging from the gold ceiling was an enormous chandelier of gold; the music was like gold; golden scotch and sodas sat before goldlit faces. A pair of golden shoes darted below the electric organ at the end of a pair of golden legs. It was a blonde with golden hair, playing. An eager-jawed Latin sang over the mike, saying: "Pichiketa-keta-pichiketa-keta!"

People glanced up and admired the suave, sleek-hair youth as he slid back Diana's chair, a ring flashing on his playboy hand. Duluoz, the drunken writer with a thousand mistresses and an apartment on midtown Madison Avenue. Duluoz sat and surveyed the room disinterestedly.

Wow! What careless poise . . .

"Isn't it restful!" declared Diana turning to Duluoz with a theatrical amazement. She fluttered her hands like Davis. Duluoz nodded with restrained approval, then glanced away in utter boredom. My Gawd!

Nothing solid here.

"Diana," said Duluoz. "There's nothing solid here . . . no foundation. No pyramid."

"Oh" sang Diana, "but how do you mean?" She fixed her glittering eyes on Duluoz as though she were looking beyond him. Make no mistake! He noticed it! He was a sensitive artist, very sensitive! He was a bored Boyer, Duluoz!

"Here," said Duluoz quietly, "there is nothing. No meaning. None of the real solid things in life. Empty! Empty!"

"Empty!" repeated Diana, glancing around to appraise the emptiness.

# Famine for the Heart

Dense clouds of cigarette smoke had long ago driven away the pure ether, so that now even the air to be breathed was necessarily evil, furious, and passionate. The blanket of smoke obscured the three-piece band, which was perched on a platform in the corner. From its general direction came the solid bounce of a bass-pedal, the scratchy, hot flutings of a clarinet, and the terrific interplay of a pianist who knew what jazz was all about. On the floor, weird figures whirled, bounced, bowed, laughed, smoked. The music grew louder. There was a din, which, though muffled by the foggy effect of the smoke, was enough to create the need to shout. It was marvelous.

Pete, seated at the bar with a long row of drinking gentlemen, produced another cigarette, lit it, and then thrust his obese, horn-rimmed face into the face of a fellow alemate.

"What do you think of the wound of living?" he asked, sheepishly drunk.

"The what? Get away, I'm not bothering you. I'll have the bartender kick you out!"

The music stopped, only to start once more at a furious, almost insane, tempo. The dancing figures gyrated madly, smoothly negotiating the favorite American swing dance, the Jive. Tall girls were held off at arm's length, scissoring their beautiful knees for an instant, and then were hurled back into male arms only to gyrate madly away once more. All the dancers bounced with the bass-pedal. Some screamed with delight.

Five soldiers from the nearby fort watched with bleary eyes. The bartender dashed about his bar, mixing drinks. Smoke clogged the low rafters. Madness ruled! Madly the dancers whirled, flinging themselves into the mist and abandon of the smoke, colliding viciously, laughing. The keen reek of beer clung everywhere. The clarinetist had picked up his tenor saxophone, hung his clarinet on a rack, and was twisting improvisations with a sweating, bursting face around the melody of "Lady Be Good."

A sailor lay sprawled across his booth table, while his girl spoke to a tall soldier. The proprietor stood at the end of the glittering bar, watching. All things were mad in this hellhole of smoke and noise and wine. Two of the Military Police entered stiffly, looking about the misted, mad scene with stern approbation.

The pianist, cigarette waiting on piano top, talked casually, as he played, to a youngster in tweed. The drummer yawned, but his rhythm was imperishable . . . his foot, with the precision of a machine, always came back to hit the bass-pedal, and the dancers, also imperishable, bounced in a body there in the rank smoke. The saxist's cheeks, blown out, glistened in the dim light. The five bleary soldiers ordered more whiskey. The little waitress dodged through the multitude. Other waitresses crossed her path, wavered and dodged on. The proprietor withdrew a fat cigar from his vest and meditatively bit off the tip. A soldier shouted something at his girl, on the floor, and had to repeat it in her ear.

"You're cute!" he informed her.

"Why corporal, what a line!" she shouted back, teeth white, eyes eager and glittering. They whirled madly, colliding with another couple, shouting pardons and laughing, inhaling the mad foggy smoke, bouncing with a rhythm.

Pete's obese face was now examining the contents of a "Zombie" drink, horn-rimmed glasses directed critically at the decorations which topped the frosted glass.

A barfly pointed, toothlessly grinning: "Talkin' to hisself. Arf-arf."

The other barfly saw two obese faces, two sets of muttering lips, two horrid sets of horn-rimmed glasses. He heard, instead of the noise of the place, the sound of the Achaeans and the Trojans, clashing in Ilium.

"Talkin' to hisself, hey?"

"Arf-arf," said the other barfly. "Arf-arf."

But outside, the quiet round moon beamed upon the lonely earth of Mississippi, illuminating the woods and fields and roads with a melancholy phosphorescence. A solitary figure advanced along the side of the highway toward the mad roadhouse, in front of which, in blazing incandescent legend, was said: "Pepi Martin's." Scores of cars were parked in the silent driveway, all of them except one bearing a Mississippi license plate—the lone stranger being from New York. The solitary figure, who now had a bottle of gin in one hand, stood swaying before the New York car and frowned at the plates.

"New York," he breathed, swaying.

Two Military Police emerged from the roadhouse, allowing a blast of smoky madness to scream in the silent night, and then closed the door behind them, trapping the inmates. Their heavy shoes crunched across the drive. A moment later, they were bouncing away in a "Jeep" car, two sad soldiers in a little brown car, moving swiftly down the road.

Our solitary figure, whom we may know as Richard, now seated himself upon the running board of the dilapidated New York car, and busied himself to uncork the bottle. It was a pint bottle, already half emptied. The music, especially the muffled bass-foot, boomed from within. Richard smirked and threw the bottle to his lips.

"New York," he gasped, letting down the bottle. "Little old New York."

A car crunched into the drive, both headlamps flinging a swath across the distant field behind the roadhouse. Richard followed the lights, saw one lonely tree, a little mist, and then the lights were clicked off. Seven persons alighted from the car, and chattering and laughing happily, made their way to the door. Once more, the door opened, the night silence was burst with revelry in Pepi Martin's; and once more, the door closed, the sad summer breeze returned to Richard's ear. Far, far away, a train whistle screamed. Richard allowed his gaze to follow the winding highway, and saw, at regular intervals, the sorrowful streetlamps.

"America," breathed the youth. "America!"

And he was lonely and alone.

Obese face, sweating over a Zombie, muttered underneath the din inside the rocking roadhouse: "Oh . . . the moon never beams, . . . without bringing me dreams, . . . of the beautiful Annabel Lee . . . and the stars never rise . . . but I see the bright eyes . . . of the beautiful Annabel Lee . . ."

"Arf-arf!"

"Hisself!"

". . . in her tomb by the sounding sea . . . ."

The proprietor's cigar billowed smoke. He beamed, as he saw the seven new customers; he beamed, like the moon in Poe.

The drunken sailor, sprawled across his cups, did not see his girl as she rose to dance with the tall soldier. He had come all the way from Louisiana to see her, on leave, and now she was dancing with a tall soldier, bouncing around the floor, laughing, colliding, smoking.

"What a lovely dive!" uttered one of the seven new customers.

"I have a hunch I won't be bored here," his girl shouted to him. She was tall, her eyes sad, her brow constantly furrowed with pity.

Obese Pete saw her from his stool at the bar, forgot Annabel Lee. The five dreary soldiers drank and drank, thinking about the War. They sat erect, with drooping eyes. They were from Massachusetts, Virginia, Florida, Utah, and Massachusetts. One of the soldiers from Massachusetts, a tall thin fellow with glasses, rose from his seat with a smile and burrowed his way through the mass of humanity. The next instant, he was on the floor with a girl, and the very next instant, they were bouncing with the beat, smiling to each other, colliding, laughing, gyrating to the din. The bartender's assistant dropped a slice of orange into a Tom Collins and dashed forward with his finished masterpiece, almost colliding with the bartender, who was dashing in the opposite direction toward the Scotch.

But outside, it was America in the night. The real, true, America, America in the night. Richard sat with bowed head upon the old running board, and far across the slumbering land, he heard the flung strains of a distant engine whistle.

And now, he heard the band in Pepi Martin's strike up the quiet blues. Presently, the introduction meandered into the strains of "Blues in the Night!"

["My mama done tol' me, when I was in kneepants, my mama done tol' me . . . Son! A woman'll sweet talk . . . and give ya the big eye . . . but when the sweet talkin's done . . . a woman's a two-face . . . a worrisome thing . . . that leaves ya t' sing . . . the Blues in the Night . . ."]

Richard looked up, and saw etched against the moon, the grief-stricken telephone wires of America. He wept in his drunkenness, alone outside of Pepi Martin's gay roadhouse in Mississippi. Wept in the Night, seated on obese Pete's old running board. Deep down in his heart, a voice tried to speak, but could not. In a welling up of tears, and music, Blues music, it said: Does the goodness of Christ shine with the moon and with the sad lamps? Does his voice moan with the train whistle? Christ returns to America, at night. Magic night is the time when wonder steals into our hearts. We know then, as never, that life is a strange and beautiful dream, and nothing else. Oh, life is bitter beauty. Oh, life is awful glory. Oh, Christ!

(What happened to Richard? Nothing. He was merely drunk, and it was America in the Night, and the Blues were playing, and the train whistle was blowing across the meadows of Night. Pity. Sadness. Dream. Love. Grief-stricken beauty. Hope of our land.)

I have traveled to distant cities, said the famined heart of Richard, and I have seen how cruel is man. Cruel wretch! I am only youth, but I swear I know . . .

"The nightingale sings the saddest song I know . . . he knows things are wrong . . . and he's right . . ."

And he wept, remembering the gaiety in Pepi Martin's, remembering the sad lamps of night. Christ! his famined heart cried, if tears shall wash away the cruelty of our years, and sow the seeds of pity in our black, broken hearts, and remind us that life is brief and lovely, not long and foolish, that it is strange and beautiful, yea as a dream, then so let it be, if it must be tears, if tears alone may serve . . .

Crack! The drummer had struck his rim-shot, and the band was off once more on a mad swing tune, and the dancers howled with delight, and smoke clung to the rocking rafters. Din! Din! Din!

The drunken sailor was sprawled across his cups, and the shouting went on all about him; and the music rebounded from beam to beam, bouncing and bouncing in steady stream.

The door opened, and in staggered Richard. The proprietor's eye hardened. Richard moiled across the little room, lost in the din and smoke, and made his way toward the Men's Room. Inside, he reeled against the wall and tried to read a penciled epitaph.

"What rhetoric!" said a horn-rimmed face beside him.

"Fragments of Milton!" muttered Richard.

He looked through the horn-rimmed glasses and saw two friendly eyes, two sad eyes.

"You've read Milton?" asked Pete.

"Some."

"Ah, . . . then, you've probably read Emerson."

"Some."

"What do you think of his essay on Compensation? My name is

Pete Miller. What's yours? I'm from New York. Where are you from? I am studying America in my jalopy. Where are you sitting?"

Richard laughed, loud and long.

"Blues in the Night," he answered drunkenly. "My name is Johnny Dreamer. Christ returns to America, in the night. Dreamer's my name."

"Well then, Dreamer, come on over and sit with me," cried Pete drunkenly. "I am studying America in my jalopy."

They left the Men's Room and pushed their way through the mass of people. At a little table in the corner, Pete ordered two drinks, and then directed his horn-rimmed stare at Richard.

"I," he began, "am writing a novel called 'The Wound of Living,' and it is my theory that Life, which begins in perfect innocence, and in relatively perfect health, ends in deep wound and deterioration. The very definition of life is the disintegration of it. That is why I fear nothing. Have you noticed that nice looking girl in the other booth? Do you write also?"

Richard looked over to the next booth, but saw nothing to speak of. The seat began to reel.

"I am not a writer," he shouted to Pete above the din. "I play tenor sax in college. I am studying nothing in particular, since I want some day to play sax for a big-name band."

"What college?" asked Pete, shouting.

"Princeton," cried Richard. "I'm home for the summer, and I feel lousy, because for some reason or other, I am bored and lonely. See?"

"I see!" shouted Pete with his honest eyes. "You've been wounded!"

The drunken sailor had by now turned over, and his drunken face was revealed to all who cared to look . . . a little mustache under a large nose. From the general direction of the bandstand, music leaped through the fogged air in great bouncing gobs, and the dancers gyrated and gyrated until Richard had to take hold of his seat or fall to the floor. Pete was shouting:

"Dreamer! I would say you were drunk!"

A waiter dashed over nervously, shouting:

"Everythin' all set boys?"

"Right," assured Richard, holding up an assuring finger.

The waiter darted off, dodging expertly.

"I'm glad I met you," shouted Pete. "I wanted someone to talk to. I'm running all around the country in my jalopy. New Orleans is my next stop."

"Glad I met you," howled Richard. "I was feeling pretty low just a moment ago. I'm drunk, you know."

Two female eyes were fixed on the eyes of Richard. He blinked, then looked carefully. Yes, she is looking at me. I shall dance with her.

Richard rose; "Excuse for a minute Pete. I am going to [take] advantage of a momentary infatuation. This girl is ogling me on."

"Bravo!" screamed Pete, raising his drink to mobile lips. He always spoke through stiff, careful lips, in deep, correct tones. "It's the girl I was telling you about. Bravo!"

Richard reeled through the smoke, toward the two eyes.

"Dance?" he said into her ear. She was one of the seven in the new party of customers.

"Hmmm," she smiled melodiously. "I certainly shall."

A moment later, they were clutched to each other, elbowing through a solid mass of dancers.

"Lovely night," whispered the girl in his ear.

"What's your name?" asked Richard.

"Annabel," she answered, breathing warmly. Everything, to Richard, was giddy and absolutely wonderful. His remembrance of Blues in the Night was vague, triumphant. He remembered also the fields that surrounded Pepi Martin's, hushed and patient in the night. And the sad lamps, and the goodness of Christ, and the warmth of Life, and the bitter beauty, and the awful glory, and his saxophone back in New Jersey moaning in trembling tremolo of the day when he should ever meet two such sad eyes and such a pity-furrowed brow. And the yielding waist.

"I have the Blues in the Night," cried Richard, triumphantly.

"I too," she whispered in his ear. Strange and beautiful dream, come to me, now. I am giddy.

Then, the next thing he knew, Richard was seated back with Pete, and Annabel was beside him, her head upon his shoulder.

Pete was talking, talking, but Richard could hear nothing. Pete's obese spectacles were rolling in slow undulations, and Annabel's head was light upon his shoulder. And in his ear, the incessant boom of the bass-pedal mingled with the rancid, beery air.

Then the three of them were out in the drive, feet crunching in the pebbles, and Richard was howling to the moon: "Alms for the Love of Allah! Alms for the Love of Allah!" The air screamed with purity.

"Allah!" echoed Annabel.

"Is your second name Lee?" asked Pete.

"Wiley!" she corrected, pinching Pete's ear.

Then they were in Pete's jalopy. The car lurched from the drive, leaving Pepi Martin's. Then the black tar road began to unwind, like a great black snake, uncoiling. Dark night winds rushed around the car, and Pete turned on the radio. Annabel sat between the two youths, singing with the music from the radio.

"What!" howled Richard drunkenly, "What circumstance, what beautiful circumstance, brings the three of us together upon this night of June 8, in this year of grace, in this little jalopy, swerving through America in the Night, with the sad meadows of Mississippi riding past in infinite wisdom? . . ."

"Secret forest of the night," shouted Pete, driving.

"What circumstance?" insisted Richard. "I shall tell you . . . it is the famished heart, the poor starving heart . . . I am alone, and drunk, and lonesome . . . and I meet Pete . . . and I meet Annabel . . ."

"Oh! the moon never beams," began Pete, "without bringing me dreams . . ."

"And Annabel meets Pete, and Pete meets Annabel. And I meet Annabel, and Annabel meets me. And I meet Pete, and Pete meets me . . . ."

". . . nor the demons down under the sea, can ever dissever my soul . . . from the soul . . . of the beautiful Annabel . . . Wi . . . Lee . . . ."

And Annabel sang with the music.

The power and glory of Bacchus!! Why, world, should it be the work of Bacchus to unburden the famined hearts of the earth? Why not you, world?

Suddenly, with the music roaring in their ear[s], and the wind flapping about the car in cold blasts, they were not riding in the road, but beside it in a field, and the tires were screeching, and the road itself had curved off to the left, a bit insultingly. Richard, arm draped over the right front door of the little coupe, suddenly realized that the car was about to turn over, and upon his draped arm. But there was no time for fear. The headlamps illuminated a large tree, which was now riding toward them very speedily, very insultingly. Every bit of the bark was plainly legible. It came near to hitting Richard's draped arm, but didn't. It rode into the car at the right front fender. There was a dull biff.

"Surely, this has happened to me before, perhaps in a dream!" thought Richard, as he tumbled slowly from the car along with the door. Then he was rolling lackadaisically in the grass, and then he was staring up at the stars and the moon. It was nothing, he thought. Death is nothing. I am dead.

But those were real stars, and that was a real breeze, chilled with night. Perhaps I am not dead. I shall see. Richard rose to his feet, and then fell on one knee. He rose again, and his legs gathered strength. From somewhere came the quiet sound of trickling water, but outside of that, there was utter silence. A door from a nearby farmhouse was flung open.

Richard reeled forward, and saw the car, which had just now been moving along in grand style, now leaning sadly and wearily against the tree, crushed within itself like an accordion. It was very sad, thought Richard. The poor sad little car, stopped and melancholy. A piece of glass tumbled within the wreckage. The water trickled on. The radio had stopped.

This had not happened, because I am Richard Vesque, and Richard Vesque was not born to be in an automobile accident on June 8. No, it has not happened, for I am Richard. Things like these happen in the papers and in the movies, but not in real life to Richard Vesque, the Princeton boy.

Richard was keenly conscious of a terrific headache. He walked around the wreckage, and the next thing he knew, he was cursing, cursing with foul words. For there lay Pete, flat upon his back, beside his little jalopy, stopped and with no more radio music. The horn-rimmed glasses were pointed stolidly toward the stars.

Where is Annabel?

Richard staggered to the wreckage, and peered into the mangled front seat. There was a patch of her dress. Richard touched it, and realized to his horror that it was her flesh he was feeling underneath that patch of dress. He grabbed, knowing then that it was her upper arm. Richard heaved, wincing as the wreckage groaned reluctantly. Richard tugged, and the wreckage tinkled, collapsed in small places, groaned. The poor flesh of Annabel, tugging against steel wreckage.

Weakly, Richard now withdrew the girl's bulk from the tangle of steel and dragged her to a standing position. Then he lifted her into his arms and with watery knees, lurched forward toward a patch of thick grass. When he had deposited her gently upon the grass, a flashlight cut into his eyes, and then fell upon Annabel's body. Someone had come.

The trickling water was not trickling water. It was a faucet of blood coming from Annabel's face. Richard reeled to one knee, and began to curse and weep all at once.

"Who was driving?" asked a voice.

"Oh, leave the poor kid alone," muttered Richard. "He's hurt."

A beam of light fell upon Pete's upthrust face.

"This one's dead,"said a woman in calm amazement.

Richard felt his own leg, and knew that it was all blood.

"What a Goddamned thing!" he cursed aloud. "Christ! Why'd you go and do that! Jesus!"

"Take it easy, boy. We've called the ambulance. That's a pretty mean wreck. It sounded like a truck wreck from my bedroom. How fast were you going?" There were a lot of people around, and cars parked across the road.

"I dunno," muttered Richard. "Get this poor girl to the hospital, will you?"

He was sick, repulsively sick with doom and tragedy and death. He could have vomited, but he wouldn't. The whole thing was too disgusting to think about. From somewhere came the dim howl of an engine whistle. Richard felt tears come to his eyes, then his hands began to shake convulsively. Screeching with the horror and agony of man, the ambulance approached through the night, siren paving the terrorized way.

The ambulance was long and sleek. It was low and racy, and could negotiate any curve without going off the road.

# [The Very Thing I Live For]

How can I deceive the very thing I live for? (writing)
(truth)
I love life more dearly, yes, more dearly [than] my
strange, dark
self, which I yet do not understand. Who am I? I can't
say . . . I
am a stranger to myself: I emerged in birth into a
strange, gray
world, and my child self was full of wonder. . .
You may wander west across the plains, across the
mountains into
the dry Nevadas, you may journey south to the sultry
Gulf, or
north to the dark pines. . .wherever you go, seek the
deepest, darkest
forest and steal into its most secluded and innermost
glade, and
there you'll find a heavy rock mouldy and dark and green
in the
green, green shade, and when you turn it over, and the
crow caws
from his secret branch, and the forest echoes and echoes,
and
the elfin deer peeps over from a hidden brook, and the
owl ruffles
his feathers in the cool shade by a virgin well, and the
tall pines
sway pointing at the passing high clouds, and from far off
you
hear once more the caw of the crow, yes, when you turn
over this

rock, there you'll find my heart. . .
When I see you and your beauty, yes, your youthful,
    laughing beauty,
my heart stirs the heavy green rock and once more I see
    a field
of violets in the May breeze and want to go out with the
    sheep
and sing by the waterfalls. . .

# The Mystery

One night, returning from work in the casual, squalid atmosphere of railroad yards, warehouses, switch towers, idle boxcars, and one lonely little lunchcart across the tracks, as I was approaching the rail crossing near the old depot that we have in my home town, I had to lean against a sagging fence (black with soot-years) for fully ten minutes while a mighty locomotive went by freighting ninety-six cars: coal cars, oil tanks, wooden boxcars, all types of commercial rolling stock. While I loafed there with a cigarette, watching each car rumble past and checking the cargoes, a thought came to me with swift and lucid impact, with the same jolt of common sense and disbelief in the scantiness of my own intelligence that I had felt when first I understood the workings of a mathematical equation. "Why," I asked myself, "does not this rich cargo, these cars, that terrific locomotive belong to me? . . . and to my fellow men? Why are they not, like my trousers, my property; and why are they not, like the trousers of my fellow men, their property? Who covets these great things so that myself and my fellow men are not heir to their full use?" Then I asked myself, "Are we not all men living alone together on a single earth?"

Then I gazed at the old depot, its aged brownstone turrets lost in clouds of steam—(steam, I thought, strangely rational puffs of steam, marks of industrial necessity each with a reason and justice behind their inception, fashioned by the common Genius of just and reasonable working men, all for sure and strong and everlastingly sound purposes)—and I wondered why the depot did not belong to my fellow men and I as well.

When the caboose finally went by, bringing up the rear of the freight train with a little glow of red light, I watched the railroad employee as he leaned on the rail of the caboose with pipe in mouth and wondered why he wasn't working for himself and for his fellow men rather than for the Boston & Maine Railroad Corporation

(its wealth as a corporation, I pondered, is measured in shares: the bulk of these scraps of paper are in the hands of a few great men of wealth, "railroad magnates" with cigars protruding from their mouths, men who are so busy others make way for them when they approach to pass . . . . and yet, I wondered, if they were the men who "ran the railroads," then where were they tonight? Where?)

I allowed my mind to imagine—I knew I was not idly speculating: I saw one of these great "railroad kings"; he was seated in the rear of a long black car, holding onto a leather window strap while his chauffeur shot the purring car like a sleek, silent cat through the streets. The car was rolling (almost floating) through the streets of West End New York, uptown along Ninth Avenue. From his plush seat, the "railroad king" saw fruit stands in the hot summer evening, peddlers pushing carts and chanting their wares, shawled women shuffling along the dirty sidewalks, unwashed children scattering suddenly from dark alleys across the street cobbles, old men seated wearily on stoops, shabby young lovers strolling, and here and there, a drunkard vomiting in his dark corner. The "railroad king" saw all this, surely, and yet he did not: he was not detached . . . . No! He was only abstracted, other things were on his mind, he was on his way to a dinner party. Who would be there, that was the question, who would be there at the dinner party? And what year champagne? Would the dinner be as exquisite as that one last night in Pittsburgh? The "railroad king's" subconscious mind was a stream of shimmering, smooth things . . . . gowns of silk, long cool drinks, natty white dinner jackets, hearty laughter beneath cigar smoke, music stealing in from concealed sources, the great head of a moose exposed dumbly and mutely above a marble wainscoting, the eyes of a woman that know; and the voices, the voices: as smooth as oil the voices will soothe confidentially, behind a cigar, the sly voices, the secret, confidential mirth, the smooth power of the clan. Yes! the smell of new things, deep-grained, walnut things, new leather, new silk, the fragrance of rich, new things. This Ninth Avenue—all in passing, something "on the way" to the dinner party, not permanent, not solid! Yes, to the "railroad king's" mind this Ninth Avenue meant only something old and corrosive and—well, to be frank—a bit on the loathsome side.

Yes! all this while the old man who controlled the wooden guards across the street from where I stood that night pulled the lever that lofted the zebra-striped guards and then went back to his little

[ 201 ]

shack to resume his reading of a Hearst tabloid by the light of a sooty oil lamp. All this . . . and Ninth Avenue, New York City. Was it evident, then, that this "railroad magnate" had no conscience, despite all that was before him to see? Could he ride through the filthy streets where the masses abounded in their rank legions and pass it off as "something on the way?" Are beasts and plants the only forms of living without a moral conscience?

It was then that I realized conclusively that this must not go on, that this must surely and would surely end, that it could not be otherwise, that the system of the world since the conquest of the last savage races by barbarians was a tumor which had somehow set in. I compared the system to a tubercle which had become inflamed by a horde of bacilli more rotten than any to be found in nature at its lush worst, and that the nature of these bacilli was powermad greed: then I knew that the inflammation would develop until the prodigy cell of society would collapse. How should this horrid tumor be eliminated? I did not know for certain. But I knew what society would be like once the corruption would be dug out. It was at once and always the most beautiful and casual revelation I have ever felt.

I saw the same freight train, the same ancestral depot with its homely turrets, the same switch towers, the same expanse of steel rail, the same old man in the shack. I, with my cigarette and shabby trousers, walked across the track and thought: "How is our railroad running tonight?" "Fine," was the answer in my thought, "the brothers are running it right, because it is our railroad. Why should it be otherwise? See, two of the brothers have stopped to chat by a switch; see the glow of their pipes in the summer darkness, see the hands that hold the lantern (look! the veinous power of their lanky hands!) Ask them how things are coming along, and they will certainly tell you. 'Brother,' they will tell you in the quiet darkness, 'our railroad is coming along fine . . . just now, a large trainload went by on its way to Boston.' 'Is that so!' I will say to them in quiet amaze, not quite able to remain calm about such a large and beautiful fact. 'Certainly,' they will answer, 'The cargo will be unloaded by our brothers in Boston to be distributed among the people . . . food from our farms, clothing and necessities and gadgets and things from our factories, oil from our wells, toys and books and little things . . . Oh! all manner of things, there is no end to it!' 'Sure,' I will say to them, smiling, 'it has always been like this.'

'And why not!' they will answer in unison. Then we all laugh, and I walk away, and there is nothing to say."

What a plain and simple fact this dream was, and is! I walked home and looked at the rich, nodding stars in the sky and it was as plain as that. When I stopped to contemplate the tree in my back-yard it was as simple as that. I could not understand what had gone wrong, and where, and at what time . . . . . it was a mystery that needed explanation. Sternly, but with a puzzled frown, I wanted an explanation.

# Thinking of Thomas Wolfe
# on a Winter's Night

Bereaved pines standing like Justice,
The cold stare of stars between;
I walk down the road, holding
    my ears,
My palms the shelters
From dry sweeps of brittle cold.

"Who has known fury?" Wolfe
    had asked,
And the critic's winter eyes,
Like these stars (between
    the pines)
Had stared, amusedly.

Come, it is warm in my house;
We shall go there;
Soon the flashing sun will
    rise up
To overwhelm the petulant
    stars.

# from The Sea Is My Brother
# (Merchant Mariner)

*Kerouac saw a rough equivalency in his World War II–era service with the Merchant Marine and the combat in Europe and the Pacific faced by his friends and contemporaries. According to the U.S. Coast Guard, Merchant Marine casualties on U.S. ships included 845 dead, 4,780 missing, and 37 dead as prisoners of war. More than 600 U.S.-flagged ships were lost. Another 500 Americans died on foreign ships under U.S. supervision.*

*The Sea Is My Brother is the most ambitious early work by Kerouac. The following is an excerpt from the third version of the novel, which is published here for the first time under the dual titles The Sea Is My Brother and Merchant Mariner. Both titles appear on the 158-page hand-printed manuscript, which Kerouac identified as follows: "Original of 1943 novel The Sea Is My Brother (which was examined by psychiatrists at Naval Hospital in Bethesda, Md. 1943)." Waiting in Lowell to report to the U.S. Navy, Kerouac told Sebastian Sampas in a mid-March 1943 letter that he was writing almost around the clock and that their friends had praised his thirty-five-thousand-word manuscript.*

*Kerouac wrote to his friend George J. Apostolos in April 1943: "And, all my youth I stood holding two ends of rope, trying to bring both ends together in order to tie them. Sebastian was at one end, you on the other, and beyond both of you lay the divergent worlds of my dual mind [. . .]—had a hell of a time trying to bring these two worlds together—never succeeded actually; but I did in my novel 'The Sea Is My Brother,' where I created two new symbols of these two worlds, and welded them irrevocably together."*

*Kerouac worked his Merchant Marine experience into various writing projects, including a story called "An Introvert at Sea," a novel titled* Two Worlds for a New One, *and a one-act play,* The Seaman. *In one of the many sea project documents from the period, Kerouac described the story as "A man's simple revolt from society as it is, with its inequalities, frustrations, and self-inflicted agonies. Wesley Martin loves the sea with a strange, lonely love; the sea is his brother and sentencer. He goes down. The story also of another man [Bill Everhart], in contrast, who escapes society for the sea, but finds the sea a place of terrible loneliness."*

*In notes for another version of* The Sea Is My Brother, *in which the worldly Wesley Martin dies at sea, Kerouac describes how Martin's friend and rookie seaman Everhart presses on alone, dealing with various characters aboard ship. He is interested in one who seems very much an individual: "[. . .] Slim is to Everhart the 'vanishing American,' the big free boy, the American Indian, the last of the pioneers, the last of the hoboes. For, in a planned economy, in the emergence of the state over capitalism, crown, and church, Slim's type is not allowed to exist without dire consequence. [. . .] Yet, Everhart is enraged by this, because he finds such humility and wisdom in the hobo, and beauty, too."*

## CHAPTER THREE
## WE ARE BROTHERS, LAUGHING

[. . .]

Wesley went to the window and glanced down the street; way off in the distance, the clustered pile of New York's Medical Center stood, a grave healer surrounded at its hem by smaller buildings where the healed returned. From Broadway, a steady din of horns, trolley bells, grinding gears, and screeching trolley wheels surmounted the deeper, vaster hum from the high noon thoroughfare. It was very warm by now; a crazy haze danced toward the sun while a few of the more ambitious birds chittered in sleepy protest from the green. Wesley took off his coat and slouched into an easy chair by the window. When he was almost asleep, Everhart was talking to him: ". . . Well, the old man leaves me my choice. All I have to do now is speak to my brother-in-law and to the Dean. You wait here, Wes, I'll call the jerk up . . . he's in his radio repair shop . . ."

Everhart was gone again. Wesley dozed off; once he heard a boy's voice speaking from the door: "Geez! Wha's dat!" Later, Everhart was back, bustling through the confusion of papers and books on his desk.

"Where the hell? . . ."

Wesley preferred to keep his eyes closed; for the first time in two weeks, since he had signed off the last freighter, he felt content and at peace with himself. A fly lit on his nose, but he was too lazy to shoo it off; it left a moist little feeling when he twitched it away.

"Here it is!" muttered Everhart triumphantly, and he was off again.

Wesley felt a thrill of anticipation as he sat there dozing: in a few days, back on a ship, the sleepy thrum of the propeller churning in the water below, the soothing rise and fall of the ship, the sea stretching around the horizon, the rich, clean sound of the bow splitting water . . . . And the long hours lounging on deck in the sun, watching the play of the clouds, ravished by the full, moist breeze. A simple life! A serious life! To make the sea your own, to watch over it, to brood your very soul into it, to accept it and love it as though only it mattered and existed! "A.B. Martin!" they called him. "He's a quiet good enough seaman, good worker," they would say of him. Hah! Did they know he stood on the bow every morning, noon, and night for an hour; did they suspect this profound duty of his, this prayer of thanks to a God more a God than any to be found in book-bound altar-bound religion?

Sea! Sea! Wesley opened his eyes, but closed them rapidly. He wanted to see the ocean as he had often seen it from his foc'sle port-hole, a heaving world pitching high above the port, then dropping below to give a glimpse of the seasky—as wild and beautiful as the sea—and then the sea surging up again. Yes, he used to lay there in his bunk with a cigarette and a magazine, and for hours he would gaze at the porthole, and there was the surging sea, the receding sky. But now he could not see it; the image of Everhart's bedroom was etched there, clouding the clean, green sea.

But Wesley had felt the thrill, and it would not leave him: soon now, a spray-lashed day in the graygreen North Atlantic, that most rugged and moody of oceans . . . .

Wesley reached for a cigarette and opened his eyes; a cloud had come across the face of the sun, the birds had suddenly stopped, the street was gray and humid. An old man was coughing in the next room.

Everhart was back.

"Well!" he said. "Done, I guess . . ."

Wesley passed his hand through the thin black mat of his hair: "What's done?"

Everhart opened a dresser drawer: "You've been sleeping, my beauty. I saw the Dean, and it's all right with him; he thinks I'm going to the country for a vacation."

Everhart slapped a laundered shirt in his hand meditatively: "The noble brother-in-law whined until I made it clear I'd be back with enough money to pay up all the half-rents and half-boards in this country for a year. At the end, he was fairly enthusiastic . . ."

"What time is it?" yawned Wesley.

"One-thirty."

"Shuck-all! I've been sleepin' . . . and dreamin' too," said Wesley, drawing deep from his cigarette.

Everhart approached Wesley's side. "Well, Wes," he began, "I'm going with you—or that is, I'm shipping out. Do you mind if I follow you along? I'm afraid I'd be lost alone, with all the union hall and papers business . . ."

"Hell, no, man!" Wesley smiled. "Ship with me!"

"Let's shake on that!" smiled the other, proffering his hand. Wesley wrung his hand with grave reassurance.

Everhart began to pack with furious energy, laughing and chatting. Wesley told him he knew of a ship in Boston bound for Greenland, and that getting one's Seaman's papers was a process of several hours duration. They also planned to hitchhike to Boston that very afternoon.

[. . .]

Everhart, busy rummaging in the closet, made no remarks, so Wesley followed Sonny into the dim hall and into another room.

This particular room faced the inner court of the building, so that no sun served to brighten what ordinarily would be a gloomy chamber in the first place. A large man clad in a brown bathrobe sat by the window smoking a pipe. The room was furnished with a large bed, an easy chair (in which the father sat), another smaller chair, a dresser, a battered trunk, and an ancient radio with exterior loudspeaker and all. From this radio there now emitted a faint strain of music through a clamor of static.

"Hey Paw!" sang Sonny. "Here's that sailor!"

The man turned from his reverie and fixed two red-rimmed eyes on them, half stunned. Then he perceived Wesley and smiled a pitifully twisted smile, waving his hand in salute.

Wesley waved back, greeting: "Hullo!"

"How's the boy?" Mr. Everhart wanted to know, in a deep, gruff, workingman's voice.

"Fine," Wesley said.

"Billy's goin' with you, hey?" the father smiled, his mouth twisted down into a chagrined pout, as though to smile was to admit defeat. "I always knew the little cuss had itchy feet."

Wesley sat down on the edge of the bed while Sonny ran to the foot of the bed to preside over them proudly.

"This is my youngest boy," said the father of Sonny. "I'd be a pretty lonely man without him. Everybody else seems to have forgotten me." He coughed briefly. "Your father alive, son?" he resumed.

Wesley leaned a hand on the mottled bedspread: "Yeah. He's in Boston."

"Where's your people from?"

"Vermont originally."

"Vermont? What part?"

"Bennington," answered Wesley. "My father owned a service station there for twenty-two years."

"Bennington," mused the old man, nodding his head in reflection. "I traveled through there many years ago. Long before your time."

"His name's Charley Martin," supplied Wesley.

"Martin? . . . I used to know a Martin from Baltimore, a Jack Martin he was."

There was a pause during which Sonny slapped the bedstead. Outside, the sun faded once more, plunging the room into a murky gloom. The radio sputtered with static.

Bill's sister entered the room, not even glancing at Wesley.

"Is Bill in his room?" she demanded.

The old man nodded: "He's packing his things, I guess."

"Packing his things?" she cried. "Don't tell me he's really going through with this silly idea?"

Mr. Everhart shrugged.

"For God's sake, Pa, are you going to let him do it?"

"It's none of my business—he has a mind of his own," returned the old man calmly, turning toward the window.

"He has a mind of his own!" she mimicked savagely.

"Yes he has!" roared the old man, spinning around to face his daughter angrily. "I can't stop him."

She tightened her lips irritably for a moment.

"You're his father aren't you!" she shouted.

"Oh!" boomed Mr. Everhart with a vicious leer. "So now I'm the father of the house!"

The woman stamped out of the room with an outraged scoff.

"That's a new one!" thundered the father after her.

Sonny snickered mischievously.

"That's a new one!" echoed the old man to himself. "They dumped me in this back room years ago when I couldn't work any more and forgot all about it. My word in this house hasn't meant anything for years."

Wesley fidgeted nervously with the hem of the old quilt blanket.

"You know, son," resumed Mr. Everhart with a sullen scowl, "a man's useful in life so long's he's producin' the goods, bringin' home the bacon; that's when he's Pop, the breadwinner, and his word is the word of the house. No sooner he grows old an' sick an' can't work any more, they flop him up in some old corner o' the house," gesturing at his room, "and forget all about him, unless it be to call him a damn nuisance."

From Bill's room they could hear arguing voices.

"I ain't stoppin' him from joining the merchant marine if that's what he wants," grumbled the old man. "And I know damn well I couldn't stop him if I wanted to, so there!" He shrugged wearily.

Wesley tried to maintain as much impartiality as he could; he lit a cigarette nervously and waited patiently for a chance to get out of this uproarious household. He wished he had waited for Bill at a nice cool bar.

"I suppose it's none too safe at sea nowadays," reflected Mr. Everhart aloud.

"Not exactly," admitted Wesley.

"Well, Bill will have to face danger sooner or later, Army or Navy or merchant marines. All the youngsters are in for it," he added dolefully. "Last war, I tried to get in but they refused me—wife n' kids. But this is a different war, all the boys are going in this one."

The father laid aside his pipe on the window sill, leaning over with wheezing labor. Wesley noticed he was quite fat; the hands were powerful, though, full of veinous strength, the fingers gnarled and enormous.

"Nothin' we can do," continued Mr. Everhart. "We people of the common herd are to be seen but not heard. Let the big Money Bags start the wars, we'll fight 'em and love it." He lapsed into a malign silence.

"But I got a feelin'," resumed the old man with his pouting smile, "that Bill's just goin' along for the fun. He's not one you can fool, Billy . . . and I guess he figures the merchant marine will do him some good, whether he takes only one trip or not. Add color to his cheeks, a little sea an' sunshine. He's been workin' pretty hard all these years. Always a quiet little duck readin' books by himself. When the woman died from Sonny, he was twenty-two, a senior in the College—hit him hard, but he managed. I was still workin' at the shipyards, so I sent him on for more degrees. The daughter offered to move in with her husband an' take care of little Sonny. When Billy finished his education—I always knew education was a good thing—I swear I wasn't surprised when he hit off a job with the Columbia people here."

Wesley nodded.

The father leaned forward anxiously in his chair.

"Billy's not a one for the sort of thing he's goin' into now," he said with a worried frown. "You look like a good strong boy, son, and you've been through all this business and know how to take care of yourself. I hope . . . you keep an eye on Billy—you know what I mean—he's not . . ."

"Whatever I could do," assured Wesley, "I'd sure all do it."

[. . .]

"Hell, man, we'll bum to Boston," said Wesley.

"Sure!" beamed the other. "Besides, I never hitchhiked before; it would be an experience."

"Do we move?"

Everhart paused for a moment. What was he doing here in this room, this room he had known since childhood, this room he had wept in, had ruined his eyesight in, studying till dawn, this room into which his mother had often stolen to kiss and console him, what was he doing in this suddenly sad room, his foot on a packed suitcase and a traveler's hat perched foolishly on the back of his head?

Was he leaving it? He glanced at the old bed and suddenly realized that he would no longer sleep on that old downy mattress, long nights sleeping in safety. Was he forsaking this for some hard bunk on board a ship plowing through waters he had never hoped to see, a sea where ships and men were cheap and the submarine prowled like some hideous monster in DeQuincey's dreams. The whole thing failed to focus in his mind; he proved unable to meet the terror which this sudden contrast brought to bear on his soul. Could it be he knew nothing of life's great mysteries? Then what of the years spent interpreting the literatures of England and America for note-hungry classes? . . . had he been talking through his hat, an utterly complacent and ignorant little pittypat who spouted the profound feelings of a Shakespeare, a Keats, a Milton, a Whitman, a Hawthorne, a Melville, a Thoreau, a Robinson as though he knew the terror, fear, agony, and vowing passion of their lives and was brother to them in the dark, deserted old moor of their minds?

Wesley waited while Everhart stood in indecision, patiently attending to his fingernails. He knew his companion was hesitating.

At this moment, however, Bill's sister entered the room smoking a Fatima and still carrying her cup of tea. She and her friend, a middle-aged woman who now stood beaming in the doorway, had been engaged in passing the afternoon telling each other's fortune's in the tea leaves. Now the sister, a tall woman with a trace of oncoming middle age in her stern but youthful features, spoke reproachfully to her younger brother: "Bill, can't I do anything to change your mind. This is all so silly? Where are you going, for God's sake . . . be sensible."

"I'm only going on a vacation," growled Bill in a hunted manner. "I'll be back." He picked up his bag and leaned to kiss her on the cheek.

[. . .]

*

## CHAPTER FOUR

*

At three o'clock, they were standing at the side of the road near Bronx Park, where cars rushed past fanning hot clouds of dust into their faces. Bill sat on his suitcase while Wesley stood impassively selecting cars with his experienced eye and raising a thumb to them. Their first ride was no longer than a mile, but they were dropped at an advantageous point on the Boston Post Road.

The sun was so hot Bill suggested a respite; they went to a filling station and drank four bottles of Coca-Cola. Bill went behind to the washroom. From there he could see a field and a fringe of shrub steaming in the July sun. He was on his way! . . . New fields, new roads, new hills were in store for him—and his destination was the seacoast of old New England. What was the strange new sensation [that] lurked in his heart, a fiery tingle to move on and discover anew the broad secrets of the world? He felt like a boy again . . . Perhaps, too, he was acting a bit silly about the whole thing.

Back on the hot flank of the road, where the tar steamed its black fragrance, they hitched a ride almost immediately. The driver was a New York florist en route to his greenhouse near Portchester, N.Y. He talked volubly, a good-natured Jewish merchant with a flair for humility and humor: "A couple of wandering Jews!" he called them, smiling with a sly gleam in his pale blue eyes. He dropped them off a mile beyond his destination on the New York–Connecticut state line.

Bill and Wesley stood beside a rocky bed which had been cut neatly at the side of the highway. In the shimmering distance, Connecticut's flat meadows stretched a pale green mat for sleeping trees.

Wesley took off his coat and hung it to a shoulder while Bill pushed his hat down over his eyes. They took turns sitting on the suitcase while the other leaned on the cliffside, proffering a lazy thumb. Great trucks labored up the hill, leaving behind a dancing shimmer of gasoline fumes.

"Next to the smell of salt water," drawled Wesley with a grass-blade in his mouth, "I'll take the smell of a highway." He spat quietly with his lips.

"Gasoline, tires, tar, and shrubbery," added Bill lazily. "Whitman's song of the open road, modern version." They sunned quietly, without comment, in the sudden stillness. Down the road, a truck was shifting into second gear to start its uphill travails.

"Watch this," said Wesley. "Pick up your suitcase and follow me."

As the truck approached, now in first gear, Wesley waved at the driver and made as if to run alongside the slowly toiling behemoth. The driver, a colorful bandanna around his neck, waved a hand in acknowledgment. Wesley tore the suitcase from Bill's hand and shouted: "Come on!" He dashed up to the truck and leaped onto the running board, shoving the suitcase into the cab and holding the door open, balanced on one foot, for Bill. The latter hung on to his hat and ran after the truck; Wesley gave him [a] hand as he plunged into the cab.

"Whoo!" cried Bill, taking off his hat. "That was a neat bit of Doug Fairbanks dash!" Wesley swung in beside him and slammed the door to.

[. . .]

"Are you sure about that ship in Boston?"

"Yeah, . . . the Westminster, transport-cargo, bound for Greenland; did you bring your birth-certificate, man?"

Everhart slapped his wallet; "Right with me."

Wesley yawned again, pounding his breast as if to put a stop to his sleepiness. Everhart found himself wishing he were back home in his soft bed, with four hours yet to sleep before Sis's breakfast, while the milkman went by down on Claremont Avenue and a trolley roared past on sleepy Broadway.

A drop of rain shattered on his brow.

"We'd best get a ride right soon!" muttered Wesley turning a gaze down the deserted road.

They took shelter beneath a tree while the rain began to patter softly on the overhead leaves; a wet, steamy aroma rose in a humid wave.

"Rain, rain go away," Wesley sang softly, "come again another day . . ."

Ten minutes later, a big red truck picked them up. They smiled enthusiastically at the driver.

"How far you goin', pal?" asked Wesley.

"Boston!" roared the driver, and for the next hundred and twenty miles, while they traveled through wet fields along glistening roads, past steaming pastures and small towns, through a funereal Worcester, down a splashing macadam highway leading directly toward Boston under lowering skies, the truckman said nothing further.

Everhart was startled from a nervous sleep when he heard Wesley's voice . . . hours had passed swiftly.

"Boston, man!"

He opened his eyes; they were rolling along a narrow, cobblestoned street, flanked on each side with grim warehouses. It had stopped raining.

"How long have I been sleeping?" grinned Bill, rubbing his eyes while he held the spectacles on his lap.

"Dunno," answered Wesley, drawing from his perennial cigarette. The truck driver pulled to a lurching halt.

"Okay?" he shouted harshly.

Wesley nodded: "Thanks a million, buddy. We'll be seeing you."

"So long, boys," he called. "See you again."

Everhart jumped down from the high cab and stretched his legs luxuriously, waving his hand at the truck driver. Wesley stretched his arms slowly: "Eeyah! That was a long ride; I slept a bit meself."

They stood on a narrow sidewalk, which had already begun to dry after the brief morning rain. Heavy trucks piled past in the street, rumbling on the ancestral cobblestones, and it wasn't until a group of them had gone, leaving the street momentarily deserted and clear of exhaust fumes, that Bill detected a clean sea smell in the air. Above, broken clouds scuttled across the luminous silver skies; a ray of warmth had begun to drop from the part of the sky where a vague dazzle hinted the position of the sun.

"I've been to Boston before," chatted Bill, "but never like this . . . this is the real Boston."

Wesley's face lit in a silent laugh: "I think you're talkin' through your hat again, man! Let's start the day off with a beer in Scollay Square."

They walked on in high spirits.

Scollay Square was a short five minutes away. Its subway entrances, movie marquees, cut-rate stores, passport photo studios, lunchrooms, cheap jewelry stores, and bars faced the busy traffic of the street with a vapid morning sullenness. Scores of sailors in Navy whites sauntered along the cluttered pavements, stopping to gaze at cheap store fronts and theater signs.

Wesley led Bill to a passport photo studio where an old man charged them a dollar for two small photos.

"They're for your seaman's papers," explained Wesley. "How much money does that leave you?"

"A quarter," Everhart grinned sheepishly.

"Two beers and a cigar; let's go," Wesley said, rubbing his hands. "I'll borrow a fin from a seaman."

Everhart looked at his pictures: "Don't you think I look like a tough seadog here?"

"Hell, man, yes!" cried Wesley.

In the bar they drank a bracing glass of cold beer and talked about Polly, Day, Ginger, and Eve.

"Nice bunch of kids," said Wesley slowly.

Everhart gazed thoughtfully at the bartop: "I'm wondering how long Polly waited for us last night. I'll bet this is the first time Madame Butterfly was ever stood up," he added with a grin. "Polly's quite the belle around Columbia, you know." It sounded strange to say "Columbia" . . . how far away was it now?

[. . .]

"Well! We're in Boston," beamed Bill when they were back on the street. "What's on the docket?"

"First thing to do," said Wesley, leading his companion across the street, "is to mosey over to the Union Hall and check up on the Westminster . . . we might get a berth right off."

They walked down Hanover street, with its cheap shoe stores and bauble shops, and turned left at Portland street; a battered door, bearing the inscription "National Maritime Union," led up a flight of creaking steps into a wide, rambling hall. Grimy windows at each end served to allow a gray light from outside to creep inward, a gloomy, half-hearted illumination which outlined the bare, unfurnished immensity of the room. Only a few benches and folding chairs had been pushed against the walls, and these were now occupied by seamen who sat talking in low tones: they were dressed in various civilian clothing, but Everhart instantly recognized them as seamen . . . there, in the dismal gloom of their musty-smelling shipping headquarters, these men sat, each with the patience and passive quiet of men who know they are going back to sea, some smoking pipes, others calmly perusing the "Pilot," official N.M.U. publication, others dozing on the benches, and all possessed of the serene, waiting wisdom of a Wesley Martin.

"Wait here," said Wesley, shuffling toward the partitioned office across the broad plank floor. "I'll be right back." Everhart sat on the suitcase, peering.

"Hey, Martin!" howled a greeting voice from the folding chairs. "Martin you old crum!" A seaman was running across the hall toward Wesley, whooping with delight in his discovery. The echoing cries failed to disturb the peace of the other seamen, though, indeed, they glanced briefly and curiously toward the noisy reunion.

Wesley was astounded.

"Jesus!" he cried. "Nick Meade!"

Meade fairly collapsed into Wesley, almost knocking him over in his zeal to come to grips in a playful, bearish embrace; they pounded each other enthusiastically, and at one point Meade went so far as to push Wesley's chin gently with his fist, calling him as he did so every conceivable name he could think of; Wesley, for his part, manifested his delight by punching his comrade squarely in the stomach and howling a vile epithet as he did so. They whooped it up raucously for at least a half a minute while Everhart grinned appreciatively from his suitcase.

Then Meade asked a question in a low tone, hand on Wesley's shoulder; the latter answered confidentially, to which Meade roared once more and began anew to pummel Wesley, who turned away, his thin frame shaking with soundless laughter. Presently, they made their way toward the office, exchanging news with the breathless rapidity of good friends who meet after a separation of years.

"Shipping out?" raced Meade.

"Yeah."

"Let's see Harry about a double berth."

"Make it three, I've got a mate with me."

"Come on! The Westminster's in port; she's taking on 'most a full crew."

"I know."

"You old son of a bitch!" cried Meade, unable to control his joy at the chance meeting. "I haven't seen you since forty," kicking Wesley in the pants, "when we got canned in Trinidad!"

"For startin' that riot!" remembered Wesley, kicking back playfully while Meade dodged aside. "You friggin' communist, don't start kickin' me again . . . I remember the time you got drunk aboard ship and went around kickin' everybody till that big Bosun pinned your ears back!"

They howled their way into the inner office where a sour faced Union man looked up blandly from his papers.

"Act like seamen, will you?" he growled.

"Hangover Harry," informed Meade. "He uses up all the dues money to get drunk. Look at that face will you?"

"All right Meade," admonished Harry. "What are you looking for, I'm busy . . ."

They made arrangements to be on hand and near the office door that afternoon when the official ship calls from the S.S. Westminster would be posted, although Harry warned them those first come would be first served. "Two-thirty sharp," he grunted. "If you're not here, you don't get the jobs."

[. . .]

But a half hour later, Wesley rose and told Meade to meet him in the Union Hall at two-thirty; and with this, he and Everhart left the bar and turned their steps toward Atlantic Avenue.

"Now for your seaman's papers," he said to Bill.

Atlantic Avenue was almost impossible to cross, so heavy with the rush of traffic, but once they had regained the other side and stood near a pier, Billy's breast pounded as he saw, docked not a hundred feet away, a great gray freighter, its slanting hull striped with rust, a thin stream of water arching from the scuppers, and the mighty bow standing high above the roof of the wharf shed.

"Is that it?" he cried.

"No, she's at Pier Six."

They walked toward the Maritime Commission, the air heavy with the rotting stench of stockpiles, oily waters, fish, and hemp. Dreary marine equipment stores faced the street, show windows cluttered with blue peacoats, dungarees, naval officers uniforms, small compasses, knives, oilers' caps, seamen's wallets, and all manner of paraphernalia for the men of the sea.

The Maritime Commission occupied one floor of a large building that faced the harbor. While a pipe-smoking old man was busy preparing his papers, Everhart could see, beyond the nearby wharves and railroad yards, a bilious stretch of sea spanning toward the narrows, where two lighthouses stood like gate posts to a dim Atlantic. A seagull swerved past the window.

An energetic little man fingerprinted him in the next room, cigarette in mouth almost suffocating him as he pressed Bill's inky fingers on the papers and on a duplicate.

"Now go down to the Post Office building," panted the little man when he finished, "and get your passport certificate. Then you'll be all set."

Wesley was leaning against the wall smoking when Bill left the fingerprinting room with papers all intact.

"Passport certificate next I guess," Bill told Wesley, nodding toward the room.

"Right!"

They went to the Post Office Building on Milk Street where Bill filled out an application for his passport and was handed a certificate for his first foreign voyage; Wesley, who had borrowed five dollars from Nick Meade, paid Bill's fee.

"Now I'm finished I hope?" laughed Bill when they were back in the street.

"That's all."

"Next thing is to get our berths on the Westminster. Am I correct?"

"Right."

"Well," smiled Bill, slapping his papers, "I'm in the merchant marine."

At two-thirty that afternoon, Wesley, Bill, Nick Meade and seven other seamen landed jobs on the S.S. Westminster. They walked down from the Union hall down to Pier Six in high spirits, passing through the torturous weave of Boston's waterfront streets, crossing Atlantic Avenue and the Mystic river drawbridge, and finally coming to a halt along the Great Northern Avenue docks. Silently they gazed at the S.S. Westminster, looming on their left, her monstrous gray mass squatting broadly in the slip, very much, to Everhart's eyes, like an old bath tub.

*

# CHAPTER FIVE

*

[. . .]

He lay back on the pillow and realized these were his first moments of solitary deliberation since making his rash decision to get away from the thoughtless futility of his past life. It has been a good life, he ruminated, a life possessing at least a minimum of service and security. But he wasn't sorry he had made this decision; it would be a change, as he'd so often repeated to Wesley, a change regardless of everything. And the money was good in the merchant marine, the companies were not reluctant to reward the seamen for their labor and courage; money of that amount would certainly be welcomed at home, especially now with the old man's need for medical care. It would be a relief to pay for his operation and perhaps soften his rancor against a household that had certainly done him little justice. In his absorption for his work and the insistent demands of a highly paced social life, Bill admitted to himself, as he had often done, he had not proved an attentive son; there were such distances between a father and his son, a whole generation of differences in temperament, tastes, views, habits; yet the old man, sitting in that old chair with his pipe, listening to an ancestral radio while the new one boomed its sleek, modern power from the living room, was he not fundamentally the very meaning and core of Bill Everhart, the creator of all that Bill Everhart had been given to work with? And what right, Bill now demanded angrily, had his sister and brother-in-law to neglect him so spiritually? What if he were a lamenting old man?

Slowly, now, Everhart began to realize why life had seemed so senseless, so fraught with folly and lack of real purpose in New York, in the haste and oration of his teaching days—he had never paused to take hold of anything, let alone the lonely heart of an old father, not even the idealisms with which he had begun life as a seventeen-year-old spokesman for the working class movement on Columbus Circle Saturday afternoons. All these he had lost, by virtue of a sensitivity too fragile for everyday disillusionment . . . his father's complaints, the jeers of the Red baiters and the living, breathing social apathy that supported their jeers in phlegmatic silence. A few shocks from the erratic fuse box of life, and Everhart had thrown up his hands and turned to a life of academic isolation. Yet, in the realms of this academic isolation, wasn't there sufficient indication that all things pass and turn to dust? What was that sonnet where Shakespeare spoke sonorously of time "rooting out the work of masonry?" Is a man to be timeless and patient, or is he to be a pawn of time? What did it avail a man to plant roots deep into a society by all means foolish and Protean?

Yet, Bill now admitted with reluctance, even Wesley Martin had set himself a purpose, and this purpose was the idea of life—life at sea—a Thoreau before the mast. Conviction had led Wesley to the sea; confusion had led Everhart to the sea.

A confused intellectual, Everhart, the oldest weed in society; beyond that, an intelligent modern minus the social conscience of that class. Further, a son without a conscience—a lover without a wife! A prophet without confidence, a teacher of men without wisdom, a sorry mess of a man thereat!

Well, things would be different from now on . . . a change of life might give him the proper perspective. Surely, it had not been folly to take a vacation from his bookish, beerish life, as another side of his nature might deny! What wrong was there in treating his own life, within the bounds of moral conscience, as he chose and as he

freely wished? Youth was still his, the world might yet open its por-
tals as it had done that night at Carnegie Hall in 1927 when he first
heard the opening bars of Brahms' first symphony! Yes! As it
opened its doors for him so many times in his 'teens and closed
them firmly, as though a stern and hostile master were its doorman,
during his enraged twenties.

Now he was thirty-two years old and it suddenly occurred to him
that he had been a fool, yes, even though a lovable fool, the notori-
ous "shortypants" with the erudite theories and the pasty pallor of a
teacher of life . . . and not a liver of life. Wasn't it Thomas Wolfe who
had struck a brief spark in him at twenty-six and filled him with
new love for life until it slowly dawned on him that Tom Wolfe—as
his colleagues agreed in delighted unison—was a hopeless romanticist? What of it? What if triumph were Wolfe's only purpose? . . . . if
life was essentially a struggle, then why not struggle toward triumph, why not, in that case, achieve triumph! Wolfe had failed to
add to whom triumph was liege . . . and that, problem though it was,
could surely be solved, solved in the very spirit of his cry for triumph. Wolfe had sounded the old cry of a new world. Wars come,
wars go! elated Bill to himself, this cry is an insurgence against the
forces of evil, which creeps in the shape of submission to evil, this
cry is a denial of the not-Good and a plea for the Good. Would he,
then, William Everhart, plunge his whole being into a new world?
Would he love? Would he labor? Would he, by God, fight?
[. . .]

*
## CHAPTER EIGHT
*

That afternoon, while Everhart sat sunning near the poop deck,
reading Coleridge's "Ancient Mariner," he was startled by the harsh
ringing of a bell behind him. He looked up from the book and
glanced around the horizon with fear. What was it?

A droning, nasal voice spoke over the ship's address system: "All
hands to the boat deck. All hands to the boat deck." The system
whistled deafeningly.

Bill grinned and looked around, fear surging in his breast. The
other seamen, who had been lounging on the deck with him, now
dashed off. The warm wind blew Bill's pages shut; he rose to his feet
with a frown and laid down the book on his folding chair.

This calm, sunny afternoon at sea, flashing greens and golds, whipping bracing breezes across lazy decks, was this an afternoon for death? Was there a submarine prowling in these beautiful waters?

Bill shrugged and ran down to his focastle for the lifebelt; running down the alleyway, he hastily strapped it on, and clambered up the first ladder. An ominous silence had fallen over the ship.

"What the hell's going on!" he muttered as he climbed topsides. "This is no time for subs! We've just got started!" His legs wobbled on the ladder rungs.

On the top deck, groups of quiet seamen stood beside their lifeboats, a grotesque assemblage in lifebelts, dungarees, cook's caps, aprons, oiler's caps, bowcaps, khaki pants, and dozens of other motley combinations of dress. Bill hastened toward his own lifeboat and halted beside a group. No one spoke. The wind howled in the smoking funnel, flapped along the deck waving the clothing of the seamen, and rushed out over the stern along the bright green wake of the ship. The ocean sighed a soothing, sleepy hush, a sound that pervaded everywhere in suffusing enormity as the ship slithered on through, rocking gently forward.

Bill adjusted his spectacles and waited.

"Just a drill, I think," offered a seaman.

One of the Puerto Rican seamen in Bill's group, who wore a flaring cook's cap and a white apron beneath his lifebelt, began to conga across the deck while a comrade beat a conga rhythm on his thighs. They laughed.

The bell rang again, the voice returned: "Drill dismissed. Drill dismissed."

The seamen broke from groups into a confused swarm waiting to file down the ladders. Bill took off his lifebelt and dragged it behind him as he sauntered forward. Now he had seen everything . . . the ship, the sea . . . mornings, noons, and nights of sea . . . the crew, the destroyer ahead, a boat drill, everything.

He felt suddenly bored. What would he do for the next three months?

\* \* \*

Bill went down to the engine room that night to talk with Nick Meade. He descended a steep flight of iron steps and stopped in his tracks at the sight of the monster source of the Westminster's power . . . great pistons charged violently, pistons so huge one could hardly expect them to move with such frightening rapidity. The Westminster's shaft turned enormously, leading its revolving body toward the stern through what seemed to Bill a giant cave for a giant rolling serpent.

Bill stood transfixed before this monstrous power; he began to feel annoyed. What were ideas in the face of these brutal pistons, pounding up and down with a force compounded of nature and intriguing with nature against the gentle form of man?

Bill descended further, feeling as though he were going down to the bottom of the sea itself. What chance could a man have down here if a torpedo should ram at the waterline, when the engine room deck was at a level thirty or forty feet below! Torpedo . . . another brutal concoction of man, by George! He tried to imagine a torpedo slamming into the engine room against the hysterical blind power of the pistons, the deafening shock of the explosion, the hiss of escaping steam, the billows of water pouring in from a sea of endless water, himself lost in this holocaust and being pitched about like a leaf in a whirlpool! Death! . . . he half expected it to happen that precise moment.

A water tender stood checking a gauge.

"Where's the oiler Meade?" shouted Bill above the roar of the great engine. The water tender pointed forward. Bill walked until he came to a table where Nick sat brooding over a book in the light of a green-shaded lamp.

Nick waved his hand; he had apparently long given up conversation in an engine room, for he pushed a book toward Bill. Bill propped himself up on the table and ran through the leaves.

"Words, words, words," he droned, but the din of the engine drowned out his words and Nick went on reading.

* * *

The next day—another sundrowned day—the Westminster steamed North off the coast of Nova Scotia, about forty miles offshore, so that the crew could see the dim purple coastline just before dusk.

A fantastic sunset began to develop . . . long sashes of lavender drew themselves above the sun and reached thin shapes above distant Nova Scotia. Wesley strolled aft, digesting his supper, and was surprised to see a large congregation of seamen on the poop deck. He advanced curiously.

A man stood before the winch facing them all and speaking with gestures; on the top of the winch, he had placed a Bible, and he now referred to it in a pause. Wesley recognized him as the ship's baker.

"And they were helped against them, and the Hagarites were delivered into their hand, and all that were with them," the baker shouted. "For they cried to God in the battle and he was entreated of them because they put their trust in him . . ."

Wesley glanced around at the assemblage. The seamen seemed reluctant to listen, but none of them made any motion to leave. Some watched the sunset, others the water, others gazed down—but all were listening. Everhart stood at the back listening curiously.

"And so, brothers," resumed the baker, who had obviously appointed himself the Westminster's spiritual guide for the trip, "we must draw a lesson from the faith of the Reubenites in their war with the Hagarites and in our turn call to God's aid in our danger. The Lord watched over them and he will watch over us if we pray to him and entreat his mercy in this dangerous ocean where the enemy waits to sink our ship . . ."

Wesley buttoned up his peacoat; it was decidedly chilly. Behind the baker's form, the sunset pitched alternately over and below the deck rail, a florid spectacle in pink. The sea was deep blue.

"Let us kneel and pray," shouted the baker, picking up his Bible, his words drowned in a sudden gust of sea wind so that only those nearby heard him. They knelt with him. Slowly, the other seamen dropped to their knees. Wesley stood in the midst of the bowed shapes.

"Oh God," prayed the baker in a tremulous wail, "Watch over and keep us in our journey, Oh Lord, see that we arrive safely and . . ."

Wesley shuffled off and heard no more. He went to the bow and faced the strong headwind blowing in from the North, its cold tang biting into his face and fluttering back his scarf like a pennant.

North, in the wake of the destroyer, the sea stretched a seething field which grew darker as it merged with the lowering sky. The destroyer prowled.

\* \* \*

# Beauty as a Lasting Truth

When James Joyce wrote "A Portrait of the Artist as a Young Man," he was asserting his belief in beauty, beauty as a lasting truth, beauty as a joy not transient but sustaining, a deeply religious feeling for beauty. In the "Portrait" he told of the beauty yet to come from Joyce; it came, in the ten-year labor, "Ulysses."

Likewise, Tom Wolfe heralded beauty-to-come in his first novel "Look Homeward, Angel." It came, in its fullest grandeur in "You Can't Go Home Again."

In both cases, the young men (Dedalus and Gant) were aliens in a world unmindful of beauty as a religion. They were, indeed, pitted full-force against the hard wall of the world's will. Like two Messiahs, they were generally crucified, yet they survived to create the beauty they had heralded in their youths.

This is a strange truth. What is beauty, then, in the Gant-Dedalus sense?

In the first place, both attained the accumulated cultures of the world; they resembled Goethe in that they undertook huge labours during which they attempted to reach all of knowledge. These were heroic men, then. They were, in every sense, Promethean.

The beauty they saw is not the sparkle found in the romantic palaver, say, of revolutionists, or parvenus of the arts, or even Londonese super-seamen and prospectors. (This can be clarified for general understanding.) In other words, theirs was not the beauty of alluring things, say the fascinating junction of Moscow bells ringing on May Day; (this, indeed, is a type of beauty which makes for the religious life of many a youth); nor was their beauty something allied, or conjoined, with, let us say, the Left Bank, an oil still moist, Parisian breeze from the Seine, and candle guttering in the garret corner—this type of thing, I have found, is the religious ambition of many young people, as it was to me several years ago; nor was their sense of beauty completely fortified within the saloon scene, the broad, rugged America scene, the back-slapping, two-fisted, whiskey-guzzling beauty. It is quite safe to say that theirs was a beauty vast and deep enough to include all of these transient entities, but it went beyond & above these in a great circumveloping pall.

Their beauty was the poet's beauty, yet I make a radical statement now when I say that their beauty went beyond the poet's art, and in my opinion, I err not. It would be difficult to explain this without taking samples from the Beauty created of Joyce & Wolfe.

Let us take Paddy Dignan, whose funeral is depicted in Ulysses (by Joyce.) What poet ever saw beauty in the death of an ineffectual old Irishman who leaves behind him a brood of Dublin gamins and an old washtub wife? More, what proof have I that Joyce saw beauty in it? True, his compassionate treatment of the death, at once coldly objective, at once sympathetic through the mourners, is well-known . . . . but, though I could hardly produce points of evidence, I am intuitively convinced of Joyce's attitude toward "poor Paddy's" death. This I know, for there are unmistakable signs that Joyce loved old Dubliners with a deep and consuming fever. No one can write of old barflies, on a sunny afternoon, with as much clarity, force, and authority as Joyce.

In Joyce's love, even for the "illgirt server" in the filthy tavern which Bloom quits with sensitive disgust, I have found love; and love dignifies, beautifies its object.

Thomas Wolfe's Charlie Green, who jumped to his death from the Admiral Drake Hotel, is the most colorless individual (and type) ever projected in Art (at least in American Art). Yet wasn't it love that drove Wolfe to his passionate contrasts with the 17th century Drake, Drake pounding his tankard in Plymouth, Charlie Green sipping his coffee in a Brooklyn cafeteria? Wasn't it love that traced Green's peregrinations through the "mobways" of New York, to the "sterile wink of Chop Suey joints" of a Sunday evening (a terrifying reality), to Brooklyn street corners on a Sunday afternoon in March (horrifying reality!) And, lastly, then, wasn't it love that gave dignity and beauty, drama and meaning, to this poor American?

These beauties, which can only evidence themselves to men of heroic proportions (Thoreaus, Melvilles, Dostoevskys) are the great beauties. They sustain and make for life—without them, a man may never know that life is truly worthwhile (divested from the time-worn shibboleths and metaphysics, those superficial attempts to rationalize our stay on earth.)

I say, these are the true meanings, the true wealths.

For this reason, I am going to try to make these sadly-written beliefs comprehensible to the world, in a series of art works. It will mean years of study, observation, and analysis. This beauty-sense which has made my life rich, ripe with meaning must be developed. My immediate object, in this life task, is not fame (though fame I most certainly do demand): it is a desire to make a world see what I see, a very egotistical sense of "guiding" a stupid child to my way of seeing things. I think men, especially those dried-up moderns, have lost hope because they are blind to beauty, and I hasten to say, to its reward.

I may sum up, and cast off confusion, by saying I see something that the world doesn't, that suggested itself to me; and was nourished by the Gants and Dedaluses of world culture when I realized I wasn't alone in my vision. I say, I am no prophet, no moralist—I am one who will draw the drapes from the room where men sit and allow them the apprehension of Beauty-sense. Equipped thus, life is glorious! And Art, which espouses Beauty, is the ultimate in, and of, Freedom.

# My Generation, My World

*In the spring of 1943 Kerouac ran afoul of military au-*
*thorities when he walked away from a marching exercise*
*and went to the base library to read. After being interviewed*
*by naval officials and psychiatrists and then transferred*
*under guard to Bethesda Naval Hospital in Maryland for*
*more observation, he was handed an honorable discharge,*
*with the qualification "indifferent character." In June 1943*
*he joined his mother and father at their new apartment in*
*New York. Writing to one of his friends from Lowell, Cor-*
*nelius Murphy, he explains "the whole farce" in Newport:*
*". . . [I]t was clearly and simply a matter of maladjust-*
*ment with military life. On this, the psychiatrist and I*
*seemed to be agreed upon in silence [. . .] And, in view of*
*my eagerness to get back to the merchant marine, I see no*
*reason for being ashamed of my maladjustment." The fol-*
*lowing three pieces relate to this tumultuous episode in*
*Kerouac's life.*

He sat on the train, looking out the window, and thought of the sad young men who dream melancholy dreams of unfound love. He was not one of them, for his love was found: it was just outside the train window.

"Our generation," he thought. "I shall pitch my heart & mind into our generation, our world. There is my love & my life."

The train was passing a defense plant housing project in Maryland. The little houses were all alike, all instantly lonely, crowded together and brooding in the coming twilight.

"Will our generation nurture this new thing, or reject it?" he thought. A long string of freights passed in a blur, going in the opposite direction. He caught glimpses of coal, oil tanks, guns mounted on platforms.

"War," he thought. "Our nation has plunged its mighty sinews into war."

The trains passed. Now he saw a small town depot: crowds of soldiers in khaki lolled.

"My generation," he whispered, "is making the sacrifice. It is suffering. Only through suffering does one learn love and fulfillment. I believe I am correct in saying so. My generation, my world is not lost."

The train rolled on. A red sun hung over distant blast furnaces. The blast furnaces discharged their thrilling and mysterious vapors. "Sinews," he whispered.

Then, green forests went by. In the clearing, a small house stood. A young man stooped tending his victory garden. A child by his side. In the train, the traveler nodded slowly.

# The Wound of Living

Living necessarily presupposes and promises hurt, degeneration, and death. Living is death. Those who live must die. Yet, life is like a battlefield: often, I have seen someone, wounded by life, moving down the street much like a hero of war, limping, medalled, carrying a cane. And thus we live and are wounded, and to that one who is wounded most, perhaps because he is least impervious to the shots and shells of the world, I proffer an accolade for outstanding gallantry.

I am young now and can look upon my body and soul with pride. But it will be mangled soon, and later it will begin to disintegrate, and then I shall die, and die conclusively. How can we face such a fact, and not live in fear?

Let me tell you: In conjunction with an article which I read today, I was and am now inclined to defend Art. A certain writer, disparaging the Humanities in the American educational curriculum, wanted to provide for a more basic dependence on science. "The arts," he minced with some deprecation (or so I trust), "are also necessary, since they have always been a source of relaxation and pleasure to man."

Imagine: Relaxation and pleasure! The very fact that he terms Art with those unimaginably puny sounds "the arts" indicates his bias against it. He is a man of science. He will renounce Shelley's world for a great test tube.

Here I will say the foundation of my knowledge of truth rests on science; but I am forced, and willing to add that my house of knowledge, its very foundation (which is science), is set in the soil of Art, or Belief, or Beauty (or religion of the spirit), and that furthermore, Art is also my roof and shields me from neurasthenic and impossible fears that assail the scientific and unhealthy psyched minds of some men.

Reading this might suggest to someone that I am a New Englander. I am a New Englander . . . . a New Englander removed. Unlike Emerson and Thoreau, my real roots are not set in New England, though I was born there; my roots come from Brittany and my people were hardy fishermen, like those in Synge and Loti. But there is something about the landscape, the weather, the face of New England, where I was born, that has brought out the Transcendentalist in me through the earlier years of my life. For this reason, I call myself of the New England tradition, because my style is New England, my muse aims at simplicity and frankness, and I love pine forests and pure thought.

June 25, 1943
Washington, D.C.
Naval Hospital

# Wounded in Action

A hospital considered the young man is a good place to remember things. He lay on his back and pondered on his private observation. More, he went on, there are a lot of things one cannot tell a psychiatrist.

The old man on the next bed, a shock victim of the last war, lay propped up on his pillows playing a game with his hands, tapping the bed with them. He had been playing this game ever since the young man had entered the hospital, two weeks ago. The old man's name was Oswald.

"How are you feeling, Oswald?" asked the young man.

"All right," said Oswald, tapping as he turned his head.

The young man returned his gaze to the white ceiling. He yawned.

It was so white and wan in this hospital. It had not been so before, two summers ago, say, when he had that job down in Virginia. Then, he stood in the hot sun covered with dust, his eyes shaded by the visor of a baseball cap, holding a shovel. The ground was burning hot and his feet blistered; his bare torso was brown and shiny in the sun. He used to glance out of the corner of his eye at a round, glistening, dark shoulder, rippling as he worked the shovel.

Here, in the white beds, everything was pale. His shoulder was so white now he could see the freckles on it.

The young man pondered a while. Yes, the hospital was a good place to remember things. He would lie here for a few months, remembering, saving something for each day.

He would remember everything except that clanging in his head when a shell hit the deck. That was something not worth remembering, because it was mostly a void in his mind. There was no room there for quiet speculation. It did not interest him anyway. Where the papers at home in Alexandria had said he was "wounded in action," to him it was not that at all . . . . it was something that had happened because that was the way it was. All the letters he received from people in Alexandria back there, people he hardly knew, puzzled him. One of them, especially, from his father's friend, publisher of the Eagle, was filled with words that sounded moving when read aloud . . . but when he would read the letter to himself, the patriotic words ended at the bottom of the page. Nothing, he thought, could explain what he knew about everything.

When the psychiatrist had asked him, upon being admitted to the hospital: "How do you feel today?" he had answered: "Fine."

Then the psychiatrist had gone on.

"Have you had strange dreams since then? . . . . Do you hear voices?"

"I had dreams."

"What kind?"

"Queer ones; I can't figure out what's going on, but I know it's something important."

"How do you mean—important?"

"Everybody is so serious," he had told him.

Suddenly the psychiatrist had changed the subject: "What do you think about things? Do you like people?"

"Sure."

"Life?"

"Sure."

"Do you like to be by yourself, alone?"

"Sure."

And then when the psychiatrist had asked why, he couldn't explain himself. The psychiatrist had given him a blank look and written something down on his paper.

Could he have told him about that brown, bare shoulder in the sun, the sight of which, back there in that lost summer afternoon, had filled him with the desire to finish his work, go home to take a bath, eat a big supper, and go boozing with the boys at night in Steve's convertible coupe? Could he explain to the psychiatrist what he thought about this white, sick silence in the hospital? And finally, could he say why it was he liked to be by himself, as now, remembering, adding up, digesting what had happened, shaping experience into new molds as yet untried, smoothing new molds, laying plans to try them . . . .

He lay there, thinking of the white months ahead of him. He would return to the sun and grow brown again, grow eager again for gin and beautiful women. He would try to add all these things up—

the curtains in his bedroom, the way the trees shushed outside in song, the sound of Steve's horn calling him at dusk (where was Steve now? Hadn't he joined the Army? Shouldn't he have joined the Navy with him?), the green fresh foliage of Virginia in the morning on the way to work, midnight when sounds would come from everywhere, the banging freights, and the long "Krooooaahoo!" of the locomotive—he would add all this up and present the sum to the psychiatrist his day of discharge.

Then he would go back home. Other things were waiting to happen. He did not mind. He would always figure things out by himself.

Silently, the hospital lights were put out for the night.

# The Romanticist

*The following statement was typed on stationery with the letterhead "Moore-McCormack Lines, Inc./ Five Broadway, New York/ American Republics Line/ American Scantic Line/ Mooremack Gulf Lines." Loaded with five-hundred pound bombs, the S.S.* Weems *had steamed out of the New York docks in August 1943, headed for Liverpool, England. Kerouac spent a few days in Liverpool and London, taking in a Tschaikovsky concert at Royal Albert Hall and visiting a few pubs. During this voyage he conceived the idea of a series of books about his adventures, the Duluoz legend—"a lifetime of writing about what I'd seen with my own eyes, told in my own words, according to the style I decided on at whether twenty-one years old or thirty or forty or whatever later age [. . .] a contemporary history record for future times to see what really happened and what people really thought."*

*Reading* The Forsyte Saga *by John Galsworthy on this Atlantic crossing had made Kerouac think further about "novels connecting into one grand tale." About a year before he had noted in an aide-mémoire titled "Recollections" that "Long concentration on all the fundamental influences of your life will net a chronological series of events that will be open to use as a novel—for a novel should have a sort of developing continuity, if nothing else." He returned to New York City in October.*

SS: George B. Weems
Port: Liverpool, England     Date: September 21, 1943

The Romanticist:
I have eaten beef stew with silent, shabby men in cheap
eateries and fingered the last two pennies in my pocket
with anger and irony . . . I have dined most sumptuously
in a spacious Park Avenue home, duck brought forth in
silver dishes by a butler . . . I have seen 10¢ movies
on Times Square, seated in the first row of the balcony
in shirtsleeves, smoking and laughing . . . Under a
lashing rain and gale, I have gazed at the angry mid-
Atlantic for a moment, pausing in my labours . . . I have
stood on a Liverpool street corner in the middle of a
drowsy afternoon and cursed the cobbles because the
pubs had closed . . . I have made love to women in
Canada, Washington, D.C., Nova Scotia, England, Greenland, New York City, Maryland, and New England . . . I
have lain drunk in the gutter of a street . . . I climbed a
mountain in Greenland and gazed down on the slim ribbon of Ikatek Fjord . . . I have toiled in the sun on construction jobs from Portsmouth, N.H. to Alexandria,
Virginia . . . I have attended cocktail parties in New York
City penthouses . . . I have worked in mills . . . I have
sold door to door . . . I have worked in garages . . . I
have worked as a reporter on a newspaper . . . I have
played football in college . . . I have starved in a cheap
urine-smelling room in Hartford, Conn. . . . I have dated
actresses, models, and social workers . . . I have brawled
in streets, in bar entrances, and in cafeterias . . . I have
heard great symphonies and been transported . . . I
have walked the streets, a lonely U.S. Navy gob, and
sought women . . . I have languished in hospitals and
shuffled cards in melancholy abstraction . . . I have written reams and reams of writings . . . And through it all, I
have always been restless, unhappy, and seeking new
horizons. What shall I do?

# The Boy from Philadelphia

*On one typescript of this story, written in 1943, Kerouac's address is 133–01 Crossbay Boulevard, Ozone Park, New York. On another copy of the story he noted: "Used by Lucien in '44 as a term paper in Composition." In 1944 Edith Parker, Kerouac's girlfriend and later his first wife, introduced him to nineteen-year-old Lucien Carr, an undergraduate at Columbia University who had grown up in St. Louis, Missouri. He became part of Kerouac's circle of new friends on and around the Columbia campus, which grew to include Allen Ginsberg and William Burroughs. By the middle of 1944 the core group of young writers whom we know as the Beat writers had formed.*

The American merchant seaman stood in the middle of the crowd outside Royal Albert Hall in London. It was getting dark fast. Across the street, in Kensington Gardens where he had just been sitting, the September winds drove the leaves scattering. It was getting so dark you could hardly see the leaves fly.

No lights came on.

Standing in the middle of the crowd, the American seaman felt lonelier than ever before in his life. He wished that he knew someone, wished that he had a girl on his arm (like the girl he had seen that afternoon on Threadneedle Street), wished that he could jostle around and kid with a bunch of pals. But he was alone, and their strange, swift talk sounded foreign. He lit a cigarette and knew that they could see his face.

What is it like, he thought, to live around here and come to the symphony on Saturday nights? What kind of apartments do they live in, what books do they read, what do they think about in this neighborhood?

The crowd surged forward as the doors were swung open.

The great hall hummed with their quiet talk. The seaman sat down and took off his black leather jacket. He looked at the program. Then he looked around. The Britishers, mostly young men and women, waited patiently with contented decorum, talking now and then in low tones. They seemed to know the value of what they were about to see and hear. The seats filled quickly.

Then Barbirolli waddled onstage and mounted the podium. After a soft applause, he raised his baton. Everyone was still. The music began, faint and sweet and distant at first, then grave with melancholy and growing louder . . .

The seaman leaned back and thought: Oh music, speak . . . Oh I am lonely, Oh I am so far from home, Oh the sea separates me from everything, Oh beautiful music speak to me.

During the intermission, the American seaman opened a conversation with the British soldier in the next seat. The soldier's name was John, like the seaman, and he carried a copy of T. S. Eliot's "East Coker."

"What do you think of it?" inquired the American.

The soldier considered for a moment. "It has fine sentiment, I think. I like it a good deal . . ."

"I do too," said the American.

When the crowd surged out of Royal Albert Hall later, the world was darker than darkness. The American seaman blinked, looking around for his new friend. His friend had a small torch. "Here I am," he called, waving his torch. "Come on. Let's go to Piccadilly. We'll have a spot of bitters."

"Swell," said the seaman. "How do we get there?"

"Oh, we'll walk. It's pleasant walking in the blackout, and I know the way well. It's only a mile or so."

They began to stride swiftly through the straggling crowds. Everywhere, small torches flashed on and then off, throwing dances of light all over. People laughed and hummed and talked and whistled and called one another, but all the American could see was darkness and the play of small lights. It smelled like an October night in New England.

"Say," he said, "I love blackouts."

"So do I," said the British soldier cheerfully. "We've come to love them now, not hate them. I suspect we'll miss them when the war is over. Rather cheerful in a way, and friendly don't you think?"

"That's just what I was going to say! Friendly . . ."

In a pub on Piccadilly, the seaman and the British soldier met an American soldier downstairs in the latrine. He was from Philadelphia, and very lonely. He had been in England for a year and a half, and he was very glad to meet the American seaman and his British friend. They went upstairs for a spot of bitters.

The pub was full of American soldiers and a few girls. They had a few glasses of black, lukewarm stout and some bitters, and then left the pub to go out in blacked-out Piccadilly. The soldier from Philadelphia was also called John. The three Johns strolled arm in arm.

In another pub, they drank Scotch and got drunk. They began to sing and shout and push one another and were gay. They swaggered down the dark, crowded streets pushing everyone and laughing with the crowd. Once, a taxicab fender nudged at the American seaman's trousers gently before moving on in the darkness. It was as though the machine itself, now that the driver could not see, had taken over in matters of traffic.

The three Johns strode down the street carrying whiskey glasses filled to the brim. The American seaman sat on a curbstone and drank his Scotch; then he got up and whistled loudly through his fingers. Everybody was talking and laughing in the darkness, flashing their torches about. When you bumped into a small, soft body, it meant a girl; and when you bumped against hard khaki, it meant a soldier. Everybody flashed their torches to see who they had bumped into, and then laughed when they saw who it was. It was wonderful.

The seaman, arm in arm with the other two Johns, bumped into a small, soft body. The girl flashed her torch in the seaman's face. He leaned over and kissed the girl and then bit her ear gently.

"Oh honey," she said.

"Ah!" cried John from Philadelphia. There were two girls, arm in arm, the blonde and a brunette. The British soldier grabbed the brunette and kissed her. Everything was fine, and John from Philadelphia began to sing.

"Let's all go to bed together," he cried. "In the same big bed!"

"In the syme baid!" gasped the blonde, as the American seaman smelled her hair. "Wot's the idea o' that?"

"What the hell!" cried John from Philadelphia. "Why not? We're all here, ain't we?"

"Oi dunno . . ." said the blonde.

"We have money," said the British soldier.

"Sure!" cried the American seaman, rifling his pockets. He threw all the tram tickets out of his pocket and pulled out a ten shilling note. "See?"

"That's only ten bob," said the blonde girl.

"What the hell's wrong with ten bobs!" howled the seaman. "Ten bobs is ten bobs!"

John from Philadelphia laughed: "It's only worth two bucks, Johnny."

"Two bucks?"

"Never mind, I have money. I have eight pounds."

"Eight pounds?" echoed the blonde. The brunette hugged the British soldier reassuringly.

It developed that the girls refused to go to bed with the whole lot of them, in the same big bed. This would not do. The three Johns did not like the idea.

But the blonde edged over to the American seaman and bit his ear hard. He offered to give her his return trip ticket to Liverpool for a night of love, but it developed that he had thrown the ticket away with the worthless tram tickets a few streets back. He was almost broke, and stranded in London. But he didn't mind that. He felt wonderful, and he wanted the blonde.

John from Philadelphia took the American seaman's hand and put five pound notes in it.

"Here's twenty bucks, Johnny. That should be enough."

"Wait a minute," cried the seaman. "What about you, John? And you John?"

The British soldier put his hand on the seaman's shoulder: "I don't like the blonde's partner," he whispered. "You go ahead with the blonde."

"Wait a minute," said the seaman. The blonde tugged at his jacket. "What about you?" he cried.

"That's all right," said John from Philadelphia. "It's not every day I meet a fine buddy like you. Take that money. She's a lovely little blonde."

"But what about you?"

"I'm glad to do you the favor," said John. "You have my address, you can send it back some day."

"Wait a minute," said the seaman.

"Go ahead, Johnny."

"But wait . . . How can you trust me?"

"I know I can," said John from Philadelphia. The brunette took the British soldier's arm and whispered in his ear. They went off a few yards away toward the alley entrance.

The seaman tried to look at the money in his hand, but he couldn't see a thing. "Come on," whispered the blonde. "Darling, I can't wyte."

Suddenly, John from Philadelphia was gone off into the blackout. The seaman called: "John! Hey John!"

He wanted to hug John from Philadelphia, but he was gone off alone into the blackout.

The next morning, the American seaman left the hotel and shuffled toward the American Red Cross in London. His hands were deep in his trouser pockets. He was broke and had a headache.

He went into the American Bar on Oxford street and bought a glass of cold beer with his last sixpence. The bar was full of American soldiers. They sat ranged along the stools, at the tables, talking quietly.

The seaman tried to remember what the blonde had looked like, but he couldn't.

A soldier was talking nearby.

"All the way from Southampton riding in the baggage car with a bunch of Aussies. Hell! Seats only in first class . . ."

"That's the way it is, Mike," said the other soldier. "But let me tell you one thing. There won't be no first class in the damned invasion . . ."

"That's the ticket, brother!"

The seaman got up and left the American Bar. He couldn't for the life of him remember what the blonde looked like. All he could remember was the face of John from Philadelphia.

# The Two Americans

*When Kerouac sent the following story to a prospective
employer in 1943, he attached a note that sheds light on
this work. He wrote: "The following short story is not at
all the one I had intended to submit to you. The story itself is interesting (and true, by the way: I witnessed such a
tableau in an English train), but to my mind it is not as
well written as the other. If, by any chance, you are not
satisfied with this one, I shall be only too glad to submit
the other story, which is at* New Yorker *at the moment. I
have no duplicate copy of that story, but should hear from*
New Yorker *within four or five days. I wrote the following story on board a Liberty ship on the way back from
London."*

*Living in New York at the time, Kerouac was looking for
a job as a script synopsizer in the movie business: "I feel it
can give me training to write scripts of my own later, and
may, at the same time, give me a sufficient footing with a
Hollywood company. The money would keep me going until I should finish the novel." He was working on* Two
Worlds for a New One, *a "remake" of his eighty-thousand
word novel* The Sea Is My Brother.

The train from London to Liverpool rolled along toward Derby
across the English countryside. A purplish-red sun sank toward the
hills charming the soft green slopes with a strange rose light.

In the dining car, the waiters cleared away the dishes, brushed
off the tablecloths, and set plates and silverware for the last group of
diners.

Two R.A.F. men entered the dining car and sat opposite one another at a table. They gazed for a long while out of the window at the

sheep grazing in the fields, at the little villages sliding past with windows aflame and streets shadowed blue, at the narrow rivers idling toward the horizon, and said nothing.

An American soldier sauntered to their table, nodded, and sat down.

The waiter placed four napkins on the table and moved on to distribute napkins to the other diners. A London-bound train flared past the window and was suddenly gone. In the brief seconds that had passed, the light in the fields had deepened.

"Nice sunset," said the American soldier, rubbing his hands together.

One of the R.A.F. men leaned over with a look of swift, frantic eagerness: "Pardon?"

"Nice sunset."

"Oh! Yes! Yes indeed!"—smiling warmly, proudly—"By all means, it is lovely."

The other R.A.F. man nodded proudly, smiling.

The American soldier withdrew a package of Lucky Strikes from his hip pocket and offered them around. Nodding assent, their faces aglow in an almost monotonous cheer, the two Britishers pulled the cigarettes carefully from the package and examined the trademarks with polite curiosity. One of them plunged for his lighter and was offering the American a light before he had had time to place his own cigarette to his mouth.

"Thanks," he mumbled, frowning and inhaling deeply.

"Lucky Strikes," read one of the R.A.F. men. "That's America's largest selling brand, isn't it?"

"I don't really know, but it's my favorite. How do you like them?"

"Oh, wonderful!" beamed the Britisher. "You are fortunate in that your cigarette manufacturers buy the best in tobaccos. Absurdly enough, you know, British manufacturers make it a policy to buy the cheapest hodge-podge mixtures available."

"Yeh?"

They all sat back and smoked, watching the sunset in a nervous, tentative silence.

A colored American soldier was standing next to their table glancing around the dining car, trying to decide where to sit for his dinner. A waiter motioned him to the nearest table. The colored soldier sat down beside the R.A.F. man who faced the other two and straightened his tie with a quick movement of thick brown fingers.

Again, the two R.A.F. men smiled warmly and eagerly. The Negro grinned around the table, but when his glance met the white soldier's, the grin faded to a look of casual recognition. Both Americans dropped their eyes, and then simultaneously turned their heads toward the window. The two R.A.F. men were lost in thought.

The waiter placed four glasses and a pitcher of water on the table. "Sausages tonight," said the waiter. "And three varieties of vegetable!" He stood by the table with sly anticipation.

"Three!?" blurted one of the R.A.F. men. "Goodness!"

The waiter winked at the American soldier: "That's right. Three! Boiled potatoes, mashed potatoes, and fried potatoes!" He guffawed, slapped the Negro soldier on the shoulder, and went off. The Britishers chuckled, and then one of them turned to the Negro and said: "That's one to take back home with you, isn't it."

The Negro shook his head in puzzled amazement: "Man, I dunno how you people can stand it. Back home we used to eat five times as much. Evertime I leave camp on a leave, I gets so hungry I cain't see!"

The two R.A.F. men laughed heartily. One of them addressed the white soldier.

"And do _you_ find it the same?"

The white soldier had been looking away, but upon being addressed, turned his head slowly.

"I say, we were just commenting on the food situation here," prompted the R.A.F. man, "and our friend here informs us that back home in the States you people eat five times as much as we do. Is that literally true, really?"

The white soldier shrugged and said: "I suppose so."

"Yes," echoed the Britisher vaguely, glancing at his companion with a small, lost look.

"Quite remarkable," his companion mumbled. They turned and fixed their attention on the countryside.

"You got small trains here," spoke the Negro. "Man, I ain't never seen such small engines and boxcars."

The two R.A.F. men grinned back quickly.

"That's so," one observed. "But there _is_ a reason for it, you know. England is a relatively tiny country, and our trains have to do a considerable amount of shuttling. Whereas in America, I understand, the distances are so much vaster and the distribution of rail so less complex. Don't you think so?"

"Yeh, I think you're right. Them old freight trains picks up the miles and lays them down, and I ain't kiddin'."

The two Britishers laughed loudly.

"Tell us," one continued, "what part of the States are you from."

"Chicago."

"Chicago! That's in Illinois, isn't it?"

The Negro grinned. "That's right."

"And where are you from?" inquired the R.A.F. man of the white soldier. Both Britishers awaited his answer with heads tilted identically for intelligent perception of this information.

The white soldier paused.

"I'm from Birmingham, Alabama."

"Indeed. Alabama. A lovely state, I am told."

"It's all right."

The two R.A.F. men glanced quickly out the window. One of them tapped his finger on the tablecloth. Both their faces had suddenly frozen into an inscrutable blankness. Outside, the contours of the purplish landscape moved past majestically, like a gigantic turntable. The sun had disappeared.

"Lucky?"

The colored soldier was holding out a package of Lucky Strikes over the center of the table. First one, then the other R.A.F. man nodded brightly and helped himself, with the one again plunging into his pocket for the lighter.

The Negro offered his pack to the white soldier, but the latter was looking away.

"Cigarette?" prompted the Negro.

The white soldier turned his head slowly, stared first at the pack, then at the Negro soldier, and then shook his head with heavy finality. He looked away again, his lips compressed, his eyes lidded.

The two R.A.F. men glanced at each other for a split second and then looked out the window.

"Light?" The Negro soldier was holding out a burning match.

The R.A.F. men stared dumbly at the unlit lighter in his hand. "Oh, yes. Thanks so much," he mumbled. The smoke rose from the table in a fragrant puff.

"Wonderful cigarette, Luckies," said the other R.A.F. man.

The Negro soldier grinned proudly.

"Come," began the other Britisher, brightening up, "tell us about Chicago. It must be a magnificent city!"

# Acknowledgments

Jack Kerouac often mentioned his beginnings as a writer. He told us about the nickel-notebook novels he wrote at eleven years old. We are indebted to him for preserving his manuscripts and papers. Of everyone I must thank for help in preparing this book, Kerouac is the first person to acknowledge; it is his book.

Under the guidance of the late Stella (Sampas) Kerouac and now her brother John Sampas, who represents her estate in literary matters, almost as many books by Kerouac have been released as were published in his lifetime. Working with Sterling Lord, Jack Kerouac's literary agent, John Sampas has overseen the publication of many Kerouac books since the early 1990s, a period of renewed critical interest in Kerouac's work. I thank him for welcoming this collaborative project and sharing his knowledge about the Sampas family, young Kerouac, and Lowell's culture. I thank Jim Sampas for his spirited day-to-day work on behalf of Kerouac's art, and I acknowledge the support of the late Mrs. Kerouac. I also thank Anthony M. Sampas for compiling the story of his late uncle Sebastian Sampas.

I am grateful to Sterling Lord for his support and essential advice and to the staff at Sterling Lord Literistic, Inc., for their assistance. I thank editor Paul Slovak of Viking Penguin, whose insight and sure editorial hand were enormously important in bringing this book to the world. Thanks also to the Viking Penguin team for first-rate production and promotion. To editor David Stanford: Thank you for your enthusiasm for this book—and my first literary lunch in Manhattan.

Working with Jack Kerouac's papers was the culmination of my thirty years of involvement with his life and literature. I first heard his name at Dracut High School in 1970 from my friend Paul Brouillette, who had asked his parents about Kerouac after the author's funeral in Lowell in October 1969. In 1954 my parents, the late Marcel and Doris (Roy) Marion, began raising me at 67 Orleans Street, on the hill of Doctor Sax, just a few doors from Kerouac's birthplace, 9 Lupine Road. We were Franco-Americans, French Canadian–Americans, sharing the same parish in the Centralville section of Lowell. My mother and Jean-Louis Kérouac had been classmates at St. Louis de France School, and my father, older than Kerouac, had attended St. Joseph's School at the same time as Jack. My parents would have been pleased to see this book, and I thank them for everything.

Several Kerouac relatives, friends, and associates shared their memories with me, some recently and others long ago: David Amram, James Curtis, Anthony Francisco, Mary Hogan, the late Robert ("Pete") Houde, Julien Marion, Stanley Polak, Roland Salvas, Demosthenes Samaras, Mary Sampas, and Anthony G. Sampatacacus (Sampas). I also thank two veteran interpreters of Kerouac: Roger Brunelle and Brian Foye.

Special thanks go to Jane Brox, Jack McDonough, and John Suiter for their editorial expertise. For professional and personal support, I thank George Chigas, Susan Kapuscinski Gaylord, Scott Glidden, Jim Higgins, Ruth Page, and Joan Ross. From the University of Massachusetts Lowell, I thank Mary Lou Hubbell and Christine McKenna, as well as faculty members Jay Atkinson, Dean Bergeron, Jim Coates, Joyce Denning, Matt Donahue, Hilary Holladay, and Charles Nikitopoulos.

For various kinds of help, I thank Clementine Alexis, Douglas Brinkley, Maurice Comtois, David Daniel, Doug DeNatale, Tom Gooden, Rev. Seamus Finn, Sister Carmen Foley, Joseph J. Foley, Laura Foley, Susan O'Brien Lemire, Armand P. Mercier, Helena Minton, Marian O'Brien, Ray and Roseanne Riddick, and the late Senator Paul E. Tsongas. For long-term encouragement, I thank Ro and Lew Corbin-Teich, Bob Dionne, Doug Flaherty, Ray and Bernadette LaPorte, Eric Linder, and Julie and Tom Mofford.

I am grateful for research assistance from the staffs of the City of Lowell's Pollard Memorial Library, the Merseyside Maritime Museum, the Museum of Liverpool Life, the University of Massachusetts Lowell Library, and the Widener Library at Harvard University; Martha Mayo of the Center for Lowell History at the University of Massachusetts Lowell; Renate Olsen of the Regis

College Library; and Rodney Phillips, Curator of the Henry W. and Albert A. Berg Collection of English and American Literature of the New York Public Library.

My wife, Rosemary Noon, was a patient listener and an insightful reader throughout. My love and endless gratitude go to Rosemary and our son, Joseph Patrick Marion, for their love and understanding. My brother Richard and his wife, Florence, and my brother David and his wife, Dianne, provided a second tier of strong support. Thanks to Eric Marion, John Marion, Philip Marion, and Stephen Marion as well. I offer special thanks to my wife's parents, Richard and Mary (Foley) Noon, whose encouragement and counsel are invaluable. Thanks also to Lionel and Rolande Patenaude, Roger and Estelle Mann, "Doc" and Rita Michaels, Joan Roy, Tom Brady, Nancy Mann, Rita Marion, and the keeper of Rosemont memories, Florence Y. Marion.